ONE LITTLE
SECRET

ONE LITTLE SECRET

A Novel

CATE HOLAHAN

CROOKED
LANE

NEW YORK

Published in the United States by Crooked Lane Books, an imprint of The Quick Brown Fox & Company LLC.

Crooked Lane Books and its logo are trademarks of The Quick Brown Fox & Company LLC.

Library of Congress Catalog-in-Publication data available upon request.

ISBN (hardcover): 978-1-68331-972-6
ISBN (ePub): 978-1-68331-973-3
ISBN (ePDF): 978-1-68331-974-0

Cover design by Melanie Sun

Book design by Jennifer Canzone

Printed in the United States.

www.crookedlanebooks.com

Crooked Lane Books
34 West 27th St., 10th Floor
New York, NY 10001

First Edition: July 2019

10 9 8 7 6 5 4 3 2 1

To Shonah Maldonado, the Bloomfield Police Department, and all the law enforcement officers who bring to work a deep empathy for the people they protect and dedication to helping folks on their worst days.

PROLOGUE

Drowning can happen in two inches of water. All the parenting books she'd consumed during her pregnancies had contained that warning, often on the first page of the bathtime section. Children could die in a kiddie pool. The sink. The toilet. Life began in an amniotic sac, but it could end in the shallows.

Her life could end in these shallows.

She clawed at the hands shoving her head beneath the breaking waves. Salt seared her nose. Her eyes burned. Still, she forced herself to scan for a weapon. The dark outline of a rock. The glint of a razor clam. Anything besides the foamy veil shrouding her face.

Air. God. Air. Watery images filled her brain: murky pictures of her kids' childhoods. She saw her oldest, Daddy's clone with those serious eyes, and her rubber band of a baby, pulled thin by puberty, vibrating with energy. The snapshots strung together like images in a spinning zoetrope. She could see her children aging. Growing up without her.

The water pulled away. She tried to breathe, but a fetid

1

backwash flooded her mouth. Coughing, she pressed her palms to the shifting ground, desperate to push herself upright before the next wave knocked her down. She had to focus. She had to breathe. To fight.

Her face slammed back into the froth. A whorling silence filled her ears. The pressure to inhale was more intense than anything she'd ever felt, stronger than the need to push during contractions. And, yet, there was a peace, a knowledge that the end would come. It was almost here, if only she'd let go.

She pressed harder against the sinking sand, digging in with her knees and fingers. Darkness swept through her brain. She had to fight. She had to breathe. She had to . . . She . . .

PART I

CHAPTER ONE

THE DAY AFTER

The room reminded Gabriella of her daughter's, sans the credit-card-sized photos thumbtacked to the white walls and the irritating poster of a tattooed action star tagged BOY-FRIEND GOALS. Like Kayla's space, it had been carved from the attic and thus suffered from a sharp triangular ceiling. A squat dresser huddled beneath a skylight cut into one of the slanted sides. Under the other diagonal, a single mattress rested on a platform so low it resembled a tatami mat.

A girl sat atop it, her head lowered over tucked knees, preventing Gabby from seeing more of her than a pair of jean-clad legs pressed to a bulky gray sweatshirt and a curtain of thick black hair. The homeowner, Dina Collette, had warned that her au pair hadn't wanted to involve the police. *But I explained that, in America, women don't let men get away with such things.* Gabby supposed that Dina, a former model whose surname changed every few years, didn't let men get away with much. But the rules were different for socialites with established wealth. Truth was, men got away with "such things" all the time.

Gabby's job was to make this time different. She tapped on the doorjamb, hoping to announce herself without startling the young woman. According to Dina, Mariel Cruz had turned eighteen in December, five months before arriving in the States. Her native language was Tagalog, though Dina claimed Mariel was fluent in English. Gabby prayed that meant the au pair read American newspapers. Though nearly everyone in the Philippines learned English in school, a typical foreign-language curriculum wouldn't cover the vocabulary for sexual assault.

She called Mariel's name from the open doorway. The girl lifted her forehead from her thighs. Even with bloodshot eyes and a reddened nose, she was pretty—her young face punctuated by the full lips that men so often equated with sex, but that Gabby couldn't see without thinking of her pouty sixteen-year-old. Sitting in her plain room, with her skin scrubbed clean, Mariel appeared even younger than Kayla.

Gabby's chest tightened. She reminded herself that the girl before her was technically an adult, even if she could pass for her daughter's classmate. Moreover, it was possible that whatever had happened had been consensual and that Dina, disgusted by the idea of some middle-aged neighbor seducing her barely legal au pair, had forced the phone call.

Gabby pressed her hand against the open door, pushing it back another inch. "My name is Gabby Watkins. I'm a detective with the East Hampton Police Department. May I come in?"

A sniff served as an affirmative response. Gabby stepped into the room, suddenly thankful for her small stature, which enabled her to slip into the cramped space without dominating it. The lack of seating, aside from the bed, meant that Gabby would need to stand for the interview. Plopping on a mattress beside a possible sexual-assault victim was even worse than lording over one.

"I understand that something happened to you last night. I'd like to help."

Mariel pulled at her sweatshirt, attempting to tuck her knees beneath the image of crossed paddles stitched into the fabric. "Dina said to call the police. She thinks somebody put a drug in my drink. But I don't know. I don't remember."

The sentences shot out in short gasps, like steam from a rusting heater. Gabby wished that the Collette family had volunteered to go out to breakfast so that she and Mariel could talk in the kitchen. A glass of water would help the young woman calm down and tell her story fluidly. Details emerged only when a conversation was flowing. And in he-said/she-said sexual-assault cases, the details often decided arrests.

"It's okay if you can't recall everything." Gabby kept her voice soft, aware that even a normal speaking voice might ricochet against the tight walls. "Let's talk about the party. How did you hear about it?"

Mariel stretched the sweatshirt over her kneecaps and rounded her back over her thighs. "From Fiona O'Rourke. She's an au pair, too. She watches a six-year-old in the gray house at the end of the street. She told me that some guys were having a pool party."

"A party where?"

"Pepperidge Lane. I don't know the house number. Fiona picked me up in a Lyft."

Gabby made another mental note. Fiona's ride-sharing app would have the exact party location.

"I thought they would be Irish students, like Fiona. But the guys were much older." Mariel released one of her arms from around her covered legs. She picked up a piece of her own black hair. "A couple were . . . I don't know how to say. *Puting buhok. Gris?* When the hair begins to lose color?"

"Graying?" Gabby thought of her own hair, pulled back into a matronly ponytail. If she shook it out, she'd find several strands to confirm what Mariel meant, though not so many that anyone would suggest a dye job. Most of Gabby's fellow forty-year-olds had yet to go full salt-and-pepper. "The guys were in their fifties, you think? Or older?"

Mariel shuddered. "Late thirties, I think. Maybe forties. When Fiona introduced me to some of the men, I said we should visit a place with younger people. But she wanted to stay." Mariel gestured to the room around them. "I didn't want to be here on my one night off."

In addition to being tiny, Gabby realized, Mariel's bedroom was stuffy, despite the air conditioning seeping from floor vents. Heat camped out in attics. Humidity was already curling the baby hairs not pulled tight by Gabby's ponytail, and she'd been inside only ten minutes.

"How many people were at the party?"

"I don't know. Maybe fifty? There were many girls like Fiona—college students on summer break. I thought I would stay for a time, and then if Fiona didn't want to leave, I could take a car with one of the other women . . ."

Gabby stepped closer to Mariel and lowered her voice to a confidential level. "But something changed your plans."

The girl nodded, dropping her chin lower with each bounce until it was nearly hidden behind her knees. "Two of the men started fighting over a girl. This big Black guy was shouting that he would call the cops. He said he'd have people arrested for drinking before they are the right age. I'd had wine." Mariel's head snapped up, revealing her wide brown eyes. "I'm allowed in the Philippines, and I only took one glass. I know I shouldn't have . . ."

Gabby offered a shy smile. "I'm not here about underage drinking."

Mariel dropped her chin back to the stretched-out sweatshirt. "I was afraid of trouble, so I went to tell Fiona that I needed to leave. She'd gone inside for the bathroom. And . . ."

A sob cut off Mariel's story. The little Gabby could still see of the young woman's face was flushed and strained. Every instinct urged Gabby to hug the girl, filling the maternal role that belonged to a woman eight thousand miles away. But Gabby kept her feet cemented to the floor. She needed to maintain perspective as she listened to

Mariel's story for the keywords of a crime. Had Mariel said no? Had she been unable to consent? Had she been trapped or forced?

"So you went into the house to find Fiona, and then what happened?"

Mariel's breaths shuddered. "I went into the kitchen and saw a couple men that Fiona had introduced me to. I told them I was searching for her and that a man was outside threatening to phone the police. One of the men ran out to talk to him. Another, I think his name was Mandy, said he'd help me find my friend. He gave me a glass of something, too. It was fruity. I was afraid to drink it and told him I was eighteen, but he said that the police couldn't enter people's private homes."

A bitter snort sprayed Mariel's top lip with clear mucus. She wiped it with her sweatshirt sleeve, creating a shimmering line atop her lips that shaved even more years from her young face. "That's all I remember before waking up."

"Where did you wake up?"

Mariel covered her mouth with her palm. She squeezed her eyes shut, forcing tears out the sides. Gabby tried again, dropping her voice to a near whisper. "Where did you wake up, Mariel?"

"In this man's bed." Mariel's voice dissolved in sobs. "I wasn't wearing clothes, and the guy that was helping me find Fiona was beside me. I don't know what I did. I don't know if we had sex. Maybe I drank too much and fell asleep and he put me to bed. I told Dina that I didn't know and I was sorry. When I explained that I couldn't remember any-thing, she said I had to talk to the police."

Gabby couldn't stop her hands from curling into fists a second time. Whether or not Mariel had been drugged or fed booze until she blacked out, the man she'd encoun-tered was a predator. He and his friends had lured a bunch of women half their age to a party in hopes of making them drunk and pliable. He'd then identified one of the weaker ones: a newly minted adult, thousands of miles from her family, unfamiliar with alcohol, and abandoned by her friend.

"I'm sure that you were feeling confused and scared, so I understand if you just got out of there. But can you tell me anything about this man, Mandy? Perhaps what he looked like and if he said anything to you this morning?"

Mariel wiped her face with the other sweatshirt sleeve. "He had blond-and-brown hair, a mix, and light eyes. Maybe green. I was too embarrassed to look close at his face. I asked him what time it was, and he said seven. He invited me to breakfast. I told him that I needed to take the twins to their tennis lessons. He got a car for me." Mariel pulled at the hair pasted to her cheeks. "If this man raped me, why would he offer me breakfast and pay for my ride home? It doesn't make sense. I must have fallen asleep."

The girl's round eyes begged the authority in the room for reassurance. Part of Gabby wanted to provide it, to assure the still-teenager that nothing more horrible had happened than her getting drunk and passing out, that she didn't need to worry her mother back in the Philippines or go to the hospital for STD screening. But a lie would be worse in the long run. Ignored wounds festered. And a rapist that got away with it would do the same thing to another young girl.

"The hospital has tests to help us figure out whether or not you were drugged, and if you had intercourse with anyone last night. Doctors can also give you medicine to protect you against diseases, if the sex was unprotected."

Mariel's pleading stare morphed to panic. "I don't have health insurance here. I earn two hundred a week. I can't afford to see doctors."

The statement grabbed Gabby's tense insides and twisted. The predator really had picked a prime candidate, choosing a young woman who would be more concerned about the cost of treatment than catching her attacker. "There are victims' funds that will reimburse you, eventually."

Mariel's eyes filled with fresh tears. "Do the tests hurt?"

The question made Gabby's own eyes sting. She tilted her head to the ceiling, forcing her emotions back into her stomach. As she did, her phone began buzzing.

Gabby removed her cell, intending to decline the call. Jason DeMarco's name dominated the screen. Detective DeMarco would have been handling Gabby's rape report had he not been pulled away minutes earlier on a possible assault. Gabby, who'd spent most of the night investigating a DUI that had totaled an SUV and a telephone pole, had been the only other detective on call—fortunately for Mariel, since DeMarco wasn't known for his sensitivity or tact. Perhaps he'd already resolved his case and was offering relief.

Gabby pocketed the phone and turned her attention back to Mariel's pinched face. "The tests are invasive, unfortunately." She slowed her East Coast speech to the speed of a Texas drawl, aware that she'd come to the part of the interview involving more technical vocabulary. "The doctors will look for fibers, like pieces of hair or carpet, and they will give you an internal physical examination, similar to what happens at a gynecologist. Many people find the tests upsetting to endure after an attack, though they can clear up what happened last night—if you had sexual intercourse with anyone and if there are any sedatives or other strange chemicals in your system."

Mariel's jaw dropped with an unspoken question. A shy knock snapped it closed. Gabby glanced over her shoulder to see Dina in the doorway, a sparkling glass of water in one hand and an aspirin in her outstretched palm. Gabby swallowed her annoyance at the second break in her momentum. For all intents and purposes, Dina was as close to a mom as Mariel had in the country. If the young woman decided to go ahead with the tests, she'd need someone.

Gabby cleared her throat before continuing. "Unfortunately, the drugs used in these kind of assaults are designed to move through the body quickly. The longer you wait to visit the hospital, the less likely they are to show up on any exams."

Dina nodded as she approached, as though she knew all about forensic sexual exams. She sat beside Mariel, placed the aspirin in her charge's hand, and then draped her arm over the girl's shoulders. "I'm so sorry. What happened was not your fault, okay? This man is a rapist. You're being so brave to hold him responsible. He can't do this to you."

Mariel hung her head, not agreeing with Dina so much as surrendering to her. As much as Gabby wanted to put Mariel's attacker behind bars, the last thing an assaulted woman needed was to feel stripped of the little agency she had left. Gabby dropped into a crouched position so she could look into Mariel's lowered eyes. "It's your decision, Mariel. Only you can make it, and no one will be angry with you no matter what you choose. If you decide to go through with it and give us evidence, though, I will do everything in my power to make sure this man is punished for what he did to you and prevented from ever doing it again."

Mariel met Gabby's intent stare. Though she didn't say anything, Gabby saw a spark of fight. The girl slipped her legs from inside her sweatshirt and pushed herself to a standing position. Dina immediately shot up, holding her au pair's arm. "I'll drive you," Dina offered. "I can do that, right?"

Gabby's pocket buzzed. "That would be good. I'll let the hospital know you're both coming." She withdrew the phone as though she intended to call ahead and not check her caller ID. DeMarco's number was on-screen again. Gabby reaffirmed the name of the local medical center with Dina and promised to alert them to Mariel's impending arrival.

Her pocket continued vibrating as she said her stoic

good-byes. Gabby waited until she'd hit the first staircase landing to answer. "Hello, Jason?"

"Sergeant."

Gabby bristled. Since her promotion, her passed-over male colleagues had taken to using her title instead of her first name. She still wasn't sure whether they intended respect or mockery. When she'd gotten the job two months prior, there'd been grumbling about the chief trying to "diversify" the ranks, as though her fawn-brown face and female parts had counted more than her ten years on the force—the past three with the detective title. "What's going on? I've been with a sexual-assault victim. Why all the calls?"

"We need you at the beach."

Gabby picked up her speed across the landing. "The assault call?"

"Patrolman Kelly used the ten-code and a new dispatcher read it wrong. A woman is dead. The coroner's office will confirm, but it's looking like she was drowned."

Gabby gripped the handrail. The Hamptons didn't get many murders, and she liked it that way. She'd applied for the job on Long Island's south fork in part because of the low rate of violent crime. Becoming a police officer had been about keeping people safe and supporting her family, not hunting armed killers. "Murders should really go to County. The call this morning is looking like a drugged date rape, and the way this guy selected his victim, I'm guessing it's not his first time. Homicide is better equipped to handle the forensics—"

"The woman's bathing suit was half torn off. The Suffolk Crime Lab folks are here gathering evidence. But if this started as a sexual assault, you have the most experience. Also the vic's friend is here. She's in a state."

DeMarco's repeated redials suddenly made sense. Handling "females in a state" was Gabby's unofficial job description. Since making detective, she'd been assigned nearly all the sex crimes and "weeping women" on the assumption that such assaults were more suited to her gender—and the realization from her peers that many of the cases devolved into a mess of allegations and recriminations that prosecutors wouldn't touch. The work was draining and the rewards often never materialized. But somebody had to try. And, as the only female detective, she was that somebody.

A surge of adrenaline chased away the prickles of fatigue in Gabby's legs. Her heels pounded down the steps. "Send the address, detective. I'm on my way."

CHAPTER TWO

THE DAY OF

Jenny had already lost her daughter. She'd been trailing Ally, keeping tabs on the head of corkscrew curls bobbing through the clogged Manhattan sidewalk at a speed intended to ditch her mother. A moment earlier, her twelve-year-old had been feet in front of her. But Ally had disappeared beyond the mosh pit of teenage boys slapping greetings and simultaneously blocking Jenny's route to the corner.

"Do you see Ally?" Jenny reached for Louis, as she always did when worried—despite him having caused the problem in the first place. Ally wouldn't have been weaving through the waiting families if Louis hadn't panicked them all about missing drop-off because of Jenny needing a few extra minutes to "put on her face."

Louis grasped her hand, using his free one to shield his eyes from the already blaring sun. "I think she found Chloe. See the pale blonde? That looks like Ally hugging her."

Jenny pushed her sunglasses to the top of her head, removing the amber filter that had blended Chloe's platinum mane with all the darker-blonde ponytail. She squinted at a group in identical camp shirts at the end of Louis's outstretched finger. Ally's auburn spirals peeked out from behind Chloe's broad shoulders. Their neighbors' daughter had inherited her mother's near-albino coloring and her father's height, enabling her to always stand out in a crowd. Jenny wondered if Chloe would ultimately find that as mixed a blessing as she did.

The sea of boys began to part in front of her. Jenny felt their eyes on her revealed face. Whispers fizzed on both sides of her, building in strength like a wave. *Is that . . . ? I think so. Dude, do you have a ball? (snickering) Dude, do you have a Sports Illustrated?* Had she been alone, Jenny wouldn't have minded giving an autograph. But this morning needed to be about bidding good-bye to her baby for seven weeks, not her second career or her husband's feelings about it.

"Where's your wedding ring?"

Jenny yanked her hand from Louis's grip and examined her long brown fingers as though their bareness surprised her. Donning all those carats to send her daughter into the Maine wilderness—to a camp with the feminist-empowerment motto "Growing Strong Girls," no less—had seemed unnecessary, if not inappropriate.

"In a lockbox. In the trunk." She hadn't been wearing the eternity band much in the past few weeks, though for their trip she'd packed it inside a portable jewelry safe for the inevitable night when someone, likely Rachel, decreed they should all go out for a fancy dinner. Jenny donned her much-practiced *everything is all right* smile, hoping to stave off a scolding about the dangers of leaving expensive, easily transported items in a garage manned by key-wielding valets. In hindsight, the decision *not* to wear it didn't seem very logical.

Disapproval flickered in her husband's blue eyes, a gas flame turned on only to be promptly shut off. Like her, Louis wanted their daughter's send-off to be negativity-free. They both shared the unspoken understanding that all potentially incendiary dialogues should wait until after Ally was on one of the buses idling on the side of the street. Still, what one person viewed as playing with fire, the other might consider a statement of mere fact.

Louis reclaimed her hand, apparently agreeing that the ring discussion could wait a few hours or, perhaps, be avoided completely. The tense energy wafting from him didn't mean he'd let the subject go, but it didn't mean he was holding on to it either. In eighteen years together, Jenny had never known her husband to give off a particularly relaxed vibe. When she'd first met him in medical school, she'd thought of a copper cable, in part because of the way the autumn sun had set his red hair ablaze, but mostly because of his presence. His body seemed formed by the twisting together of muscle and sinew, each internal fiber conducting its own heat and electricity.

Jenny pulled Louis through the path made by the staring boys. As soon as they cleared the group, he tugged back on her palm. "I don't think she wants us hovering. Teenage girls."

Her husband might as well have pointed out the color of the sky. Ben and Rachel had apparently decided it was fine to leave Chloe by herself before boarding the bus. Of course Ally would want to demonstrate the same level of independence, especially given the presence of older boys destined for the brother camp. But Ally was only twelve, and Jenny wasn't about to let her pretend to be more mature the morning before spending a summer away from home.

Seeing her daughter giving the boys sly glances as Chloe whispered, Jenny wanted to grab Ally and transport them both back to a time before puberty and secrets. Sometimes Jenny wished she could rewind a full five years to when she'd still been home with an elementary schooler, working just two days a week in a sports medicine clinic and once a month or less commenting on injuries for ESPN. At that time, Louis had still been a trauma fellow laboring under eighty-hour hospital shifts, so she'd had Ally to herself most of the week. Her daughter had loved and admired her then.

Jenny mentally scolded herself for being so negative. She and Ally had been close until recently. If not friends, certainly more than simply a mom and daughter who loved each other. Until six months ago, Jenny would have said that Ally genuinely liked hanging out with her. Evidently, turning twelve-and-a-half flipped some internal teenage switch, triggering the raging-bitch years her mother had warned her about.

Jenny pulled from Louis's hold. "She'll have seven weeks without me. She can deal with another hour of my existence."

Louis followed Jenny's lead, remaining a step behind so it would be apparent that "Mom" had demanded the embarrassing reunion. Her husband wouldn't dare do anything to risk his favored status with Ally. Somehow he'd remained insulated from the hormonal back draft that blasted Jenny each time she tried to talk to their daughter. Daddy was still given pecks on the cheeks and promises to return home before curfew. Ally even shared the occasional frustration with him, like her difficulty with one crush that had thought her too "different looking"—aka "ethnic."

"Ally," Jenny called to her, as though seeing her daughter for the first time since arriving. If Ally had been pretending to be unchaperoned, she could save face by claiming that her parents had been parking the car.

Ally looked over at them and then rolled her eyes toward her best friend. Chloe tossed her near-white mane in agreement, a filly swatting a fly. "So, are you two all ready for seven weeks?" Jenny smiled despite her daughter's irritated expression. "I don't know what I'm going to do without you both hanging in the kitchen all the time. The house will feel so lonely."

Ally tilted her head to emphasize her incredulous stare. "I'm sure you'll manage."

Jenny reached for her daughter's hand. "But I'll miss you."

Ally sidestepped the attempt at physical contact. She

21

looked over Jenny's shoulder to Louis. "Dad, make sure Mom doesn't have too much alone time."

The condescension couldn't have been clearer. *Dad, Mom is complaining about something again. You fix it. I can't be expected to deal with her.*

Jenny didn't consider herself a whiner. She supposed she could be critical sometimes, especially when she felt Louis had been getting away with too much. But all things considered, Jenny thought herself rather adept at keeping her problems to herself.

Louis landed a loud smacking kiss against Jenny's cheek. "Don't worry, sweetheart. I'll take care of your mother."

Ally's nose wrinkled in disgust.

"Camp Nova!" a growling female voice blasted through a bullhorn. "If you are in Camp Nova, form a line along that wall. We will be boarding in a couple minutes."

The chatter on the sidewalk swelled into a chorus of good-byes. Chloe gestured with her head to Ally and started toward the brick side of the building. Ally held back for a moment, allowing Louis to pull her into both of them for a final embrace. Jenny felt Ally bristle against her chest.

"Chloe. Wait. Chloe!" Ben's bark broke through the din. Their neighbor jogged from around the corner, his wide shoulders and six-foot-five frame overshadowing the other dads. The crowd parted for him as it had for Jenny. He ran through the space and tackled his daughter in a bear hug.

Like Ally, Chloe seemed to suffer through the embrace. She didn't wrap her arms around her father's chest or offer any reassuring pats. When he released her, Ben looked about as disappointed as Jenny felt. "Sorry. Saying good-bye to your brother took a little longer than expected." Ben rubbed the back of his neck. "We love you, kiddo. And we're going to miss you. But I know you're going to have a great time."

Chloe glanced around her father's broad sides. Rachel's heels clapped up the sidewalk. Had it not been for the sound, Jenny might have mistaken the woman in the crowd for one of the teens. Her slight, jean-clad figure blended in with the other narrow-hipped girls.

Before she reached all of them, Rachel opened her arms toward her daughter. Chloe went running, shattering all of Jenny's gender- and age-related justifications for Ally's atti-tude. If near-thirteen-year-old girls hated their mothers, then why was Chloe hugging hers like she might forgo camp altogether if Rachel asked that she stay? Why the tears in both their eyes? Why was Chloe lingering by her female parent while Ally had already staked out a spot in the boarding line?

The loving sight sickened Jenny with jealousy and self-doubt. She really tried to be a good mother. But clearly she was doing something wrong. Save perhaps for the three weeks of March Madness, Rachel worked longer hours at her law firm than Jenny did in the television studios. Jenny attended more school events than Rachel. Jenny was the parent who had taught Ally to read and write and had learned the new Common Core math to help with home-work. Yet her only child despised her.

Jenny wrested her attention from the knife-twisting scene. "I guess we should go."

Louis squeezed her to his side and stepped toward the line. "We'll grab one more hug."

Ally leaned against the building with a wide stance, saving space for her best friend. As they approached her, Ben bounded over to them, seemingly happy to focus on something besides the tender mother-daughter moment from which he'd been excluded. Jenny pulled from Louis to accept a hello hug. Her neighbor's height forced her to look up as he bent down to brush his face against the side of hers, bringing his lips within grazing distance of her cheekbone. It was the American version of the French greeting kiss, made more intimate by the tilted heads. Louis, in turn, received a masculine nod of acknowledgment. Ben gave Ally a neighborly wave.

Her daughter stared at Chloe's dad like he'd intruded on a sleepover party, eyes wide with revulsion. Jenny cleared her throat to communicate her disapproval at the gawking. It was one thing for Ally to be rude to her—parents had to accept a certain amount of boundary testing—but she couldn't let her kid insult another helicoptering adult just because Ally wanted to pretend to be a big girl. "Say hi to Ben, Ally."

Ally glared at her. "Hi, Mr. Hansen." She folded her arms across her chest. "Mom, your makeup is melting."

Jenny swiped at the corner of her nose. Her finger picked up a brownish-yellow glaze from the foundation she'd layered on earlier. The amount of cover-up required to hide the purplish blur beneath her left eye had necessitated heavy makeup.

She faced Louis. "Am I all right?"

Her husband's smile thinned as he gave her skin a clinical once-over. "Yeah, you're good." He chuckled. "Paparazzi prepared."

Ally snorted. "Thankfully someone will keep an eye on her."

The exchange didn't strike Jenny as amusing, despite Louis's laughter. Humor, she knew, was often a mask for frustration. Her husband had never been comfortable with her move from orthopedist to ESPN injury analyst to full-time CBS sports commentator. He often grumbled that she was known in town as "the attractive Black woman from TV" rather than his preferred titles of Mrs. Murray or Ally's mom. And he'd railed in the past about her minor celebrity threatening to make them all tabloid fodder.

Before Jenny could join in the laughter at her own expense, Rachel came up arm in arm with her adoring child. She released Chloe into the line and then stood beside Ben. Rachel's head didn't quite reach his shoulder.

The woman with the megaphone announced for a second time that the campers should line up and head toward their labeled buses. Chloe and Ally began shuffling forward. Jenny waved to the girls, even though she knew from her daughter's turned head that her good-bye would go unacknowledged. They all watched in silence as the kids stepped onto the bus, turning back only after Ben had confirmed from his higher vantage point that their children were seated.

"Are you two heading out now?" Rachel sniffled. Jenny didn't know whether she really cared about the answer or simply wanted to distract herself from the bus taking away her daughter.

Louis shrugged. "Might as well beat Friday traffic."

Rachel's tongue clicked against her teeth. "I wouldn't rush. Susan and Nadal still have to drop Jonah at his camp, and I am guessing that will take a bit." She lowered her voice. "He had an issue this morning."

Ben cleared his throat. "It wasn't that bad."

Rachel pulled her chin to her neck. "You had to carry him out of the crowd, hon. You said he was hitting himself." She turned to Jenny. "I was saying good-bye to Will, so I didn't see the whole thing. But I gather it was pretty awful. When I got there, Jonah was rocking back and forth beside a building."

Ben shot Rachel a disapproving glance. Louis scratched his forehead. It was his doctor move, one Jenny had seen many times during their emergency room residencies. When thinking about medicine, Louis rubbed his frontal lobe, as if massaging his differential diagnosis into the language center of his brain. "They should really try him on risperidone. It works wonders with self-harm in autistic kids."

Ben tilted his head in Jenny's direction, seeking a second opinion. She'd heard that the drug could make kids sluggish, but she wasn't in a position to comment. Her medical license was only for maintaining the MD in her television moniker and writing personal prescriptions. Moreover, she didn't want to pontificate about either of her new neighbors' twins. Though she knew Jonah's diagnosis, Susan had never discussed it with her in detail. In fact, their relationship had yet to progress much past polite chatter about school functions. Jenny assumed she and Louis had been invited to go in on the Hamptons house simply because any place on the water would have been prohibitively expensive for two couples alone.

Rachel tossed a hand in the air. "Maybe they don't like the drug's side effects."

Louis shot Rachel the same exasperated look that Jenny gave her fellow anchors when they tried to diagnose Achilles' injuries from instant replays. "Or maybe," he said, "they're having difficulty finding a doctor willing to prescribe it. Doctors are gun-shy when it comes to autism. The anti-vaxxers made us all afraid of some lawyer taking us to court for developmental delays."

Rachel returned Louis's irritated expression. As a personal-injury attorney, Rachel was more likely than not to be *some lawyer*. "Doctors don't need to fear providing drugs that are FDA approved to treat particular diagnoses. If the physician has the problem correctly pegged, then he's in the clear. Unless he's been specifically alerted to another ailment that would result in a complication."

Jenny felt Louis's energy change beside her, his vibrations intensifying like a tuning fork struck twice. "Well, we should get on the road." He gave a curt wave and whirled in the opposite direction, announcing his aggravation with the conversation.

Jenny offered what she hoped was an apologetic smile. "See you at the beach."

Louis echoed her statement over his shoulder. "See you . . ." Jenny caught up to him as he trailed off, grumbling the last word under his breath. To Jenny, it didn't sound like *beach*.

CHAPTER THREE

THE DAY OF

"Do I have the right address?"

The incredulity in her husband's tone startled Susan awake. She'd drifted off watching the repetitive green blur outside the passenger window, exhausted and emotionally drained from the morning. The foliage outside had since ceased moving, but her view still seemed out of focus, a shaking Polaroid yet to reveal a real image. All she could see clearly was Jonah sprawled on the dirty sidewalk, his flailing legs enforcing a circle of personal space, and the gawking onlookers who had surrounded the two of them, all staring as though her son had been some kind of break-dancing street performer and not a child breaking down.

Susan blamed herself for Jonah's flare-up. She should have known that the combination of the humid morning, dense crowd, and seeing his brother taking off with his new best friend, Will, would prove too much for her hypersensitive nine-year-old. But she'd convinced herself that witnessing Jamal's excited departure would ease Jonah's anxiety about his own week-long stay at "camp." As a result, Jonah had displayed the worst of his symptoms in front of their neighbor's boy and countless other families, many from their new town.

"Is this it, honey?" Nadal leaned over to inspect the screen on the SUV's console and the waving red flag announcing they'd reached their destination.

Susan shifted her fuzzy attention to the windshield. A grayed cedar structure loomed at the end of the clamshell drive. Her stomach dropped. *No. This can't be it.*

She called up the address in her text-message history and compared it to the number on the mailbox at the property's edge. It matched, though it shouldn't have. The timber-clad saltbox before her with its long rectangular sides and slanted roof was not a "luxury farmhouse." It was a barn. A plain, simple, $3,000-per-night barn.

She imagined her new friends' reactions to the building in front of them. Ben would be a good sport, as always, and she didn't know Jenny and Louis well enough for them to be anything but polite. Whether or not anyone said anything explicit, though, they'd all be thinking the same thought pulling up her husband's right eyebrow: *Why on earth did she book us here for a fortune?*

"Location is everything, right?" Nadal tried to cover his quizzical expression with a smile.

The cliché had been their real-estate agent's refrain when they'd been searching for houses ten months earlier. The woman had taken her and Nadal through a series of tiny Tudors on lots measured in square feet, each listed in the same price range as multiacre estates back home. "This isn't Washington State, sweetheart," the realtor had said when Susan had balked at the listings. "This is Westchester. You're sixteen miles from Manhattan on a commuter train line. Basically, you're moving to Mecca."

The agent had said that last part smirking at Nadal, as though her analogy had contained particular relevance for the almond-colored man considering kitchen appliances. Susan had informed her that Boston-born and -bred Nadal believed Mecca was where the Sox played. "Living twenty minutes from Yankee Stadium doesn't have the same attraction," she'd said.

Quip notwithstanding, they'd purchased one of those overpriced homes in the "right" locale. And, Susan reminded herself, so had all their new neighbors. Perhaps Nadal was right. The *barn* before her was nestled in the Amagansett dunes with direct access to the Atlantic Ocean. Surely the others would know not to expect much curb appeal, exorbitant cost aside. Wouldn't they?

Nadal turned left and let the car roll toward the forest marking the edge of the property and the inverted L-shaped driveway. Shells rattled beneath the chassis until the vehicle finally pulled parallel to a white gate leading, Susan supposed, to the backyard. She exited and squinted at the structure, hoping that the late-afternoon sunlight would illuminate some redeeming feature. The house appeared just as dour as it had through the windshield, however. Rain had weathered the siding to a drizzly gray.

The windows were small, squinty insect eyes atop a gaping barn-door mouth. The smallest panes, tucked beneath the ski-slope roof, appeared to wink at them. From the front, the home hardly seemed large enough to accommodate three couples. "It looked so much bigger on the website. Didn't it?"

A beep answered. Nadal disappeared beneath the SUV's rising hatch. He grunted from the weight of something that Susan knew couldn't be their suitcase. Her husband prided himself on his fitness regimen. Weights multiple times a week. Cardio on weekends. He woke at five daily for the gym—a fact that had once impressed her though lately had made her resentful. She couldn't squeeze in regular workouts between caring for the twins and the house. Her CEO husband was becoming even more handsome (and wealthy), while she was letting herself go.

"It has three bedrooms, three baths, an outdoor shower, a pool, and is on the beach in the Hamptons, honey." Nadal emerged, a vein pulsing in his left bicep from carrying the massive cardboard boxes cradled in his arms. "If it were any larger, it would have only been available for the full summer and cost the down payment on our house." He braced the wine cases against his chest and headed toward the door. "Don't worry," he called behind him. "Everyone knew what they were getting into."

A shrill ring emanated from Nadal's pocket. Her husband's lips parted. For a moment, it seemed he would try to shift the weight onto one arm to answer the phone—an act almost as insane as leaving a wife with a screaming child to answer an office call, as he'd done that morning.

"Honey. I know work is crazy right now." Susan forced a lightness into her voice so that Nadal wouldn't realize how angry she still was about his earlier disappearance. "But let's try to be present this week. It took a while for me to plan this, and it's important for our family to make some real friends in the area. Jonah needs people that will look out for him like we had back home, and we have to foster that. He's not Jamal."

Nor, Susan thought, was she. Though both her boys were tall, dark, and handsome, like their father, only their neuro-typical son had inherited Nadal's attractive personality. Jamal, like her husband, came across as smart *and* affable, the kind of person others welcomed onto their team and into their homes. Susan, like Jonah, was shier—or, at least, she'd become that way since her recent fiasco. To make friends, she had to plan vacations for the neighborhood.

Nadal readjusted the weight in his arms. "I know, *honey.*" The stress on the nickname turned it sour. "And I'm sorry. Again. Something came up right before we left, and I still—"

"You're the CEO of a tech start-up. Something always comes up." Susan felt the scowl parting her lips. She forced a tight smile. "It would mean a lot."

"I already promised and I mean it." Nadal returned her smile like a tennis volley. "I won't let anything spoil this week."

He started toward the house. Susan retrieved their duffle from the trunk. She slung the bag over her shoulder and then stretched to shut the hatch. The overhead motion released the acrid odor in her armpits. Stress sweat stunk worse than regular perspiration. Maybe, she thought, she could freshen up before the others arrived. Apply some makeup. Slip into a sundress. At the very least, she could assess whether or not the barn's interior measured up to the online photos. If it didn't, she couldn't back out of the rental. But she could preempt complaints with her own.

Susan hurried toward her husband as he closed in on the entrance. "I'll get the door."

Nadal wouldn't wait. He raised a knee and shifted the liquor boxes onto his left side, freeing his right arm to retract the sliding panel mounted on a thick overhead track. Behind the barn door stood another, though this one was glass, coated with a dark film to cloud the view inside. A round electronic keypad had been bolted above the handle.

Susan jostled in front of her husband to deal with the lock. As she touched the black screen, numbers appeared. She tapped in the four-digit code, an easy-to-recall "1492," the same year "Columbus sailed the ocean blue." A green light flashed around the high-tech device, followed by a welcoming tone and a whirring noise like an electric can opener.

A rattling overwhelmed the sound of the lock. Susan turned to see a familiar cherry Range Rover crunching down the driveway. She pressed the door handle. Showering before saying her hellos was out of the question. Still, perhaps she could glimpse the inside before the Murrays.

"Hey, hold the door for us?" Jenny called as she climbed out of the Range Rover. "I forgot the code you emailed. I've no head for numbers."

Susan pushed back the tinted glass in front of her. A glance inside the house revealed only a narrow hallway and the glow of a distant window. The online photos had shown a ton of natural light.

The clink of bottles called her attention back to the threshold. She turned to see the wine cases at Nadal's feet and his arms around Jenny as they said hello. "How was the ride?" he asked.

"Can't complain." Jenny separated from Nadal and extended her toned arms toward Susan. The three-hour-plus car ride had done nothing to dull Jenny's cover-girl appearance. She wore a flowing, off-shoulder shirt that displayed her pronounced clavicle and raw linen shorts revealing her long, chiseled legs. Her makeup, which Susan could tell included foundation from the uniformity of her caramel skin color, was flawless beneath her Jackie O sunglasses. If a paparazzo jumped out of the bushes to ask whether the Giants' injured running back would play next season, Jenny would be ready.

Susan's discomfort deepened at her own haggard appearance. She forced a smile and leaned into the waiting hug. "Sorry. I'm a bit sweaty from the ride up."

Jenny grinned. "Who isn't?"

You, Susan thought. Unless, of course, Jenny's natural

BO smelled of gardenias. Susan half suspected that it did. Jenny Murray was the Mary Poppins of neighborhood moms. She was TV beautiful with a body like sculpted glass, and an encyclopedic knowledge of both the human body and sports. To boot, she was painstakingly pleasant. Not once, in the ten months Susan had lived next door to her, had she ever seen Jenny evidently stressed. She'd never heard her snipe at her spouse in the backyard, snap at her daughter, or betray a hint of sarcasm in her tone, let alone raise her voice as Susan did, too often. Practically perfect in every way.

"You look great." Susan brushed the sleeve covering Jenny's bicep. "I love this blouse."

Jenny winced. The reaction made Susan feel catty for the compliment, as though she'd intended to shame her neighbor for being too done up in a casual setting. Susan hoped that hadn't been her motivation, though she couldn't be sure. Insecurity with a pinch of marital anxiety and a dash of jealousy, whipped together by a stressful morning, was a recipe for bad behavior.

Susan tried sweetening her comment. "The Hamptons is preppy chic, right? It's the perfect top for out here." She gestured toward her jeans–and–T-shirt ensemble. "I plan to shower and change into something more appropriate after we get settled. Put on a little makeup myself. We're on vacation, right?"

Jenny pushed her sunglasses to the crown of her head, revealing her soft brown eyes. "You don't need all this paint to look good."

And that, Susan thought, was why she'd invited Jenny to the Hamptons, even though she didn't know her that well and her sons would probably never befriend the Murrays' preteen daughter. Jenny, unlike so many of the other moms she'd met in their new town, didn't act as though she was too good for anyone—even though she, out of all the people in the neighborhood, could have gotten away with it.

The social hierarchy of East Coast suburban moms, Susan had learned, mimicked high school. Stay-at-homes who regularly ran out the door without their hair brushed, as Susan so often did, were the wallflowers of her new world. Harried working moms were the nerds, begrudgingly respected though not particularly admired or envied. *Ladies who lunched*, aka stay-at-home moms with staff, were the popular girls who planned lavish charity events and shared all the relevant gossip. At the top of the ladder, however, were the women like Jenny who somehow juggled successful careers and still showed at school functions and fund-raisers looking like they'd spent all day at the salon. They were the prom queens.

"Let's get the booze out of the sun." Nadal was again cradling the cases in his arms. Susan became aware of her dry throat. A glass of wine would surely take the edge off her house tour.

She held her breath as she entered with Jenny steps behind. Plasterboard, painted the stark white of a gallery, narrowed the small foyer into a tight corridor. On Susan's right, two oak slabs hung from a track like long slabs of meat. Jenny slid back the first door, revealing a crowded bathroom. The second door had been left half covering the opening, possibly because the room behind it would have made anyone claustrophobic otherwise. It barely appeared large enough for the full bed inside.

Susan caught Jenny's nostrils flare beneath her cat-eye sunglasses. "This will be fine for Nadal and me," Susan said. She'd booked the place, after all. If she'd done a horrible job, the least she could do was agree to take the worst bedroom.

Susan headed deeper into the house, her fear that she'd fallen for a scam increasing with each step. Perhaps the owners had posted images lifted from a realty site and populated their rental page with fake reviews. Could she get everyone's money back if she could prove fraud? She hadn't read the fine print on the agreement. "The photos showed a ton of windows. Where are—"

The house responded to Susan's unfinished question, opening into a great room with a double-height cathedral ceiling and a far wall constructed almost entirely of glass. Tall French doors composed the base of the transparent expanse. Above them, trapezoidal panes of graduating sizes met at a pentagonal center window. Beyond the wall, a deep sapphire pool sparkled in an emerald setting. Relief flowed through Susan's tightened throat like a good glass of cabernet.

"It's beautiful. Louis," Jenny yelled over her shoulder, "come take a look at this!"

Susan couldn't stop looking. Beyond the lawn, a patch

of scrub forest separated the backyard from a blue field of sea and sky. The beach was right there, as promised.

A doorbell rang. Nadal's voice reverberated in the high ceilings from somewhere behind her. "I'll get it."

Susan wrested her gaze from the view to take in the rest of the house. The furnishings in the great room were sparse, but elegant. A U-shaped sectional faced a brick fireplace pressed against what appeared to be the barn's original stone wall. Behind it stood a farmhouse dining table in the same pale oak as the ceiling beams. The kitchen, identifiable by its white cabinets and stainless-steel appliances, hid behind the dining area at the front of the house. It was separated from the great room by the plasterboard wall that had made up one side of the cramped hallway and a low ceiling supporting the second story.

Most of the upstairs had been left open, a loft tucked beneath the elongated slope of the saltbox's roof. Two glass panels, each of which stopped at chest height, cordoned off a furniture-less mezzanine leading to what Susan assumed were the second-floor bedrooms.

"Susan, look at this place." Ben Hansen emerged from the hallway, the strap of his bag slung between his large pectorals. He opened his arms toward her, offering a hug. She dove in for one, suddenly overwhelmed by the resurgence of her earlier gratitude when he'd carried Jonah—in full meltdown mode—from the crowd. A second into the embrace, she realized how her enthusiasm might look to Ben's wife and pulled away, awkwardly double-tapping her neighbor's back to decrease intimacy. Ben had a face that called for a camera: perfectly symmetrical with a strong nose, diamond jaw, and dark-blue eyes that appeared deeply interested in whomever they focused on. Such handsomeness made any congeniality from the opposite sex appear coquettish—probably because, on some level, it was. Susan needed to be extra careful around him, especially around alcohol. Acting too friendly, a glass or two in, had gotten her into enough trouble back in Seattle.

"So, how are we doing the sleeping arrangements?" Louis set a wine box on the kitchen counter and then huffed over to the staircase. With white steps the same shade as the walls and a single glass side topped with a near-invisible metal banister, the freestanding structure seemed to float above the concrete floor.

"We don't know." Nadal reentered the great room with Ben in tow. "The only claimed space is the wine fridge."

Louis gestured upstairs with his chin. "I'll toss these anywhere, then."

He hustled up the steps at a pace that made Susan nervous, given the staircase's open side. When he reached the mezzanine, he turned a sharp left toward the smaller of the two bedrooms, which offered an ocean view.

"Um, maybe we should ask what everyone wants to do," Jenny shouted up the stairs.

Louis looked down at her over the railing. "I want to ditch the bags, Jen. What did you stuff in here, anyway? Five outfits for every day of the week?"

Jenny's red lips pursed.

"Well a girl's gotta be prepared for anything," Susan said, gesturing to the large duffle at her hip, as though it contained only her clothing and not also all of Nadal's things. "Who knows what we might get up to? Dinners in town. Dancing. Celebrity house parties." She nudged Jenny, making clear that the celebrity to which she referred was already in the house.

"I do love my celebrities." Louis grinned at his wife, eliciting an eye roll from Jenny along with a small smile that said he'd been forgiven. Susan recognized the exchange as the kind of thing that passed between her and Nadal all the time. Someone said something to annoy the other one, the aggrieved party arched his or her back like a hissing cat, and then both people moved on. Marriage was like a poker game in that the stakes increased the longer each player sat at the table. After a dozen years with the same person, the pot became so large that no one could walk away over anything less than a monumental display of cheating. All other grievances had to be shrugged off.

"So, what are we drinking?" Rachel's voice snapped Susan's attention back from the second floor. Her neighbor strode into the great room on heeled espadrilles like a native New Yorker in midtown, oblivious to the sights around her. When she reached Ben, she made pointed eye contact, as though he were the designated bartender. "I need a large glass of something. That call was brutal."

Ben pulled the strap of his weekender bag over his head. "I'm going to put our stuff in the downstairs bedroom. My bum knee has been acting up lately. Makes stairs a pain."

Rachel grimaced at her husband's leg and then turned toward the rest of the group. "Jen, maybe you can give him another cortisone shot."

Jenny frowned. "Doctors really shouldn't inject the tissue too often. And I really shouldn't be giving shots at all since I'm not technically practicing at the moment. There's a bit of a liability issue."

Rachel doubled-slapped her husband's thigh, a jockey sending a stallion on his way. "That's why I like having you treat him. If anything happens, I know you're good for it." She headed into the kitchen. "So, what's on tap?"

Nadal crouched beside the cabinets, unloading bottles into a wine fridge. "Pick your poison, guys," he shouted. "Sauvignon blanc, Riesling, rosé. Red. Whiskey?"

The mention of a drink made Susan's mouth water. Since the move, cabernet had become her antianxiety medication. Without a hefty dose, she'd keep thinking about the twins and worrying about the bedroom sizes, obsessing over whether her husband's determined focus on the wine bottles—and not on Rachel striding toward him—was because he found their neighbor disconcertingly attractive.

"We brought champagne." Rachel glanced behind her, perhaps for Ben with their suitcases. He'd already disappeared down the hallway, though he'd left a pink-and-green-checkered bag on the coffee table that looked suspiciously like it held a bottle of something.

Red relaxed Susan best, but she knew most people didn't drink it on sunny days. "How about the rosé?"

Nadal pulled a bottle of pink wine from the open box. "Wölffer Estate it is. This is a good one. Local." He pulled a corkscrew from a drawer and slashed the paper at the top of the bottle.

Susan realized she should be making conversation and not ogling the wine like a dehydrated man before a mirage. She was a former lawyer and Rachel was still one. There was common ground to explore. "So, Rachel, you had a work call? Big case?"

Rachel was also watching Nadal. She turned her focus from him as he jammed the screw into the stopper. "I'm not out for blood or anything, but it could be. I'm hoping to settle it amicably before it goes to court and ends up a big thing in the papers."

Nadal yanked the cork out like he was mad at it. "Honey, grab some glasses."

Susan opened the cabinet above the wine fridge, the obvious location for them. A line of thick wine glasses stood on a bottom shelf. She grabbed one, realizing as her nails struck the stem that it had been constructed out of plastic. Susan slipped the stems of two glasses between the fingers of her right hand and then reached in for more. "A big thing in the papers, huh?" She raised her voice so that Rachel could hear her. "Did someone get really injured?"

Rachel groaned. "Died, actually. A nine-year-old boy."

Susan's breath caught in her chest. She imagined her sons' faces from that morning, Jamal's winning smile and Jonah's searching eyes. The wine no longer seemed appealing. "Oh my God. That's horrible." She turned her full attention back to Rachel. "What happened?"

Nadal set the bottle on the table with a hard thud. The cork was in his hand, speared through by the screw. Rachel glanced at him and then quickly shifted her gaze back to Susan. "I shouldn't even be talking about it. Attorney–client privilege. And we're on vacation, right? No work talk."

Discussing dead children, admittedly, wasn't a way to start a vacation, but Susan *did* want to know what had happened to the poor little boy. Hearing about the case had set her mind racing with all the dangers facing nine-year-old kids—dangers that she, hundreds of miles away, couldn't protect either of her twins from.

Susan set four glasses on the counter beside Nadal. "Sorry to bring up work. It's just, God, that poor boy. His poor mother . . ."

Rachel's irises blurred into a watery blue. "I know." She sniffed. "Every time I talk to her, I think of Will. It's—"

"So, vacation!" Nadal said it with forced enthusiasm, an umpire calling a strike. He lifted the wine dramatically and began filling the row of glasses. "Some view, huh?"

Rachel murmured her appreciation as Susan returned to the cabinet for two more glasses, resigned to dropping the subject. She'd asked Nadal not to bring up work. Grilling Rachel on her new case wasn't exactly playing fair.

"No wine for me yet." Susan looked up to see Jenny hovering by the wall of windows.

"I'm going to check out the beach," Jenny continued. "Tell Louis?"

Before Susan could answer, Jenny was through the French doors in the glass wall. The sound of them shutting was followed almost immediately by the slide of the first-floor bedroom door. Ben's heavy footsteps thudded on the concrete floor. The house carried sound throughout the great room, Susan realized. She hoped it wouldn't make sleeping difficult.

Susan brought a fifth glass from the cabinet, in case Louis also wanted a drink when he came downstairs. Nadal stopped pouring and handed her a glass. He grabbed his own and raised it in the air.

"To my wife." His mouth spread in a sappy smile. "I know this year hasn't been easy with the move and not having the right school for Jonah or the family help that we're used to—not to mention me working around the clock to expand the company. Yet you still planned this vacation for all of us. I hope you have a chance to truly enjoy it and relax. You deserve it."

The saccharine speech embarrassed Susan. Nadal knew that she didn't enjoy being the focus of attention. Rachel was staring at her with one of those gluey grins. Susan might have planned the trip, but Rachel—like Nadal and Jenny and Louis—had worked to pay for it.

Susan said a quick thanks and raised her own glass. "To new friends and taking a leap of faith going in on this sublet with us for the week. I hope this vacation is the first of many."

Rachel's real smile unlocked as their plastic glasses tapped together. Nadal set his untouched wine back on the table. For a second, Susan could have sworn she'd caught her husband scowling at her toast. "I should see if Louis needs a drink."

CHAPTER FOUR

THE DAY AFTER

The shore was a surreal place for a crime scene. Something about the reflection of the sky in the encroaching ocean, the way the unbroken blue above shimmered at the water's mirrored edge. It disoriented Gabby, made her feel flipped upside down.

Police tape, neon yellow in the white morning, pulled at spikes cordoning off a square area in front of a wall of black boulders. The jetty extended into the sea like the enormous fin of some prehistoric whale. Detective Jason DeMarco stood outside the designated area, identifiable, despite Gabby's distance, by the black hair shining like sealskin atop his skull. His head bobbed along to the gestures of two khaki-clad officers semi-camouflaged by the sandy landscape. County had apparently sent a forensic team.

Gabby's clunky pumps sank into the loose sand as she tried, and failed, to jog toward her colleague. Each step kicked hot grains up beneath the hem of her pants. It would have been easier barefoot. But she couldn't show up to her first murder looking like a misguided tourist.

By the time she reached the trio of officers, her calves itched from the sand pasted to her skin. She ignored the feeling as Jason introduced her to the County team as "Detective Sergeant Gabby Watkins." The addition of her full name added heft to the title, as did the authoritative tenor of Jason's dropped voice.

Neither forensic officer shook her outstretched hand as they provided their names and ranks. Gabby dropped her arm without taking offense. Both men wore bright-blue latex gloves, and touching her bare, sweaty palm could unwittingly transfer her DNA onto the body.

"She was killed late last night." Captain Dennis Lee remained standing for his explanation while his partner crouched to snap photographs of the scene with the massive digital SLR hanging from his neck. Lee was evidently the elder statesman, with his gray-streaked black hair and hooded, downturned eyes, the skin at the corners exploding with lines as he squinted in the bright sun. He also outranked Gabby by two degrees, which meant she shouldn't interrupt his update with questions.

Gabby pulled out her notebook from an interior pocket of her navy suit jacket, along with a pen. She flipped over several pages, skipping the scrawled thoughts she'd jotted down earlier that morning in Dina's house, and stared at Lee, ready to take dictation.

"We can't determine the exact time of death yet," he

went on, "because we don't know how long she was in the water. The ocean would have brought down her body temp pretty quickly. Given her location, I figure she was killed a couple hours before high tide when there was water here. So, say around midnight. Certainly no later than one."

Gabby turned her attention from Captain Lee to the victim. The woman was petite, more the size of a girl than a grown adult. She was propped up against the jetty, her head drooping as though she read an invisible book on her lap. Her silvery-blonde hair gleamed in the sunlight, long dried from whenever she'd been underwater. If police tape hadn't surrounded the woman, Gabby might have passed her by, assuming she'd simply nodded off while sunbathing in her white one-piece.

Closer inspection, however, betrayed that something was very wrong. One strap of the victim's white bathing suit had been snapped from her shoulder. Her fair skin had been rendered near translucent with faint blue lines, like cheap notebook paper. Gabby took a step toward the other side of the body in hopes of spying the signs of a water death that were so apparent to Lee. The victim's thighs, she realized, were porcelain only on top. An eggplant color crept from underneath where the blood had settled.

"Did you detect water in the lungs?" Gabby asked.

Lee said something to his younger, stockier partner in medical terms too fast for Gabby to fully comprehend. The man put his gloved hand beneath the victim's chin and raised it an inch. So many red and purple splotches dotted the neck that the pale skin between looked like a baroque pearl necklace.

"She was clearly asphyxiated, though determining whether from drowning or strangulation will have to wait for the autopsy. Judging from the size of the neck bruises and the abrasions on her knees, she was likely held underwater by a larger—or at least significantly stronger—assailant standing behind her with his palms pressing on the clavicle and fingers against her windpipe." Lee transferred his attention from the body to Gabby. "Unfortunately, she's only about your height and obviously petite, so that doesn't narrow the field much. The average American man is five foot ten and the typical female is still a couple inches taller than the victim. Overpowering her wouldn't have taken much strength."

Lee nodded decisively, as if to dismiss her. Gabby turned toward her fellow detective. Jason had been listening to the forensic expert while grinding his bottom lip beneath his top teeth. He glared at the victim as though she'd ruined his afternoon.

"Who placed the call?" Gabby asked.

Jason rotated toward the grass-covered dunes dividing the houses from the beach. A man stared at the crime scene from the sand in front of the vegetation. He was dressed for a run in a T-shirt and tight bike shorts. Gabby put his height at over six feet. His size, coupled with his apparent athleticism, heightened her senses. The man could be a threat if he wanted to be. He could hold a woman underwater.

"Nadal Ahmadi," Jason said. "Says he's renting a house with the victim, her husband, another couple, and his wife—the woman Officer Kelly is over there watching. She was pretty worked up."

A few feet behind Nadal, the shorter uniformed patrolman was sitting with a woman who must have been *the wife*. She had long mouse-brown hair and skin that was reddening in the sun. She wore shorts and a T-shirt. Her head was drooped toward her lap, perhaps to avoid seeing her friend's body.

"You said they found her on a jog?" Gabby started toward the couple, knowing that the sooner she spoke with them the better. It wasn't unusual for people who called 911 to be guilty of something, or to know more than they'd told the dispatcher. She needed to talk to them before they conferred about their story—assuming they hadn't already.

"I gather they went out around eight." Jason pointed in the opposite direction of the people. "Their rental is about a quarter mile that way."

More grains of sand sprayed Gabby's calves as she moved away from the packed sand towards the victim's friends.

Jason withdrew his own notebook from the duty belt visible around his hips. Most detectives didn't bother with the heavy getup, opting to clip their gun holster and cell phones onto a regular leather belt and pocket a couple of zip ties for emergency arrests. But Jason seemed comfortable with all the artillery around his waist, despite the added weight and the overbearing heat. Gabby was secretly glad one of them could stand it.

"The victim is Rachel Klein," he said. "The man is Nadal Ahmadi. He claims he checked for a pulse on the neck and didn't find one. His wife, Susan Ahmadi, has calmed down from earli—"

Jason abruptly stopped talking as they drew within ten feet of the pair. Gabby copied the names into her notebook, peering over her colleague's bent arm to check spelling. When she finished, she tilted her head in Susan's direction. Women often did better talking to other women, particularly when they were afraid. "You take the husband."

Gabby made eye contact with the uniformed officer and pointed to Jason, indicating that he should follow his lead. She then continued toward Susan, holding her notebook out to deemphasize the gun strapped to her hip. "Ms. Ahmadi, I'm Detective Gabriella Watkins. I'd like to ask you some questions."

The eyes that met Gabby's were noticeably dry, though the red lines snaking from the woman's hazel-green irises suggested she'd shed tears at some point. Gabby thought her attractive in a kind of girl-next-door-got-married-and-had-a-couple-kids way—the same way Gabby considered herself attractive. She and Susan didn't have the dewy complexions and Pilates bodies of many of their Hamptons counterparts. But they'd been born with a certain appeal and had more or less maintained it.

"I understand that the victim is Rachel Klein. How do you know her?"

"She's our neighbor." Susan pressed her fingers into her temples and slowly circled them, massaging away a headache. "Her son, Will, and my boys are friends. We're all renting a house together."

"You and who else?"

"Jenny and Louis Murray, our other neighbors." Susan kept rubbing her forehead.

"You all live on the same block?"

Susan lifted her left sneaker from the sand and stamped the sloped ground in front of her. She leaned over to carve an *X* with her index finger into the grains. "We moved here." She scrawled another *X* in the sand beside it. "The Murrays, Jenny and Louis and their daughter, are there." Behind the second letter, she made another mark. "Rachel and Ben live behind them with their two kids. Our backyards all touch." She coughed and covered her mouth, taking a moment before continuing. "We thought, with the kids all in camp, we could pool resources and get a house on the beach for the week."

"When was the last time you saw Rachel?"

Susan unfurled her folded legs and placed a hand on her stomach. With her limbs stretched out, Gabby could tell she was tall. If Susan stood, she'd tower over her. "Rachel was with us all last night." Susan took a deep breath. "She went out for a walk around ten."

"Alone?"

"She was—"

A second cough interrupted her, followed by a loud internal gurgling. Susan flipped onto her knees and pressed her palms to the ground, arching her back. A harsh retching followed. The sound of his wife vomiting worked like an alarm for the husband. Out of the corner of her eye, Gabby saw him shoot between the two officers, his hands already reaching for Susan. Detective DeMarco jogged to catch him.

"She's sick." The husband didn't exactly yell, but his voice was elevated. He glared at DeMarco's hand as it gripped his shoulder.

"The sergeant will handle it."

Gabby put up a hand, urging both of them to stop. She dropped her notebook and gathered Susan's brown hair off the back of her neck, keeping it from the stream of thick yellow bile splattering the sand. The sour smell reminded her of the yeasty sweat that stunk up the jail Sunday mornings.

After a minute of hurling, Susan settled back onto her haunches. "I'm sorry." Her face cracked like a porcelain doll's. "I'm so sorry."

Gabby released her hair. "I'm sorry for your loss."

Susan gazed at her as if the platitude surprised. She slumped back on the slope of the dune. "God, Will is only nine. And Chloe adores Rachel." She wiped the heel of her hand beneath her watering nose. "Ben will have to break it to them, and he doesn't even know."

Gabby dipped down to reclaim her notebook and pen from the sand. She wrote Ben's first name and then asked for the spelling of the surname *Hansen,* along with the name of the town where they all lived. Years of handling sexual-assault calls had taught Gabby that violence against women was often perpetrated by intimate partners. She'd have to check Ben Hansen for prior violent arrests.

"He'll have to get his kids from camp." Susan rubbed her sandy hands beneath her eyes, streaking grit across her cheeks. "They're in Maine."

"Ms. Ahmadi." Gabby hardened her tone. She needed the woman to stop with the kids and start in on the parents. "You said Rachel went for a walk last night around ten. Did she go alone?"

Susan put a hand over her mouth, as though she might be sick again. "Yes," she said, once she'd settled. "We thought it was a safe area."

"Her husband didn't go with her?" Gabby let a note of incredulity into her voice. Safe neighborhood or not, most of the men Gabby knew wouldn't feel comfortable having their petite spouse trekking along a strange beach, at night, by herself. Gabby's husband certainly wouldn't want her doing it—and she carried a gun.

"Ben had gone to talk to her earlier, but he'd already come back by then." Susan pointed toward the jetty propping up the victim's body. "I saw Rachel still out there while I was cleaning up the dinner plates in the yard."

Gabby continued writing, even as she realized that Susan's statement indicated something unfortunate had occurred between Ben and his wife. "What time was this?"

"Maybe just before midnight? I'm not positive."

Gabby wrote twelve AM as the "last seen" point in her notebook, along with a question mark. "So, Ben left Rachel out there?" She didn't try to hide her suspicion. If Ben had given his friends an excuse for that, she wanted to know what it was before grilling him.

Susan's greenish eyes begged for a break in the questioning. Footsteps shuffled behind her.

"They'd had an argument." The husband, Nadal, stood between Detective DeMarco and Officer Kelly. Both cops looked at him as though he'd defied orders. He ignored them, gesturing with an open palm toward his wife. "She should know, Susie, or else it won't make sense." He faced Gabby. "Ben and Rachel got into a disagreement at dinner, and then Rachel went out to the beach for some air."

Gabby checked her notes. "For two hours?"

"I think they were both embarrassed at having argued publicly," Susan said. "Ben went out to apologize. I assume Rachel wasn't ready to hear it."

"What was the fight about?" Jason asked.

"It—" Nadal started, but Susan cut him off.

"You would have to ask Ben." Susan pushed her right hand into the sand to help her up. Standing, she kept all her weight on her left foot.

Gabby tried the question again. "But you heard them argue . . ."

"That doesn't mean we know what it was *really* about. Married couples fight. You should ask Ben. I'd only be guessing, and I'd rather not."

Gabby made a note to return to the subject with Susan

later, after she'd talked to Rachel's husband. "And you saw Ben return to the house after trying, unsuccessfully, to make up with his wife?"

Susan wrapped her arms around herself. "I think so. I saw him go around to the driveway. Their bedroom's on the first floor, near the front door. I'm sure he just got something from his car before going to bed." Susan looked over her shoulder toward the dunes, shielding her eyes from the sun to see her rented house. She pointed toward a line of homes visible behind a strip of scrub forest. "He's probably there now."

Gabby asked for the address and made another note on her pad. The house was one of the handful of properties grandfathered into occupying the dunes themselves. Only people with a ton of money could afford those houses. A murdered woman in the Hamptons was already newsworthy. A murdered, wealthy, blonde mom would be a front-page story. Gabby felt her jaw tighten at the thought of the attention. Rachel Klein's kids would be going through enough without the media speculating about what their dad had done. To spare them, she'd have to solve this quickly.

"You can't think Ben had anything to do with this, can you?" Susan's face crumpled like a plastic bumper in a collision. "She's his wife. It must have been someone who saw her on the beach alone and thought . . ." Susan's brown hair swished around her face from her vehement head shakes. "You saw how we found her. Her neck? Ben couldn't have. He wouldn't. God, I should have checked on her . . ."

"We have to inform him." Gabby placed her notepad

back in the interior pocket of her jacket. As she lowered her hand, she let it graze against the bulge of the Glock. She'd never pointed her gun in the line of duty, let alone shot it. But she'd also never tangled with a murderer.

Gabby waved the men toward them before gesturing to Susan. "Please, take us to the house."

CHAPTER FIVE

THE DAY OF

The Atlantic Ocean spread out in front of Jenny, a mattress topped with a rumpled sheet of blue, green, and silver. In her peripheral vision, she watched an invisible hand grasp the silken edges at the shore and raise the fabric. Each time, the cloth settled more wrinkled than the last, forcing the frustrated hand to keep lifting and lowering it. The repetitive rustle of these waves echoed the thud of Jenny's feet. Routine was the solace of the endurance athlete. She could endure anything as long as it followed a pattern.

Jenny ran along the shoreline, restoring her energy through her favorite activity. The outgoing tide had packed the sand into a semifirm clay that kept her sneakers from sinking in with each stride. As she advanced toward the jetty, the anxious energy that had accumulated in her muscles drained from her limbs. Her legs loosened. Her heart rate normalized. Her breathing steadied.

This was her release. Since childhood, the act of putting

one foot in front of another, of moving away from whatever had come before, had always made her feel better. She'd turned her coping mechanism into a competitive sport, racing long distance in high school and college. Medaling had never been her primary objective, though. Jenny ran to remember herself and regain control.

"Jen!" The sound of her name distorted the rhythm of her footfalls. She stopped and whirled toward the call. Ben emerged from a path cut into the scrub forest on the side of the house, just beyond the view of the glass wall. He cradled a paper grocery bag in his hands.

Jenny cursed under her breath. Either her neighbors were toasting and Ben was calling her back to clink glasses, or he wanted to discuss what had happened after she'd given him that last injection. The thought of doing either made Jenny want to sprint in the opposite direction. Alcohol was prohibited on her pain medication. She couldn't confess that fact, however, without also fielding questions about why she was taking pills in the first place. And that was between her and Louis.

Ben set down the brown bag to wave her over. She filled her lungs and walked to where he stood beside the bent trunk of a pine tree. "Hey." Jenny tried to sound happy to see him.

"I was wondering where you'd run off to." Ben's thin lips parted in a half smile. It was the controlled expression of a person pleased about something, yet trying to keep that beneath the surface.

Jenny turned up her palms. "You found me."

"I did. I thought after all that time in the car with Louis, you might need to settle your nerves with a run."

Jenny felt her own lips press into a line. It was one thing for her to complain about her husband—in confidence, during a moment of frustration—but it was quite another for Ben to bring it up. "Louis drove fine, actually. No weaving in and out of traffic or blasting the horn."

Ben's smile receded. "For once."

"I really only wanted to stretch my legs."

His eyes ran from her calves up to the several inches of exposed thigh. The brief look made her painfully aware of how little her husband would appreciate her seemingly sneaking off to chat with the neighborhood's "Magic Mike," as Louis referred to Ben behind his back. Ben's "job" taking care of his two kids and self-publishing mystery novels, Louis insisted, was a cover for his real role of looking attractive for—and catering to—his wife.

The sun beating down on Jenny's head seemed to get stronger. A droplet of sweat ran down the back of her neck. "Well, I should get back inside." She started toward the house.

As she passed, she felt a soft pat on her bare shoulder. "Hey, Jen."

She faced Ben, willing him not to ask what he'd been gearing up to with the pleasantries. His dark-blue eyes probed her expression. As they did, his brow pinched above his Roman nose. "Is everything all right?"

The unexpected question made Jenny feel suddenly exposed. Despite Louis's dismissal of Ben as a pretty boy toy, he wasn't shallow or unintelligent. He was strangely empathetic, in fact, with an uncanny ability to pick up on body language. She'd personally witnessed his eerie ability to read people before. Jenny forced a smile. "I'm fine."

His eyes narrowed. "Beneath your eye, Jen."

Her hand flew to the spot, betraying that she knew exactly which eye had the problem. The heat was apparently melting her makeup. She needed to slip back into the house and reapply before anyone else noticed. "Oh, that." She yawned. "All the camp packing kept me up the past few nights. Dark circles."

Ben hunched his shoulders and lowered his head to meet her gaze. "Jenny. That's not from being tired."

She was tempted to tell Ben *it* was none of his business. But she didn't want to start an entire week on a confrontational note with one of her housemates. The vacation with the neighbors, which Louis had wanted to go on so badly three months earlier, would be difficult enough without her making things any more awkward.

"Well, I don't know what you're seeing. I should run to the bathroom and check it out." She brushed past him and began jogging to the house, knowing he couldn't catch her with his arthritic knee. With luck, Jenny thought, she'd make it to her room before anyone else spied the truth written on her face.

CHAPTER SIX

Susan should have stuck with wine. Like any good Catholic, she'd first tasted it at age eight, forcing the bitter sip down her throat like expired cough medicine to satisfy her parents. She remembered her mother tapping the tip of her wrinkled nose and giggling. *It'll make you feel better in the future.* That future had arrived long ago.

Wine had become the dessert in Susan's regular diet. Since moving East, she'd gotten into the habit of uncorking a red every other day. Right after tucking in the boys, she'd fill a goblet, sit on her couch, and alternate between sipping and swirling the viscous liquid until only dregs remained.

Wine was her companion all those evenings when Nadal worked past nine. It quieted her when she really wanted to talk to someone about Jamal's impossible-to-explain "new math" work sheets, or Jonah's latest space model, or how much more taxing homeschooling an autistic child was compared to her former career as an attorney.

As her mother had promised, wine definitely made her feel better.

Champagne was not wine. Bubbles ruined the experience. They acted like out-of-control electrons, charging the liquid's surface so that it prickled her tongue, sapping the juice of its sugary, sedative qualities. Half a glass in, Susan could already feel the carbonated alcohol fizzing in her brain.

She listened to Nadal, Rachel, and Louis chat in the kitchen, painfully aware of the IQ points dissolved by her drink. What could she contribute to a business conversation between people who measured their worth in quantifiable dollars? She knew nothing about the economy anymore. She barely read the newspaper. The year at home, focused on elementary homework and imparting basic social graces, had reduced her to a simpleton.

"It's definitely not imminent." Nadal eyed Rachel as he responded, though it had been Louis who'd asked whether he'd be traveling soon for an IPO roadshow. "We're considering some investment bank bids for a future offering—that much has been reported. But we're not pouncing on anything. It's been helpful to be in New York and get a real feel for how Wall Street views the company as opposed to tech investors. Those guys can be a bit exuberant when it comes to anything they can slap a *disruptive* label on. I still have to see how some things shake out before I make any moves."

"Like the insurance thing." Louis sipped his drink. Susan couldn't tell from his tone whether he'd made a statement or asked a question.

Nadal shrugged and splashed more scotch into his

tumbler, an unusual act for him given the relatively early hour. He brought his drink to the fridge, pulled back the freezer door, and palmed a couple of oblong cubes from the ice tray. Susan couldn't blame him for discussing work. Though Nadal had tried to change the subject several times, Louis and Rachel had kept bringing it back to his firm.

"I think the insurance question has pretty much been decided." The freezer shut with a decisive clap. "Doc2Go is a tech company, not a medical group." Ice cubes clinked in Nadal's glass. "We're like a ride-sharing service, but our drivers are physicians willing to make house calls. Essentially, they're independent contractors operating under their own malpractice policies. Our riders are patients willing to pay cash up front and seek later reimbursement from their health insurer."

Nadal swirled his whiskey as he answered. When he finished, he took a long sip.

"Those companies cover their drivers when they're working," Rachel quipped.

Louis raised his glass in her direction. "There you go."

Nadal set his drink back on the counter. "Bad analogy, then. Think of Doc2Go as an interactive directory or online marketplace." Though Nadal sounded measured as always, Susan caught a flash in his dark eyes as he stared at Rachel. "Doctors who use it have their own malpractice insurance to compensate for any unintentional pain and suffering."

Louis stared into his glass as if tea leaves had settled into the bottom. His eyebrows shrugged as he took a swig.

"Doc2Go also helps the whole system by keeping people

with minor issues from clogging emergency rooms." Again, Nadal gestured to Louis. "You're in the ER. You know that—"

"Hey, you don't have to convince me of the premise. I've used it, as you're well aware." Louis set his glass down and drummed his fingers against the sides. "I think, though, in the rare instances when something unforeseen happens, the company that matched the doctor and patient should share the cost of remedying the situation, the way a hospital does. Doc2Go *is* taking part of the doctor's fee, after all."

Nadal rubbed the side of his nose with his knuckle. Susan understood the scratch to be a display of annoyance. Doc2Go was Nadal's other child, conceived without her and, Susan suspected, loved more because of the lack of outside input. He'd invented it, coded it into existence, and established all the necessary relationships to set it up in the world. Even with nearly a hundred people working for him, it operated according to the rules he'd programmed into its DNA and the connections he'd forged. It was as pure a legacy as anyone could ever have. As a result, he tended to take criticism of it (or the amount of time he spent with it) as a personal attack.

"Speaking of fees, this place doesn't have any for the beach." Susan walked over to her husband and wrapped an arm around his waist. "Anyone want to check it out? Jenny's already there, probably getting even more bronze." She glanced at her exposed arms, made whiter beside Nadal's brown ones. "I need some color, right, hon?"

Rachel glanced over her shoulder. "Is Ben out there?"

Susan realized she hadn't been the only person not

contributing to the conversation. Ben hadn't returned after slipping outside to retrieve more stuff from his car. "Maybe he's—"

"How much of the cost, Louis?"

Susan had been about to suggest that Ben had left to buy food. But Nadal's terse question shifted talk back to his company. "We're charging a flat fee of fifty dollars to set up the visit and process the payment," Nadal added. "That's less than ten percent of what the doctor typically makes. Hospitals, on the other hand, claim far more and often employ the physicians."

The back door opened with a whoosh of air. Susan breathed the incoming scent of the ocean and exhaled. The presence of somebody else uninvolved in the tense discussion would help break it up. Jenny or Ben could easily swing the topic toward some safe, guy-friendly arena like the NBA finals or professional golf.

Jenny stood in front of the wall of windows, pixelated by the bright sunlight streaming behind her. "It's gorgeous out there." Her backlit form doubled over to untie her sneakers.

Susan pounced on the new topic. "It's supposed to be one of the best beaches in the Northeast. Not too hot. And not too crowded, since you have to be in one of the houses to gain access."

Jenny didn't comment on whether Susan's research was right. Instead, she finished removing her shoes and headed toward the stairs, her tall, athletic form coming into focus as she strode further into the room. Still, having stared at the bright windows, Susan's eyes struggled to adjust.

Louis stood from his seat at the breakfast bar and opened his arms. Chivalry withstood a decade-long marriage, Susan supposed, when the wife looked like Jenny. She needed to make more of an effort to spruce up around Nadal.

"Hey, honey," Louis said. "How was the run?"

Jenny stopped several feet from her husband, at the edge of the staircase. "Good. I'm sweaty though. I should shower."

"Did you see Ben out there?" The change in Rachel's relaxed expression told Susan something was wrong. Rachel's eyebrows had squeezed together, deepening the lines that stamped all women past a certain age. "What happened to your eye?"

Jenny's fingertips fled to her left cheekbone. "Oh. Is it swelling?"

"It looks bruised."

Susan strained to see the cause for concern. Jenny's hand covered nearly the whole left side of her face, and she had dropped her head, too, swinging her hair over her eye like a brunette Jessica Rabbit. "It's the silliest thing. I was running and—"

"Let me see." Louis walked over to his wife, partially blocking Susan's view. He held Jenny's chin and tilted it upright. She let her hand drop, revealing a shimmery yellow patch on her brown skin that faded into a violet swath.

Instinctively, Susan pivoted to the freezer and withdrew a handful of ice. Raising twin boys had turned her into a triage officer. "Are you okay?" She scanned the kitchen for a paper towel roll. "Did you trip or—"

"That looks like a really bad bite, honey." Louis released her chin. "Maybe a mosquito or a spider. Your skin is so sensitive."

Jenny nodded. "I should put some anti-inflammatory ointment on it."

Rachel took several steps toward Jenny for her own examination. "You wouldn't think the beach would be so buggy in June. I mean, to get bit on your face? While running?"

"It's not teeming with insects or anything." Jen retreated from Rachel, withdrawing into her husband. "I'm sure I just, um—"

"It probably happened earlier and you're only now having the reaction. Blood flow and heat always makes any skin injury worse." Louis brushed his wife's hair from her face. "You should go upstairs, babe. Wash off any irritants that might be exacerbating the reaction. There's Benadryl in the front pocket of my suitcase. I'll bring you a cold compress."

Jenny bolted toward the stairs. A loud crack stopped her as she reached the mezzanine. The front door was opening.

"Hey, everybody. I got dinner." Ben's voice reverberated in the hallway.

The sound seemed to hasten Jenny's sprint to the second floor. Susan winced as she watched her run up the modern staircase, hand barely brushing the thin metal railing affixed to one side. The cement floor would not forgive a fall.

Nadal started toward the front door. "The bags might be heavy."

Susan remembered the ice freezing her palm. A roll of paper towels peeked from behind the swan-necked kitchen faucet. She peeled off a sheet, dropped in the cubes, and then twisted it into a little pouch. "I know an ice pack would be better." Susan passed the makeshift satchel to Louis.

"Thanks." He accepted it with a shake of his head. "Her skin blows up at the slightest thing."

"She does get a lot of bruises, Louis." Rachel's arms folded across her chest. "Perhaps you should look into why."

Louis started toward the stairs. "Maybe an iron deficiency, or too little vitamin C."

"Does Jenny need orange juice?" Susan shouted after him. "I can grab some in town."

"That bug must have been a big sucker. Beneath her left eye is all swollen and black." Rachel's mouth drew into a line. She gave Ben a pointed look as he came into the kitchen, communicating in the silent language of long-term partners. Susan couldn't interpret what had been said, but she knew information had been exchanged.

Paper rustled. Ben clenched the sides of the grocery bag as though it threatened to slip from his hands. He called up to Louis on the landing. "What bit her, Louis?"

"I'm an ER surgeon, not an entomologist." Louis mimicked the cadence of Dr. McCoy as he delivered his one-liner. The quip failed to elicit a chuckle from any of the concerned faces in the room. Louis shrugged like a comedian used to some jokes falling flat and headed toward the bedroom. The door clicked shut behind him.

CHAPTER SEVEN

THE DAY AFTER

Gabby followed Susan down a thin path carved through the scrub brush. Although the woman led with her right foot, her left sneaker stamped deeper impressions into the sand, emphasizing the limp that Gabby had previously noted. She wondered if the uneven stride was something new, brought on perhaps by a blister from her beach run or some injury sustained after stumbling upon Rachel's body.

The path opened up onto the side of a well-manicured lawn with a sparkling lap pool. The jewel of the property, however, was truly the house. Rhomboid and rectangular panes of glass made up the entire waterfront wall, providing an unobstructed view of the beach and, Gabby reminded herself, the approaching officers. Thankfully, there didn't appear to be anyone watching. Through the windows, she could see straight through to the kitchen, as well as the entirety of the second-floor hallway. The interior was sparsely furnished, leaving clean sight lines. There weren't many places for a grown man to hide other than in the bedrooms.

"Any guns in the house?" Gabby brushed her hand against her hip as though she were adjusting her jacket and not reminding herself of her service weapon.

"No." Susan's matter-of-fact denial surprised Gabby. Usually, New York suburbanites reacted to the question as though Gabby had asked if there were starving children handcuffed to the basement radiator. Susan's eyes went to the black grip poking out of Gabby's open suit jacket. "Please break the news gently to Ben. Whatever problems he and Rachel had, he can't have done this."

Gabby tried to see beneath Susan's apparent nausea and nerves to whatever emotion fueled her continued defense of Rachel's spouse. In Gabby's experience, relationships between heterosexual married couples divided along gender lines, with wives befriending the other women and the husbands making nice with the guys. But the way Susan was acting, it seemed that she cared more about Ben than her dead friend.

"Where is everyone sleeping?" Gabby directed the question at Nadal.

He pointed to a tiny balcony with two Adirondack chairs overlooking their position. "Jenny and Louis have the upstairs bedroom facing the water. Ben is in the downstairs bedroom, off the first-floor hallway."

Layout provided, Gabby started toward the windowed wall, skirting the lap pool. Before she reached the door, she noticed a red stain on the stone coping. She stopped beside it, then crouched for a better look. The thinness of the crimson smear didn't look like any blood Gabby had ever seen, but she couldn't be sure. She scanned the area for more. About a foot from the blemish were several squashed blades of grass, dyed a thick red. She waved DeMarco over. "Tag these," she mouthed.

DeMarco pulled a pad of Post-its from one of the pouches on his belt and bent beside the two red blotches.

"That's mine," Susan said as Gabby crouched down. The woman's already wan face seemed to turn green. "I was walking around barefoot and cut my heel."

A foot injury explained the slight limp, Gabby supposed. Though a kick to the back of the leg during a struggle would excuse it as well. She gestured to the round smart lock atop the back door handle. "What's the code?"

Susan reached over Gabby's head to the keypad. As she did, the curly hairs on the nape of Gabby's neck seemed to coil tighter. Susan was certainly tall enough to overpower a woman Rachel's size.

"One, four, nine, two." Susan paused between announcing each digit, like a lotto worker reading off the winning numbers. She expected, Gabby supposed, that someone would be jotting it down. But none of the officers, Gabby included, wanted their hands occupied with a notebook and pen when entering a strange home, one that more than likely housed a murderer.

The door swung back with a whisper, as though nothing stronger than the wind had pushed it open. Gabby's blunt heels were not as subtle. Sharp claps announced every step as she crossed the concrete floor. Officer Kelly's footfalls sounded even louder thanks to his regulation boots.

Gabby expected the noise bouncing between the ceiling beams to call all the house occupants into the main area. Instead, she was greeted with a humid quiet, as if the air were weighed down. Beneath it, she heard the hiss of water rushing through pipes, a steady respiration in the near-silent room.

"He could be washing off evidence." Gabby couldn't distinguish whether DeMarco or Kelly had spoken. Their voices were distorted, muffled by her heartbeat and the blood pounding in her head. Ostensibly, she was just notifying the next of kin, she reminded herself. She needed to calm down.

She started toward the first-floor hallway, one of the few areas of the home not illuminated by the sun pouring through the windows. As she walked, she waved for DeMarco to tail her with one hand while signaling Officer Kelly to stay back with the other. Water stopped surging through the pipes. The house seemed to hold its breath as both she and DeMarco hustled toward the closed bedroom door.

"Hello, Nadal? Is that you? Who's here?" The avalanche of questions tumbled down onto the officers. Gabby spun around to track the motion on the mezzanine. A wiry redhead had stepped into the upstairs hallway. He wore a long-sleeved dress shirt and plaid golf shorts, the picture of a prep-school product on vacation. His sun-reddened complexion paled at the sight of the uniformed officer below.

"What's going on? Susan? Nadal?" He shouted toward the bedroom door.

"Louis," Susan shouted up at the second floor. "It's about Rachel."

Louis pivoted toward the door he'd exited moments before. "Jenny, the police are here. Come out."

"The police?" The woman's voice sounded high and timid.

"If you would come downstairs." The cathedral ceilings amplified DeMarco's normal speaking voice. "We would like to speak with you."

Louis squinted down at them. "What's this about?"

"We can talk once you're both downstairs." DeMarco said. "We—"

A rumbling, like a train rushing down a track, interrupted them. In Gabby's peripheral vision, a door in the hallway slid open. She whirled toward the motion, her right hand reflexively reaching for her Glock's grip. A wall of a man ducked under the doorjamb and entered the narrow hallway.

In the dim light, Gabby couldn't see his face, but she could estimate his size: six foot five or six and around two hundred forty pounds. Loose gym shorts dangled around his knees and a white crew neck clung to the lines of his muscular torso, as if wet. He hadn't toweled off from his shower.

"Mr. Ben Hansen." Gabby hoped she got the name right in spite of her nerves. There'd been so many thrown at her in the past twenty minutes. "I'm Detective Watkins, and with me is Detective DeMarco and Officer Kelly. We'd like to talk to you."

The massive man placed a hand on the wall, steadying himself while effectively blocking her from passing. He stepped in her direction. "What? Wha—What's going on?"

His words bubbled out like his brain had not yet fully surfaced from a deep sleep. Gabby stepped back and tapped her fingers against the Glock's handle. "Let's go into the living room where we can sit down."

Gabby retreated two steps into the great room. She turned to the side, giving Ben an opportunity to pass, and allowing her and DeMarco to subtly flank their suspect. As he emerged from the hallway into the light, Gabby caught the look of confusion marring his clearly handsome face—a face, she realized, that had recently been in a fight. A red bump bulged from the center of Ben's thin bottom lip, making him appear to pout. A purple bruise glowed on his forearm, as though it had taken the brunt of a punch.

"What's this about?" Louis's question echoed above her. He was demanding to know what the police were doing in "his house."

"We'll discuss it down here, sir." The calm in Gabby's voice relieved her. She didn't sound at all like how she felt. "If you would come down."

Louis stepped toward the staircase. Before he reached the banister, a woman hurried from the open second-floor door. The first thing Gabby noticed was her skin, a bronze with a yellow-brown undertone that hadn't come from any self-tanning solution. Black people stood out in the

Hamptons because there were so few of them, particularly on the South Fork. Since moving for work, Gabby often went days without seeing anyone that resembled her.

Jenny, as the man had called her, appeared to have just woken. Her dark-brown hair was uncombed, half curly with straight pieces falling at the sides. The tee hanging over her leggings looked as though it had been scrunched into a ball. To make up for it, perhaps, she'd thrown a scarf around her neck, as if the red tie somehow made wearing yesterday's clothing "French" and therefore stylish.

Gabby shifted her attention to Louis. Though he was complying with her demand to descend the stairs, he still exuded arrogance. His head was cocked at a skeptical angle. His lips were pursed in a nervous yet disapproving kiss-off.

"It's Rachel." Susan's voice sounded even higher and thinner that it had moments before, a violin string about to snap. "We found her on the beach."

Ben squinted at the wall of windows. "Still? She can't have stayed out all night."

Though Ben didn't seem to register Susan's implication, the couple upstairs clearly understood. Louis's mouth fell open while Jenny clutched her husband's arm. "But I saw her from the upstairs balcony last night." Jenny's tinny voice trembled. "She was on the jetty."

"Come down," DeMarco repeated. "Both of you."

Louis grasped the railing with his right hand. His left remained in the air as he headed to the first floor, continuing to signal his surrender. Jenny followed him as if on a delay, descending one step to every two taken by her husband. As she reached the middle of the staircase, Gabby saw that the hand gripping the banister was yellowed at the knuckles from the force of her squeezing.

"Rachel?" Ben called up the staircase where Jenny stood, statue-still, several feet from the bottom.

"I saw her from the upstairs balcony last night," Jenny repeated, her voice stronger. "She was sitting on the jetty, watching the ocean."

"What time was this?" Gabby asked.

"I . . . I don't know. It was night. There were waves. Big swells dashing against the rocks. Could she swim?" Jenny covered her mouth with both hands. "I'm not sure that she could swim."

Ben's eyes darted from Jenny to Louis to Jason to Gabby, as though he couldn't discern friend from foe. "She *can* swim." He faced DeMarco. "She must have gone to a hotel. Did you check the local hotels?"

Gabby didn't know what to make of Ben's reaction. On one hand, he seemed genuinely distraught and discombobulated. But then, he did have a face for acting.

Gabby cleared her throat. "Your wife is dead, Mr. Hansen."

Ben raked his fingers from his temples down the sides of his cheeks. He looked at Gabby as if she'd failed to understand some self-evident truth. "No, Susan just said she saw her, and Jenny—"

"We saw her body on the beach, Ben." Nadal said. "I'm sorry."

Ben reached out to grab on to something. He stumbled as his hand clawed air on the staircase's open side. His mouth fell further open, baring his teeth. "No. No. This isn't right. It can't—"

"She was wearing the same swimsuit from last night." Susan made a hiccupping noise, half gasp, half swallowed tears. "She didn't respond when we called out to her. Nadal took her pulse."

Ben yelped like an injured animal. "No. She was right outside. How?"

"We intend to find that out." Gabby stepped beside Ben, asserting her lead of the investigation. "We'll need everyone to come down to the station and tell us when they last saw Ms. Klein, and anything else that you can remember from the prior night."

"But she was just here." Ben spoke with his hand covering his mouth. "How could—"

"Enough, Ben." Louis's pointed at the grieving man's chest. "You know how Rachel died. We heard her admit she'd been cheating. We saw how upset you were when you came back from talking to her."

Ben's mouth hung open, showcasing the scabbing back of his busted lip. His eyes widened like a choking victim.

Louis glared at him. "Just admit it. You went back out to that beach. You went out there, and then you killed her."

CHAPTER EIGHT

THE DAY OF

Jenny placed her purse in the pedestal sink, removing the pill bottles and face creams to unearth her cosmetic bag. She withdrew the tattoo concealer, purchased six months earlier to cover a nasty splotch on her shoulder, and then pulled off the top. With the compact in her left hand, she dug in the canvas satchel with her right for the smooth handle of her makeup brush. Finding it, she scraped the bristles across the compact's creamy surface. The hue on the tip reminded her of the custard pies her grandma used to make. Nothing covered a black eye like yellow.

She swapped the brush for a foam wedge and patted the color from the purple swath outward over the larger red area, stopping at the welt's chartreuse outline. Jenny fished in the bag for a small bottle of lavender face primer. She pumped a dime-sized amount onto the tip of her pointer finger and massaged it over the bruise's tender edges where the yellow concealer had not touched. The purple lotion dulled the biliverdin-tinted skin into a honey brown akin to her natural tone. Yellow to blend red and blue. Purple to blur green. She finished with a full-coverage foundation and a setting powder that was supposedly waterproof—though she now doubted it, given the failure to outlast her late afternoon jog. She'd have to be more careful about regularly freshening up in the heat.

Jenny examined the results in the mirror, smiling in spite of herself. Practice had improved her cosmetology skills. An intense examination might reveal that the skin beneath the right eye had a grayer undertone than the rest of her face. But no one would see the bruise.

A door popped open in the adjoining bedroom. Her semi-pleased reflection vanished from the mirror. In its place stood a stranger with worried eyes and a mouth pulled like guitar wire.

Louis entered with a pouch of ice and tube of arnica cream, the right choice for skin discoloration. Her husband was a good doctor—she had to give him that. He placed the paper towel of ice in the sink, beside her bag, and then wrapped his arms around her waist. His chin nestled atop her healed shoulder. "I'm so sorry, babe."

Jenny examined her husband's reflection. His fair skin had become so lined since she'd first met him in medical school. There were wrinkles on his forehead, formed from years of punctuating statements with his eyebrows; a pair of lines around his pursed lips, two parentheses highlighting the emotions that he tried to discard; and, her favorites, the starbursts that exploded from his half-moon eyes when he was happy or sad or, like now, concerned.

Facial lines told a story, Jenny thought. So many couples traded each other in as that story started to emerge, when they finally knew one another well enough to read each other's faces. Her parents had been that kind of couple, divorcing—despite two kids—simply because they'd become annoyed with one another for aging, resentful of seeing their disappointments etched into their spouse's skin. They hadn't contemplated what would come after their separation: how her mother would entertain guy after guy, none of them interested in settling down with an older woman with children, even if she did look good for her age. Nor how her father would suffer a string of divorces, each new woman robbing him of half his wealth until he'd become destitute, relying upon checks from the kids to purchase booze for uninterested barflies. Her folks hadn't cared that the routine they'd found so boring was what had made their children feel secure. They hadn't worried that that their kids might grow up feeling alone, uncertain, and abandoned, desperate to recreate the stability they'd once known.

She and Louis were not like her parents. They valued their child and their routine. Their shared history. When Jenny stared at Louis's reflection, she saw the med student with whom she'd worked through organic chemistry and the college kid who had taught her how to ice skate. The young man with whom she'd managed to furnish an apartment on a resident's budget. The husband and father who had worked twelve-hour shifts and then, as soon as he'd finished his residency, watched a toddler so that she could complete her program. She saw her daughter Ally's lanky body and auburn curls twisted with copper highlights. She saw the love of her life . . . and the man she'd betrayed.

It was so easy to convince oneself that history didn't matter, that whatever was out there was better than whatever had come before. But seeing her husband, smelling the sandalwood of his familiar aftershave, observing the concern for her in his creased skin, Jenny knew she'd made a mistake. Another man would never measure up to Louis. She couldn't leave him.

"What can I do for you?" he asked. "How can I help?"

She turned from the apparition in the mirror to face the real McCoy. "Nothing. I'm good now."

He gave her a smile that failed to crinkle his cheeks.

"No, really." She looked into his eyes, blue laced with gray like gathering stratus clouds, and tilted her head. Louis saw the signal and pressed his mouth to her red lips. Caramel flavors from the whiskey lapped at her tongue. His warm hands slipped under her shirt, grazing her stomach. He kissed her harder as he grasped the blouse's fabric and pulled it upward.

She wrenched back. "I just did my makeup, and folks will want dinner soon."

Louis bit his bottom lip and wagged his brows.

"Later," she said.

"Promise?"

"Promise. Now go." Jenny pushed his chest. "I need to fix my lipstick."

CHAPTER NINE

THE DAY OF

The flat side of the knife was reflecting the late-afternoon sun into Nadal's eyes. Susan shifted the cutlery's angle before severing the top of the strawberry in front of her, sending the glare into the center of the deck table. She sliced the fruit into four thin pieces and then scraped them into the metallic bowl overflowing with raw spinach.

She was tempted to taste one before dinner was ready, but she fought the urge and grabbed another plump strawberry. Ben had found some decent produce in the farmer's market off the highway. Given the surroundings, she supposed she shouldn't be surprised. Even the backyard where she sat, nestled in the sandy dunes, had a lushness to it. A mossy green lawn, flanked by scrub oaks, surrounded the long pool and small patio. It stopped at a swaying line of ornamental grasses, the green stems morphing into rose-colored plumes, mimicking the ombré of the house's grayed timbers behind her. Beyond it, the sea rushed toward the dunes, the large swells drawing ever closer to the undulating grass.

Susan wondered whether it would rain at some point. The air, still humid despite the waning sun, had the heavy feel of a coming storm. It had the smell of one too. There was a clean odor, as if the atmosphere had been laced with some green herb. The scent mingled with the smell of the lemon Ben had squeezed over the side of halibut roasting atop a foil bed on the grill, beside some husked corn and the baby potatoes she'd quartered.

Susan breathed it all in as she resumed cutting the remainder of the strawberries and half-listening to Louis holding court. He was relating an ER story about a man who had come in with an unknown injury. In the short time she'd known Louis, she'd heard at least half a dozen stories with the same theme. Most were interesting, though they all had the same ending of *Dr. Murray saving the day.* That was a good thing for all involved, Susan guessed— though it did make Louis seem a bit of a braggart.

As Louis talked, Susan heard the back door pop open. She looked over her shoulder to see Jenny enter the yard. Even with the sun's amber glare on her neighbor's face, Susan could see that Jenny had freshly applied her makeup.

"Hey everyone," Jenny called out. "Oh, did folks get into bathing suits?"

While Jenny had been dealing with her bug bite, they'd all donned swimwear, responding to Rachel's suggestion that they enjoy a soak in the hot tub after dinner. Susan was somewhat relieved that Jenny wasn't wearing her suit. The sporty bikini that Susan had shimmied into no longer fit as well as it had the prior year, and she wasn't eager to shed the sundress she'd layered over it, especially not after eating. Rachel, on the other hand, was clearly itching to get into the hot tub. She wore a white one-piece with a cut-out side that advertised her svelte form, despite the translucent, floral kimono hanging open off her narrow shoulders.

"I still need to put mine on." Louis waved Jenny over. She walked across the grass to the tiled area where they all sat. Instead of scooting a few inches to make room beside him on the bench, Louis yanked the belt loop of his wife's shorts, pulling her onto his lap in a playful, possessive way that Susan couldn't help but envy. It had been a while since Nadal had publicly showed the same need to have her physically near.

"I was telling them the detergent story." Louis grinned as if the so-far tame tale was a bawdy one.

Jenny groaned. "Really? Why?"

"It's one of my more amusing ER war stories."

"Horror stories."

Louis kissed the side of her temple. "It's a good thing you switched to television. You're too sensitive for emergency medicine."

"I just think it's gross."

"I've already started it." Louis turned his attention back to Rachel at the head of the table. She sat catty-corner from Nadal, whose shoulder, Susan noted, barely brushed her own even though he sat beside her.

"So, as I was saying," Louis continued. "Here we all are thinking compound femur fracture because of the way this guy is grasping his thigh through his pants and howling about a hit, you know? The *heet*. The *heet*, right?"

Susan winced at Louis's poor Mexican accent, which sounded more like Tattoo from Fantasy Island than anything remotely Spanish. She looked to Jenny to see if she took any offense. Her mouth was tight, either in disapproval or anticipation of a cringe-worthy punch line. Susan stopped dicing the strawberry, just in case the conclusion of Louis's "war story" was shocking enough to make her slice through her finger.

"So"—Louis clapped his hands together—"we get him on the table and start to cut away his jeans, sure we'll see a bone fragment protruding from the leg. Instead—get this— what we see is a third-degree burn. I mean, huge patches of white carved into this guy's thighs. The skin burned through to layers without any melanin. It's awful. And we realize this man's been talking about heat, not a hit."

In the corner of her eye, Nadal's nose flared like he smelled rotting seafood. She tilted the cutting board over the bowl and scraped the remaining fruit into the salad. "That's terrible. Poor man."

Louis shrugged, either disagreeing with her assessment or not caring either way. "We stopped the burning and saved his leg. Ultimately, he had to be transferred to a burn center for recovery. But we got the chemicals off."

"How did he get a chemical burn on his thigh?" Rachel asked.

Louis squeezed Jenny's shoulder. "Well, that's the funny part. His wife, apparently, worked as a maid in some hotel. She'd discovered him cheating and coated the inside of his jeans with an industrial-strength alkaline laundry powder." Louis suppressed a laugh. "Sure showed him. If it weren't for his boxer shorts, she would have burned his balls off."

Rachel snickered. Susan followed suit out of a sense of politeness, despite failing to find the humor in a man nearly losing his leg. Her halfhearted snort clearly wasn't convincing, because Jenny began shaking her head at her husband. "See? You turned everyone's stomach. Right before dinner."

Louis's stormy eyes shimmered. "Oh come on, babe. It's a crazy story. Tarantino couldn't make that up."

Ben frowned, and pointed at Louis with a metal spatula. "Spousal abuse is a real riot, Louis. I hope the perpetrator ended up in prison."

"Hell if I know." Louis stifled another laugh. "I was busy saving the cheating bastard's leg from amputation."

Rachel rose from the table to grab the near-empty bottle of wine at its center. She tipped it upside down into her glass, adding a swallow to the drop above the stem. "Oh, lighten up, Ben. You should be taking notes for your mystery series." She gulped the last bit and then smacked her lips together. "I bet that story would fly off the shelves. *Death by Detergent* by Ben Hansen. Inspired by true events."

"I want a cut," Louis laughed.

"Well, it would only be fair," Rachel said, smiling. "The woman can't profit from her crime. Son of Sam law. The doctor and his author neighbor, on the other hand . . ."

"Fish is ready." Ben pulled the salmon off the grill and plated it on a waiting plastic platter. "Hopefully some of you still have an appetite."

Rachel traded her wine glass for the empty bottle. "We should refresh this. What goes with fish? A nice white, right?" She waved the recycling at Nadal. "Help me pick one?"

Nadal glanced at his own empty glass. "The California Chardonnays are all fair game. I brought a white Burgundy that's better for later in the week."

Rachel pointed the bottle at Nadal like a rifle, staring down its slender neck. "The fact that you can distinguish between Chardonnay and white Burgundy alone proves that you, sir, should be in charge of picking the bottle for dinner."

Nadal's hand glided atop Susan's own, resting on the cutting board. "Hey, hon. You know the dif—"

"Your wife's busy chopping strawberries, for goodness' sake." Rachel's tone switched from teasing to scolding.

Nadal looked down at the bench that he straddled. Reluctantly, he set his whiskey on the table. Rachel's smile stretched into a Cheshire cat grin. "We'll be right back."

Susan watched Rachel strut back to the house with Nadal in tow. Rachel couldn't really need that much help with the wine. Though she might not be able to distinguish between a California Chardonnay and a French Burgundy by taste, Rachel could certainly discern the difference between a label reading PRODUCT OF CALIFORNIA versus one proclaiming PRODUIT DE FRANCE. So why had she wanted Nadal to come with her so badly?

Susan glanced at Ben for clues as to the real reason. He watched his wife reenter the house, deep-set eyes shadowed by his lowered brow. Was he concerned? Was Rachel trying to make him jealous? Susan silently chided herself for the thought. She'd never make friends if she let her insecurities keep her on the lookout for flirtation. Given her own history, she was probably projecting anyway.

"Bring out some balsamic vinegar, too? I think I saw some left in the fridge door," Susan shouted over her shoulder, keeping her tone nonchalant. "If it's expired, maybe grab the olive oil and mustard Ben bought, and a fork? I can whisk it together with a splash of white wine to make a dressing."

"Will do," Nadal answered.

A spinach leaf folded over the edge of the mixing bowl in front of her. Susan plucked the piece from the side and popped it into her mouth. It tasted like green cellophane.

"What are the boys doing at camp?" Jenny asked.

Susan made eye contact with her, acknowledging the question while pointing to the salad bowl. She covered her mouth with her hand, not wanting to treat her neighbors to the view of mashed spinach undoubtedly between her teeth. "Every sport on the planet for Jamal, including water skiing. Jonah has water skiing and some soccer practice. His camp also focuses on occupational therapies—social interactions, team building, that kind of stuff. It'll be good for him."

"Occupational therapy can really work wonders." Louis's voice dropped a decibel, as though he were giving her a diagnosis.

Susan didn't want to hear one. She plucked another baby spinach leaf from the lip of the bowl, distracting herself from the line of questioning. Someday, she hoped people would ask about Jonah in the same way they inquired about Jamal, focusing on the things he did well and not the ways he could improve.

"Do you think you'll keep homeschooling?" Louis asked.

"I don't really have another option at the moment." Susan rubbed the spinach stem between her thumb and forefinger, twirling the leaf like a pinwheel. "The private schools here won't take a child with an autism diagnosis. And the public school would place him in special education classes, which would be a disaster for him. He's well above his grade level academically. He just gets overwhelmed from too much stimuli. He can't handle too many strangers or loud noises. But he's working on it. They'd mainstreamed him when we'd lived outside of Redmond."

Louis nodded, his face a mask of seriousness and concern. "Is he taking risperidone?"

Susan closed her eyes for a beat so Louis wouldn't see them roll. The moment he'd started asking about Jonah, she'd known the conversation would turn to medications. Doctors thought pills and scalpels could solve nearly any problem. "It makes him very sleepy." She spun the spinach leaf into a blur. "He has such an active mind, and we didn't want to sedate it to mush."

"Maybe a mild—"

"He's a great kid," Ben interjected, shutting off the grill's

gasoline. "Bright. Will's always saying he'll be first to colo-
nize Mars."

Ben Hansen to the rescue. Again. Susan allowed her
eyes to travel up his superhero physique to his chiseled face.
She grinned at him. Finally, someone was willing to treat
her kid like a human being and not a medical experiment.

"I'm not used to talking about Jonah's diagnosis with
non-family members." She let the leaf tumble to the table.
"But it's important for our friends to understand so that
their kids get where he's coming from and can overlook
some of his difficulties to see what he's really great at. I
appreciate how nice your children are to him." She looked to
Jenny. "Ally always waves to him in the backyard and asks
about his day. She treats him like a younger kid next door,
which he is." She transferred her attention back to Louis.
"That's really all he's looking for. All we're looking for."

Louis pulled his thin lips into a tight line. Susan gathered that he wasn't accustomed to his free medical advice
not being appreciated. But people—with or without a medical license—needed to understand that her son should be
accepted for who he was, not who she or anyone else might
want him to be.

A broken air seal shattered the tension. Nadal closed
the door behind him with his free fingers. He carried a
stack of paper plates topped with cutlery in one hand. The
other held a wine bottle. "I'm starving." He dropped everything on the table save for the Chardonnay. That he placed
in the middle like a centerpiece. It had already been
uncorked.

Had he shared a glass with Rachel inside? Again, Susan admonished herself for worrying about flirting. So what if he had? It didn't matter. What mattered more, she told herself, was that he'd forgotten the dressing. The spinach salad would be inedible without it. That, she told herself, was the reason for the tightness in her chest.

Ben glanced toward the backdoor. "Where's Rachel?"

"She got a call from Chloe, said to start without her."

Ben scratched at the shimmer of gold along his jawline. "Is something wrong?"

Nadal settled back into his former seat. "First-day jitters, maybe?"

Worry drew down Ben's mouth. He tried to cover it with a forced smile as he brought the fish platter over to the table and sat down on Susan's other side, opposite Jenny.

"Be right back." Susan used her husband's shoulder for leverage as she rose. "Somebody forgot the dressing."

"Rachel was supposed to bring out the rest," Nadal said.

"Well, since she's on the call, I'll just grab it." Susan headed toward the house, stopping for a moment at the back door to punch in the lock code. As she entered, she could hear Rachel's voice rising and falling in the hallway.

"Who is it, though? Did you see her?"

Susan shifted her weight to the pads of her feet before continuing toward the kitchen. There was a harshness to Rachel's tone reminiscent of how Susan sounded right before she shouted or started mentally ticking off the minutes until five o'clock *happy hour*. She knew better than to interrupt the person making that voice.

"What do you mean, you didn't see her? You saw the kiss, didn't you? How could you really not see her face?"

Rachel sounded even louder in the kitchen. Susan could hear her pacing on the other side of the wall, her sandals slapping the concrete floor. Susan opened the pantry door like it was the electrical panel of a bomb, pulling it back a centimeter at a time to avoid it squeaking.

"All right. No. Honey. You're right. I don't mean to get upset with you. I'm not upset with you. I'm glad that you told me. You were right to do that. It's just upsetting to hear."

A stuttering inhale penetrated the wall. Susan froze with her hand wrapped around the dark bottle of balsamic. Was Rachel crying? Did Rachel do that? Everyone did under the right circumstances, Susan supposed, though she couldn't imagine what those circumstances might be for a woman that seemed to have it all: healthy children, handsome husband, high-powered career that even helped people. She grabbed a bottle of olive oil and began looking for a small glass dish to whip her dressing in, excusing her eavesdropping as a desire to be of use. If Rachel needed someone, she could offer a listening ear. Being there for someone when it was uncomfortable or difficult was the difference between friendliness and real friendship.

"You think she's a mom at school or just in town? Uh-huh. So you've never seen her at any of your school events? Maybe? Well, what is it, Chloe? Is it that you don't want to tell me?" Rachel's voice raised to a decibel below a shout. "No. I know. I'm sorry. I love you. I love you so much, you know that, right, honey? This isn't about you. It's about your father."

The back door slammed shut. Nadal strode into the room, an annoyed look on his face. Susan grabbed a glass dish and closed the cabinet door. "Sorry. It took forever to find this balsamic." She said it more for Rachel's benefit than to give Nadal an excuse for her delay.

Nadal went to the cabinet by the wine fridge. "I should probably bring out a few more wine glasses, too."

Susan squirted the balsamic atop the pale-green oil she'd poured into the glass bowl. As she did, she gestured with her head to the wall. Instead of Rachel's voice, she heard the harsh rumble of someone pulling the sliding bedroom door. "Rachel's crying," Susan mouthed.

Nadal's eyebrows pinched together. He shook off the expression and resumed grabbing glasses from the cabinet.

"Should I—"

Nadal interrupted her murmured question with a sharp shake of his head. He started toward the back door. "People are waiting to eat. Let's go before the food gets cold."

CHAPTER TEN

THE DAY AFTER

The police station had only two interview rooms. After fingerprinting all the houseguests—ostensibly to rule out any prints not belonging to Rachel's *unknown* assailant—Gabby told Detective DeMarco to place Ben Hansen in "Interrogation One." The room was a closet-sized space with gray walls, griege carpet, two chairs, and a single slate-colored table bolted to the floor. The desk had two handles on it for cuffing suspects to the furniture—though the detectives didn't typically advertise that fact to "visitors" without bracelets. Gabby figured she might mention it to Ben. Since Louis had publicly accused him of murder, there was little point pretending that he wasn't a prime suspect. He'd be anticipating a grilling. She might as well show him just how hot the fire could get.

She led the other couples to the "soft" interrogation room. A homely space, it had been modeled after a family sitcom set in hopes of putting victims and their loved ones at ease. The room contained a taupe couch and a floral easy chair, probably picked up at an estate sale. The walls were nonthreatening neutrals.

Gabby didn't plan to interview the neighbors as a unit. But she did think it all right—perhaps even beneficial—to leave them as a group under the glare of Officer Kelly and a mounted camera. If they talked about the case, she'd have everything recorded.

Gabby pulled back the door and waved the foursome inside, hanging back to watch how they chose their seats. Louis entered first, holding his wife's hand. He led Jenny to the sofa, subtly guiding her to the inside seat against the armrest, furthest away from Officer Kelly's position by the door. As Jenny assumed her designated place, she hung her head low so that her hair fell into her face. Louis stood beside his wife, partially blocking her from view, as Nadal and Susan perched on the opposite side of the couch. When they sat, Susan leaned into her husband as though she might not be able to hold herself up. He put his arm around her shoulder and squeezed her to his side.

"We would appreciate if you all would stay here while we talk to Mr. Hansen," Gabby said. "I will be back shortly to answer as many questions as I can."

Louis stood straighter. "You're not going to let Ben come back to the house with us, are you? He's a murderer."

Gabby held up a hand. "If there is any evidence to support that Ben hurt Rachel, he'll be arrested. But we have to talk to him first."

Louis patted his wife's shoulder, apparently satisfied by

the statement. Jenny shuddered at the touch, or, perhaps, at the possibility that she'd been sleeping in the same house as a murderer. She adjusted the bizarre scarf around her neck so that it covered nearly to her chin.

Gabby made eye contact with Officer Kelly and then glanced up to the corner of the room with the camera, reminding him they would be recording all interactions. He followed her gaze a little too obviously, though without eliciting an apparent reaction from the group. Louis was, thankfully, still gazing at Jenny's lowered head, and Susan's face was nearly buried in her husband's side. Only Nadal was staring at the officers as though anticipating his coming interview.

As she pushed the door shut, Gabby's phone vibrated against her leg. She checked the caller ID while striding down the linoleum hallway to Interrogation One. "Bae" was calling. In spite of the seriousness of her circumstances, Gabby felt a smile crack her stern expression. She'd altered the nickname for her husband several weeks earlier to tease her daughter, who'd been using the moniker to refer to the baby-faced ballplayer who had escorted her to junior prom. As Derrick often joked: *Teenagers. If you can't beat them (and you really can't nowadays), mortify them.*

"Hey, Deuce." Gabby had called her husband by that nickname since high school, when he'd been on the baseball team playing under the number two. As terms of endearment went, it wasn't much more mature or original than Kayla's "Bae." But she'd chosen it at eighteen, and it had stuck. Derrick had even had the number tattooed on his bicep. "What's up?"

"When you getting home tonight?"

Gabby felt her smile fade as she strode down the hallway. "The way things are going, I'll be lucky to make it home at all. A woman was found dead on the beach this morning. It's looking like murder."

The speaker crackled with Derrick's exhale. "Man. Okay then. We'll discuss it later."

Gabby stopped walking. Summer was the busy season for Derrick's landscaping company. He wouldn't have called her in the middle of the day to talk unless it was important. "What's up? Did something happen with Kayla or Dan?"

A heavy sigh confirmed her suspicion. Gabby felt the surge of motherly panic that always accompanied phone calls about her kids. Police work had made her hyperaware of the threats to women, particularly young ones who pretended to act grown like Kayla, as well as the dangers of binge drinking, which college sophomores like Daniel were apt to do. "What happened?"

"Don't worry. I don't want to bother you while you're dealing with all this. Just know that Kayla is fine and under house arrest. We can discuss appropriate sentencing later."

The panic receded. Kayla was home and Derrick was handling it. No doubt their daughter had lied about something boy-related. Derrick had always been strict when it came to dating and curfews, but he was particularly so with

Kayla, allowing her only on group dates to public places. Her husband remembered too clearly how he'd gotten Gabby pregnant the summer before her freshman year of college, leading her to defer acceptance to the University of Michigan and ultimately withdraw.

Gabby resumed walking. "She went on a solo date or something?"

"Remember how she said she was going to Zoe's house? I found her at this party." Derrick's voice rose on the other end of the line, his anger at their daughter's lie returning. "But don't worry. You have enough on your plate. We'll talk later. Love you."

She turned left from the hallway into the room of gray cubicles and computer screens where the detectives filled out their paperwork. The door to Interrogation One was at the end of the room, closed and locked like a jail cell. Derrick was right. She had to focus on the possible murderer behind that door and not her teen's latest indiscretion. "All right, later. And love you too."

Gabby pulled back the door. Ben sat behind the bolted desk positioned perpendicular to the exit. The handlebars for the cuffs flanked his free hands. His eyes were bloodshot, even more so than earlier. Gabby thought his split lip looked worse, too, as though he'd reopened the wound by chewing on it.

She glanced at the camera mounted in the room's far corner, above the edge of a one-way mirror facing the desk. The camera sent a live feed to the adjacent room where Detective DeMarco sat behind a television-sized monitor, watching the proceedings that he could also see live by gazing through the window. They'd agreed that she'd take first crack at Ben. If her tactics didn't get him talking, DeMarco could relieve her.

"Mr. Hansen." Gabby assumed the seat across from him, adjusting it so she wouldn't directly block DeMarco's view. "Obviously, your neighbor made some pretty serious accusations earlier that we need to discuss."

Ben folded his hands together. "It wasn't like Louis said."

"Well let's get this over with, then, so you can tell me what he got wrong. You have the right to remain silent. Your custody officer has informed you of your Miranda rights, correct?"

Ben rolled his eyes.

"You have to speak aloud for the camera. Do you understand these rights?"

Ben looked over her shoulder to where the camera was positioned. "Yes. I understand my rights."

Gabby shifted in her chair, turning slightly sideways so that her legs wouldn't brush Ben's far longer ones. "You understand your rights. Good. Now, tell me about this argument with your wife."

"Louis is lying about me going back to the beach." Ben leaned over his folded hands. "He started the whole fight, actually. Maybe that's why he's saying these things. He's angry that—"

Gabby held up a palm. An interrogation was not an exchange of information between equals. She couldn't let

Ben settle into storyteller mode and ramble on about some beef he'd had with the neighbor. It was necessary to interrupt him. Throw off his rhythm.

"How did the fight start?"

Ben mashed his lips together. "I don't know. Jenny had something on her face that . . ." Ben ran his right hand over his forehead. "It doesn't matter. The point is, I didn't hurt my wife. I would never have laid a hand on Rachel, or any woman." He looked directly at her, dark-blue eyes pulling like a riptide. "I am *not* an abuser."

Gabby shrugged. "I don't know what you are, Mr. Hansen. But I know what your neighbors think you did. They say you got into a public argument with your wife, one devastating enough for her to run out to the beach, by herself, and stay there for hours. Afterward you went out to talk to her and she sent you away. Then, you tried again—"

"No, I didn't. Louis doesn't know anything." Ben leaned farther over the table. "I went out once to talk to Rachel a bit before midnight, when Louis and Susan saw me. I left my wife, alive, on that beach. I swear. I'll take whatever lie detector test you need to prove it."

Gabby motioned for him to settle back down into his seat. "Where did you go after talking to her?"

"I drove to a bar called Pharaoh's Place, down the block. Had a drink."

"How long were you there?"

Ben's eyes shifted from her. "I don't know."

Gabby settled back into her chair, as though *I don't know* were a completely acceptable murder alibi. "Well, that's all right. I can check with the bartender there and the traffic cam in front of the place. I'll see how long you were at that bar, and if you left soon after arriving. It won't look good for you if you did, though. It'll seem like you were trying to create an alibi. It'll seem like you planned everything."

Ben made a grunting sound like he'd been tackled to the ground.

"You know that saying, *Intent is nine-tenths of the law*," Gabby continued. "There's some sympathy for a crime of passion. Husbands and wives argue. Emotions run high. Sometimes, things get out of hand. I'm married. I get it. Premeditated murder, though." Gabby winced as though she could see the dirty prison cell Ben would soon be occupying. "That's life imprisonment without parole. Even the death penalty. New York still has one, you know."

"I didn't hurt my wife," Ben said firmly.

Gabby gestured to his split lip. "How did you get that?"

He shook his head.

"You don't know again? That's okay. I have a theory. Your wife admitted during the course of an argument, in front of your friends, that she was sleeping with someone else. You went out to talk to her, maybe get her to apologize and beg your forgiveness. But it didn't go that way. So you walked off, hoping to calm down. Maybe you even went to the bar, thinking a drink would take the edge off. But it didn't. She'd slept with someone else. That's a huge betrayal. I get it. So you went back out there to really lay into her. And things got out of hand." Gabby pointed at Ben's puffy bottom lip. "Maybe she popped you in the mouth, and you saw red. Maybe she was defending herself—"

"I didn't hit my wife!" Ben's shout broke his composure. Sobs shook his broad shoulders. "I was in the bar for twenty minutes. Some Irish college girls started chatting me up, said there was a party." He rubbed his hands over his reddened cheeks. "I shouldn't have gone. But I was thinking, well, if my marriage is over, then what's stopping me?"

Ben puffed his cheeks and exhaled. The blood rushing to his face gave him a boozer's complexion. "I get to the party and start drinking. About an hour in, I'm talking to this attractive woman. She's young, but I'm thinking twenty-one, at least. Next thing I know, this guy, almost as big as me, is grabbing my arm and throwing a punch, shouting that she's sixteen. He's threatening to have me thrown in jail for serving minors, like it was my party." The flush on Ben's face deepened. "My daughter's thirteen, so I get where he was coming from. But this girl didn't look her age, I swear."

Gabby felt her tongue start to protrude from between her lips, the way it often did when she was puzzling out a connection. Mariel had told her about two men fighting at a party and a man threatening to call police about underage drinking. It seemed Ben had gone to the same place. "Was there a pool at this party?"

The bones in Ben's neck bulged beneath his skin. "God, I can't tell my kids what I was doing while their mother . . ."

"Was there a pool at this party?"

Ben looked confused, as though she'd suddenly asked

his astrological sign. "Yeah. I was just talking to girls. I never touched that teenager, either. Once the guy told me, I left. I was back at the house before two AM. Rachel wasn't there, but I thought she'd gone to a hotel or maybe gotten a car service back home. I never . . ."

A cough cut him off. Ben covered his mouth and rubbed his knuckles beneath his nose. As he did, Gabby examined his hair. It was dark blond and silvering on the sides. Graying—or *gris* as Mariel had said. She wondered whether Mariel would be able to identify him as one of the men at the house.

"Where was this party?"

Ben sniffed. "A few blocks from where we're renting. Pepperidge Lane, I think. I don't remember the exact address, but I'd know it if I saw it."

Gabby didn't need Ben to show her the house. If the party really was the same one Mariel and Fiona had been at, Fiona would be able to tell her the address. She pushed her chair back from the table. "I'm going to check on your alibi, Mr. Hansen. And you're going to hang tight here while I do." Gabby gave Ben a hard stare as she stood. "For your children's sake, I hope you're telling the truth."

She locked the door behind her and then moved into the neighboring room. DeMarco rose from the single chair behind the monitor. "You believe him?"

Gabby didn't know how to answer. Ben seemed distraught and confused, but maybe he was simply a good actor. "You need to interview the others, individually," she said, ignoring the question. "They'll probably claim to have been sleeping with their spouses all night, but press them on the timing. We need to know whether they all went to bed around the same hour or if they staggered in at different times. We need to know how much folks drank and get a sense of how aware they would have been of their environment—if anyone heard, or would have heard, the front door opening and closing. Tell Kelly to babysit the others in the chief's office while you're doing the one-on-ones." Gabby held up a finger. "And, most importantly, don't let anyone leave."

DeMarco's near-black irises reminded her of coal briquettes. They seemed to smolder as he dragged a hand over his slicked hair. "While I'm interviewing everyone, what are you going to do?"

The attitude fueling his question was evident. She was handing the junior detective a lot, and a ton of subsequent paperwork. But his job wouldn't be as difficult as hers. His interview subjects, after all, were already in the station house.

"I'm going to track down that party, detective." Gabby met DeMarco's steel stare. "I'm going to confront a possible rapist. I'm going to uncover every detail about that fight. And I'm going to determine whether Ben Hansen could have killed his wife."

CHAPTER ELEVEN

THE DAY OF

Jenny watched Nadal head in for more wine glasses, wishing she had some excuse to keep him outside. Three was an awkward number of people to leave together, especially when two of them were Ben and Louis.

"Nice piece of fish." Louis's compliment conveniently left out Ben's effort in preparing it. He grabbed the spatula from beside the dish and cut into the center of the halibut. Steam released, carrying the scents of lemon and salt as he placed a slice on Jenny's plate.

"Perfectly prepared," Jenny added.

Ben acknowledged the compliment with a slow blink. "I heard you got a bruise?" he said to Jenny.

"Bug bite." Louis didn't look up from plating the white fish. But Jenny caught Ben's eye roll.

"Strange. It's near dusk now." Ben gestured to the gold-tinted scenery. "I have yet to feel a mosquito."

Jenny returned Ben's probing stare. "I was on the beach."

"You'd think they'd breed in there." Ben indicated the scrub forest on the side of the property. The squat oaks twisted between each other's limbs, linking to form a dark-green privacy hedge. Ben was right. If there'd been biting insects, they'd have swarmed from the side yard to feast on them already. As it was, Jenny couldn't detect any bugs save for cicadas, the hum of which was barely audible beneath the ocean's crash.

"Well, sand flies breed in sand." Louis brought a forkful of fish toward his mouth.

Ben served himself a section of the fillet while continuing to stare. Jenny could feel his eyes scraping the layers of foundation from her skin. "Does it hurt?"

"It's fine." Jenny eyed her fillet like it was a cadaver. She carved off a piece with the back of her fork. "I'm sure it looked bad because I was flushed. I don't feel anything."

The back door opened again, and air filled Jenny's lungs. The presence of the other houseguests would distract Ben from his interrogation. "Hey," she said, "you have to try this." She turned to see Susan and Nadal striding past the pool. "Ben's a grill master."

Louis tensed beside her. In her effort to distract Ben from her face, she was flattering him too much. Jenny brushed Louis's leg with her bare calf, apologizing for overdoing it with the suggestion of coming physical affection.

Nadal placed several wine glasses at the center of the table. He then stepped over to the far end of the bench and sat, stretching to dish out some fish. "I never became proficient with the grill," he said, cutting off a decent chunk of the plated halibut. "Susie's the grill master, baker, and salad creator in our family."

Susan carried a small glass bowl to the table. Gelatinous blue-black blobs of balsamic floated in sparkling oil. In the amber glow, the concoction reminded Jenny of the lava lamp in Ally's room. She'd gifted the psychedelic light to her daughter on her last birthday, a glowing middle finger to the pastel decor Louis had selected for his little girl.

"I'd happily relinquish my titles to anyone that wants to take them over." Susan slid onto the bench beside Nadal and then scooped a large portion of salad onto her plate. She drizzled the oil over the spinach leaves. "I taught Jonah and Jamal how to bake recently. Edible science class."

Susan's motherly presence calmed Jenny. She felt the muscles between her shoulders loosen and her blood pressure recede. Everything would be fine. They'd talk about the kids for an hour, and then, as soon as everyone finished eating, Jenny would excuse herself, blaming her early exit on the antihistamines to reduce her bite's swelling. Everyone knew that Benadryl wiped folks out.

"Did you need to take painkillers?" Ben's voice. The blood rushed back to Jenny's head like she'd stood too fast. She felt Ben's gaze pulling at her, an outgoing tide dragging her down. "I mean, any bruise that requires painkillers is a bad injury, right?"

Louis stabbed a potato, his eyes finally focused on their neighbor. "Fortunately, she's married to a doctor."

"Fortunately, I am a doctor." Jenny glared at Ben. "And I'm fine."

"Fine." Ben pushed back from the table, moving the entire bench with Nadal and Susan on it. "I need another drink." He looked to Nadal. "Want anything?"

Susan's eyes darted from Ben to Jenny to Louis, then to the full wine bottle on the table. "I've probably had too much already." She chuckled. "The dangers of day drinking."

Ben didn't laugh at her attempt to lighten the mood. He started toward the house, body puffed up like a linebacker looking to throw someone to the ground.

"Hey, Ben." Louis chuckled as he called out their neighbor's name. Jenny braced herself for whatever words came next, aware that no interruption on her part could block their assault. "Maybe when you go inside you should ask Rachel if *she* wants anything. You know, pay attention to your wife, instead of staring at mine."

Glass shattered. Ben stepped to the side as though Louis had thrown something at him other than the insult. As he did, Jenny saw Rachel. She stood on the strip of tile separating the pool and the lawn. Dark splotches stained her light-colored kimono. Shards of glass shimmered on the pool coping beside her sandaled feet.

"Don't move." Susan shot up. "I'll grab a broom."

If Rachel heard the instruction, she didn't show it. She charged ahead, refusing to stop despite the broken wine bottle in the grass. "What's going on?"

Jenny's heart raced. Rachel was on the attack.

"Are you okay?" Ben stepped toward his wife.

"You're flirting with Jenny now?"

Ben's chin retreated to his throbbing Adam's apple. "What are you talking about? You're misunderstanding."

"No. I think I understand perfectly." Rachel looked at Ben as though he were rotting in front of her.

"I was looking at Jenny's brui—"

"I don't care!" Rachel shouted. "You know what? I don't care about any of it. I don't give a shit who you look at, or what you do, or who you did. I don't. Because you know what I realize, Ben? You don't do a damn thing for me."

"Are you kidding me right now?"

Rachel rushed toward her husband, stopping centimeters away. Spitting distance. She tilted her head up, a furious David daring Goliath to use his height and weight against her.

"Nothing," she sneered. "You do nothing for me. I support our entire family while you're at home doing God only knows with—"

"What are you talking about?" Ben retreated from his wife. "Did you drink too much or something?"

Rachel's kimono billowed behind her. "Me! Drink too much. You think you can blame—"

"I'll tell you what I do for you, Rachel. I care for our family while you are at work. I take the kids to school and to activities and complete a million other tasks on your to-do list."

Ben threw his hands out, shifting from defense to offense. Louis jumped up, but Jenny grabbed his arm. Her husband taking Rachel's side would only make things worse. Ben wouldn't hit his wife, Jenny was sure of it. But he'd relish socking Louis.

"You've taken advantage of me for far too long," Rachel shouted. "Leeching off of me while—"

"I'm your husband. I took the hit in my career so that you—"

"Your career? What career?"

"Writing is a career, Rachel. Not everything is about money. A marriage isn't about money."

Rachel pushed both her hands into Ben's chest. "No. It's about give-and-take. And you just take. Ever since you failed at being a football star, it's all been taking and taking from me, you ungrateful asshole."

Ben stared down at his diminutive challenger, clenching his fists. Nadal stood from the table and walked toward him, palms up, arms extended, a crisis counselor approaching a man on a ledge. He glanced back at Susan. "Hey, I think we should all calm down—"

Ben focused back on Rachel. To Jenny, he looked like a man about to lay bare everything weighing on his mind and his soul. *Please, shut up.* She tried to project her thoughts into Ben's brain, to urge him to step back from the fight and let them all try to somehow salvage the vacation.

"You know what, Rachel? I'm sorry." Ben shrugged. "I don't make you happy. Maybe you're right. I take from you and don't give back what you need. It's not fair. It's not. So feel free to go ahead and give someone else a try. It's summer. The kids are at camp. We can take a vacation from one another. Maybe it'll make the heart grow fonder. Or maybe it'll tell us something else."

Rachel stumbled back from her husband, blinking as though she'd been sucker-punched.

"We should probably all call it a night, huh?" Susan's voice sounded an octave higher than normal. "We all woke up super early to get the kids to camp this morning, and then we had those long drives. We've been in the sun all day, drinking. I barely know my own name, let alone what I'm saying right now. We should all get some rest."

Everyone was standing—except for Jenny She rose as slowly as possible, her heart threatening to break through her rib cage.

"Dr. Louis." Susan's operatic voice trembled with vibrato. "What's your professional opinion? Sleep, right?"

Louis grabbed Jenny's hand. Too rough. His fingers dug between her knuckles. She looked up at him, searching for facial clues to explain the pressure. He kept his eyes trained on Ben. "I'm all for turning in early," he said.

Rachel stepped toward her husband, a fighter returning to the ring. "Do you know what, Benjamin Hansen?" She imitated Ben's speech pattern, patently mocking him with the rhetorical question as he had done before. The way she spat his full name turned every syllable into a four-letter word. "Maybe I'll take you up on that offer." She strode to a lawn chair, ignoring the possible glass chips in the grass. She grabbed her handbag off a cushion. "Maybe I already have."

The comment hit Ben hard. Jenny watched his eyes widen in surprise, his jaw hang open. "What?"

Rachel didn't respond. She stormed toward the path leading to the beach, stomping a straight line from the lawn through the scrub grass. The setting sun turned the swath of sand between the bushes into a gold rivulet, running toward the ocean. Rachel strode atop it without a glance back for her husband. For any of them. Jenny couldn't help but feel a swell of female pride for her. Rachel didn't give second and third and fourth chances. To Jenny, she looked as though she walked on water.

PART II

CHAPTER TWELVE

THE DAY AFTER

Fiona O'Rourke was the kind of girl Gabby had warned her kids about. She looked innocent enough, thanks to a youthful, round face and rash of cinnamon freckles beneath her prairie-blue eyes. But the defiant swish of her long hair as Gabby explained Mariel's shaken condition told a different story.

"I saw her before I left. She looked fine." Fiona stretched an arm out to lean against the doorjamb, further barring Gabby from entering the modest gray house on the mansion-lined block.

Gabby hadn't demanded an invitation inside. The potential for gossip about Mariel's case was high enough given Dina's notoriety without alerting more local homeowners to the allegations. Even so, Gabby didn't relish standing on the slight porch in the afternoon heat, her hushed interview at the mercy of an easily slammed door.

"Completely fine," Fiona repeated, her head tilted at an

annoyed angle over the strap of a too-tight tank top. The door moved a centimeter forward.

Gabby placed a hand on her hip, pulling back her suit jacket in the process to bare the sergeant's badge pinned to her belt. "What do you mean by fine?"

"Grand—not like she wanted to go home." The young woman cocked her head to the other side, implying that Gabby was dense. "Mariel was clinging to one of the guys renting the place. Andy, I think. Green eyes. Brown hair. Fit."

The description was similar enough to the one Mariel had provided, Gabby thought, and *Mandy* could very well have been Mariel's mishearing of his name. The au pair could have committed the American name to memory with a Pinoy twist.

"When you say 'clinging,'" Gabby asked, "was Mariel walking along holding his arm, or hanging on him like she couldn't stand up by herself?"

Fiona glanced to the right, either trying to remember how Mariel had looked or struggling to invent a description that wouldn't highlight how she'd callously abandoned her friend. Pupil movements, as much as psychologists touted them, rarely revealed lies—at least in Gabby's experience. Hands, however, often betrayed nervousness, and Fiona's knuckles were white as she gripped the doorjamb.

"They were wearing the face off each other, to be honest. Kissing and groping in front of everyone." Gabby caught the spark of schadenfreude in Fiona's eyes before her dark lashes batted it away. "I was a bit surprised, since Mariel had only met him an hour earlier. Some girls are like that when they come here, though. They think they've got a temporary visa to behave wh—"

Gabby raised her eyebrows before Fiona could finish suggesting that her supposed friend slept around. The girl cleared her throat. "Wanton. You know, since no one back home will hear about it, they think it's okay to be that way."

Gabby suspected Fiona was really talking about herself. "But you were still surprised at the public display of affection because Mariel didn't seem the promiscuous type, right? She'd even suggested leaving the party? She'd thought the guys were too old?"

Fiona snorted. "Well, that didn't last long, did it? An hour and a glass or two of wine."

Gabby gave the woman a warning look. Abandoning a younger friend at a party with older men that were likely to take advantage, after said friend had expressed concerns about staying, was bad enough without the added snark. If Fiona continued to imply that Mariel had gotten what she'd asked for, Gabby might threaten to charge her. Fiona had known her fellow au pair was too young to legally drink, but that hadn't stopped her from bringing the girl to a booze-fest. At a minimum, she'd contributed to the delinquency of a minor.

Fiona's smirk faded into an obstinate frown. "If I'd thought she'd been smashed, I would have interrupted. But I'd been outside with her the entire time and hadn't seen her have more than a few sips of wine. I was in the queue for the loo five minutes, tops, and out in ten. That's not much time to get drunk. As soon as I rejoined the party, though, she was pressed against Andy like a wetsuit."

What Fiona had apparently viewed as Mariel's sudden change of heart, Gabby saw as a clear sign of drugs. Out-of-character actions were typically evidence of outside influences. "So you really didn't find it at all odd that Mariel would go from barely drinking to making out with a guy that she'd complained was too old for her an hour earlier? She hadn't appeared at all inebriated?"

Some of the pink drained from Fiona's face. She glanced over her shoulder, perhaps checking to see if her bosses would be coming in from their backyard pool soon to investigate why their au pair was taking so long with the deliveryman. Fiona's hand dropped from the doorjamb. "Mariel might have seemed unsteady." Fiona lowered her voice to a near whisper. "She *was* stumbling and hanging on Andy, kind of giggling and telling him nonsense. I overheard her saying that his eyes looked like snails' shells, all green and spinning. But I thought she was doing the drunk thing for show. If she acted sloshed, then Andy might not dismiss her in the morning as that kind of girl."

As she talked, Fiona pulled at a necklace resting at her clavicle. The pendant was a Trinity knot. One of Kayla's friends had the intertwined triangles etched on the back of her shoulder. She'd told Gabby that the symbol had originally represented the cycles of a woman's life: mother, maiden, and crone. The Catholic Church had taken it over, though, and morphed it into a representation of the Holy Trinity, hence the name. Was Fiona worrying it, Gabby wondered, because she felt like a bad Christian for leaving Mariel or a poor female friend?

"Lots of girls do that, you know. Pretend to be drunk." Fiona's blue eyes begged to be believed. Gabby looked away. She didn't really trust that Fiona had thought Mariel's tipsiness an act. The girl had convinced herself that Mariel was behaving loose because she'd been jealous. That was why envy ranked up there with wrath, Gabby thought. Coveting sapped people of human compassion.

"I need the address of the party." Gabby folded her arms across her chest, signaling that she wouldn't budge from the porch until she got it.

Fiona started to shake her head. "I know those guys, and it was at their private—"

"Of course, I could charge you as an accessory to date rape." Gabby reached into her pants pocket as though prepared to withdraw cuffs. She stepped toward the open door, assuming her full height and the authority of her badge.

"How? I didn't—"

"You brought an eighteen-year-old to a party with copious amounts of alcohol, even though she wasn't of drinking age." Gabby took another forward step, pretending that she really had the evidence to do more than threaten the girl. "Maybe you knew Andy liked them young and inexperienced and thought she'd be his type, once she was all liquored up."

Fiona's jaw dropped to her chin, a puppet with a snapped string. Her eyes took on a glassy quality. "I didn't serve her. I—"

"Does Andy ask you to bring him girls, Fiona? Maybe you get a tip for every pretty young thing that you entice to come over? Maybe you even know how he likes to mix drinks."

"No." Fiona's face froze with fear. "I had nothing to do with it. You have to believe me. Mariel looked *into* him. I'd never have left if I'd thought she'd been drugged. I'm not a—"

"Then help her," Gabby interrupted. "Help your friend instead of protecting a rapist."

Fiona pulled in her lips, trying not to cry. She withdrew an outdated cell from the pocket of her jean shorts and tapped in a six-digit passcode. Gabby watched as she called up the Lyft application and hit the purple icon. "It's not far," Fiona said. "542 Pepperidge Lane."

Gabby pulled out her own phone and inputted the address in her map program. She started toward the black Dodge parked at the curb.

"Please." Fiona's voice cracked behind her.

Gabby glanced over her shoulder, prepared to hear the girl plead that she not mention her name to the party boys. Fiona clutched the Celtic knot on her neck. "Tell Mariel I'm sorry. I thought we'd have fun in a mansion with some cute guys. I wasn't bringing anybody anyone. I thought Andy was hot, so I assumed she did too. I really didn't know."

Gabby turned back to the car without promising to relay the message. Fiona didn't seem stupid. On some level, Gabby guessed, Fiona had known that she was leaving Mariel in a dangerous situation. Jealousy had simply convinced her that her friend had deserved whatever was coming.

CHAPTER THIRTEEN

Anger had sobered Louis. He strode through the great room, spine steel-straight despite all the wine and scotch at dinner. Part of Jenny wished he'd drunk more. Inebriated, Louis might not have noticed anything unusual in Ben's attention at dinner. He might have assumed that the interest in her bruise had stemmed solely from friendly concern. He might even have convinced himself that Ben, unhappily married to Rachel, simply couldn't help looking at *his* beautiful wife. *Let him look*, liquored-up Louis might have teased as she undressed for bed. *He can look. Only I can touch.*

But the pressure on her hand as Louis led her toward the open staircase made clear there'd be no laughter later. Her husband had picked up on the pointedness of Ben's questions, and now he would have some of his own. Why had Ben not believed his bug bite story? Why had he asked about the painkillers? Why was Ben more concerned about her cheek than his own crumbling marriage?

She couldn't answer the last one. Jenny tried to prepare explanations for the others as she followed Louis up the stairs. Her precarious position on the steps kept distracting her. Louis held her left hand, forcing her to the staircase's open side, her feet inches from the empty air and the waiting concrete below. Her legs trembled with each step. Still, she didn't ask Louis to let her stop and steady herself. She wouldn't dare.

When she reached the landing, she nearly dropped to her knees. Louis noticed the shift in her weight and tugged her arm, keeping her upright in front of their friends and urging her forward. He pushed back the bedroom door and held it open, releasing her hand to let her walk through first. Jenny glanced over her shoulder, wondering if any of their neighbors had noticed her husband's aggressive behavior. Ben sat on the couch with his back to her, a scotch glass in one hand and the bottle in the other. Susan and Nadal gave her small smiles and mouthed good-nights.

Jenny supposed she couldn't blame her new neighbors for not doing anything. From the first floor, Louis's door-holding would appear chivalrous. They couldn't see her husband's jailor stance as he ordered her inside, or the red bracelet of fingerprints around her wrist from their hand-in-hand ascent to the loft.

"Thanks." Jenny forced a smile as she passed her husband. She knew from experience that he was watching her behavior, looking for things to add to the list of transgressions justifying his anger. She wouldn't let him call her unappreciative.

The door shut behind her. It didn't slam. Louis was smarter than that.

Jenny scanned the room for an escape hatch, some way of avoiding the altercation. The sunset sneaked through a pair of balcony doors on her left. Its reddish light stained the edge of the white duvet atop the bed.

"Interesting conversation at dinner." Louis feigned a kind of gossipy camaraderie. *Let's talk about the weirdos next door.* He liked to pretend that his actions weren't premeditated. It made him feel more normal to start a casual conversation that would become heated and then "out of control."

Jenny tried to use his tactic to her advantage. "Ben and Rachel hate each other. What's new, right?" She hurried to the balcony doors and flung them back, acting as though she only wanted to exorcise the oppressive air. Two gray Adirondack chairs sat side by side, facing the beach. She rounded them and pressed her torso to the wooden railing. "Baby. Check out this view!"

Jenny didn't bother looking at the ocean. Instead, she searched the backyard and beach for witnesses: neighboring renters, couples strolling along the shore, late-night surfers, anybody whose presence might keep their fight from becoming too violent. Strangers were more likely to report Louis's behavior than people they knew. Friends and family members, Jenny had learned, feared upsetting their social circle too much to intervene.

She imagined her neighbors downstairs justifying whatever they saw or heard during the trip. *Jenny tumbled off her mattress, poor thing. She must have scratched that bug bite and increased the swelling. Well, I bet she had a good time last night with Louis, given all that shouting.* As long as Jenny didn't publicly accuse her husband of hitting her, the neighbors would avoid the inconvenient truth about their friends.

Except, of course, for Ben. He'd seen through her excuses six months ago.

The backyard below reminded her of a high school party abruptly shut down by the cops. Half-empty wine glasses shone in the dim light. Food scraps littered abandoned plates. Bottles rolled back and forth in the breeze. No one was sitting in the yard, but that didn't mean someone wasn't lounging outside on the neighboring property, able to hear her shouts.

"Jenny." Louis said her name in a singsong manner, like there was something amusing about it—or what he intended to do.

"You picked a great room." She aimed for a childlike mix of sweetness and awe, the way Ally sounded when she was excited. Louis had never hit their kid.

"Come inside." A growled tone replaced the musical tenor. He wasn't asking. Jenny continued playing like she was too dense, or drunk, to pick up on his anger. She looked out over the water and described what she saw, or what she would have seen were it not for the tears clouding her vision. "There's this beautiful shade of violet on the horizon. I think I can see the moon rising."

Motion pulled her gaze to the jetty stretching into the

water a quarter mile past the yard. A small figure walked atop the boulders. Jenny rubbed away her tears to make out the individual's feminine outline and the billowing kimono behind her. Rachel stopped a third of the way to where the waves swallowed the jetty's edge, a few feet beyond the shoreline.

"I want to talk to you," Louis said from right behind her. Jenny turned to see him blocking her exit, pressing the balcony door to the wall with an outstretched arm.

"Rachel is on the beach." She pointed to the jetty, a last-ditch effort to entice Louis outside.

"Who cares? She's a bitch."

The epithet had preceded enough violent arguments to trigger Jenny's fear response, despite its direction at someone else. Moisture evaporated from her throat. Her pounding heart picked up its already frantic rhythm.

"I'm more interested in the conversation *before* Rachel came back to the table," Louis went on. "Ben kept asking about the spot beneath your eye. He seemed convinced that it couldn't be a bug bite. That I was a liar." He smirked, as though he found Ben's impression of him funny.

"I don't know what was up with him," Jenny scoffed, trying to sell her disdain. Sports commenting hadn't taught her enough about pretending. Whenever she tried to fake an emotion, she overacted like a cast member in a nineties telenovela. "I mean, to say those things to Rachel, in front of everyone? He must have been plastered."

Louis tilted his head side to side, performing nonchalance. He was so much better at faking it.

"I guess we should get ready for bed," she said. The words came out like she'd pressed them through sandpaper.

Jenny tried to smile as she walked into the room. Louis caught her as she passed the threshold. Thick fingers wrapped her bicep like a blood pressure cuff. She tried to pull away, but Louis held on, his nails digging into her flesh. He twisted her forearm behind her, pulling her back against his chest.

"Stop, you're hurting me!" Jenny screamed in spite of herself. She knew that yelling would only make Louis angrier, that he'd accuse her of trying to alert their friends. Still, she couldn't hold it in. She couldn't go through this again after the horribleness last week that had resulted in the black eye. Louis was usually on his best behavior for months after a bad fight. She was supposed to get recovery time.

"Quit with the role-playing, babe." Louis directed his normal speaking voice over his shoulder, out the open balcony doors. "People might get the wrong idea."

Jenny tried to kick at Louis's shins as he carried her into the room, but he clamped down harder on her arms, cutting off the circulation. With one foot, he hooked the door and pulled it shut. He lifted her higher, until suddenly she was hurtling forward.

She landed facedown on the bed with enough force that even the foam mattress didn't fully cushion the impact. Her nose throbbed as she pushed onto her hands, intending to crawl off the bed and run from the room. Before she could move, Louis grabbed a hand from under her and flipped her onto her back. He straddled her torso, pinning her arms to her sides with his thighs. Jenny knew she wasn't strong enough to push him off her. She struggled to lift her hips regardless, to jam her pelvic bone painfully into his groin.

"When did you tell him?"

"What?" Her question sounded hollow. "I didn't say—"

"So, you talked to Rachel then? What, you picked the girls up from a playdate and decided to have a midday bottle of wine?" He leaned forward, pushing his chest against her own, constricting her lungs as his weight crushed her diaphragm. "The big celebrity hadn't had enough admirers with basketball season over. Huh, that it? So you decided to play the victim for some extra attention. You sobbed to Rachel so she could go blabbing our private business to Ben and God only knows who else?"

She shook her head, able to move it an inch despite the closeness of his face to hers.

"I know what you're doing. You want to emasculate me." His low voice wriggled in her ear. "To control me. You already make more money, even though I'm the one saving fucking lives. All you need is to turn our friends against me. You think you're so fucking smart."

He sat up, releasing the vice on her chest. Jenny filled her lungs with as much oxygen as possible. "I didn't say anything. He must have guessed."

Louis let go of one of her wrists. Before she could use it to pull herself from beneath him, he cupped her throat.

"You're smart enough to lie, Jen. But not to me." His voice raised to a near shout. Spittle sprayed her face. "I know how women scheme. And I'm not going to let you control me."

The pressure on her throat made her want to gag, but her muscles couldn't move enough to execute the reflex. Tears, hot as blood, filled her eyes. She knew Louis had to be satisfied at the sight. Each drop was a form of compensation for the embarrassment she'd caused him. All the pain was really just to make her pay.

Louis retracted his hand. A heaving followed Jenny's every inhalation, as though she breathed in water with air. "I'm sorry," she sputtered. "I'm sorry. I'm sorry."

She repeated the words like a waving flag, whispering them over and over. Fighting his accusations would only make Louis continue to battle with her physically. And she couldn't win that fight. Louis was thin but sinewy. A pulsing cord of muscle and testosterone. He was stronger and far angrier. Moreover, he already knew she'd lied. Ben, obviously, had known the origin of her bruise. But at least the explanation Louis had invented for that was better than the truth.

"I'm sorry," she continued whispering. "I'm sorry. I'm sorry."

Louis's thumb scraped beneath the left side of her face where her bruise was still healing. She closed her eyes, bracing for him to slap the wound. He could suggest that the swelling had worsened overnight. Ben and Rachel, he'd assume, would be too busy with their own relationship issues to worry about anyone else's, and Susan and Nadal wouldn't know any better. The Ahmadis were the couple Louis really cared about, anyway. When Nadal's company eventually went public, his family might be worth many multiple millions. Someday soon, Nadal could need a doctor for a prominent C-suite position, perhaps to handle the medical troops when they got restless from all the unpaid travel. Her husband would think himself perfect for such a role and the equity that came along with it.

Louis's hot breath enveloped her ear. "You're not sorry yet."

Jenny's eyes snapped open. She didn't have any more apologies in her. "I swear, Louis. You hurt me anymore and I'll scream so fucking loud that Ben will come rushing in here, and then everyone will know what you are. You think Nadal will want to talk shop with you after? You think Susan won't call the cops? What's your hospital's rule on hiring doctors that beat their wives, huh?"

For a moment, Jenny thought her threat had scared Louis enough to stop the fight. His eyes widened as though he were seeing his future self: jobless, reputation in shreds, booted from their home.

Then both of his hands went to her neck.

The edges of Jenny's vision blurred, leaving only Louis's wild eyes. His irises seemed to melt into his pupils, two black holes rimmed with dying stars, sucking the light from the room, pulling her into darkness. Jenny felt her consciousness rip from her body. Silence filled her ears. Louis faded to black.

CHAPTER FOURTEEN

THE DAY OF

"That was some fight, huh?" A loud spatter punctuated Nadal's words, followed by the sound of a running faucet. Susan kicked a leg from the milky liquid in the freestanding bath, letting the splash answer for her. They'd both witnessed the blowup, so Susan felt no need for a deep dive through the wreckage. In fact, she was certain that the only way to rescue the vacation she'd painstakingly planned for weeks was to blame the argument on alcohol and hope everyone tried to forget all about it.

Nadal shut off the faucet. "You don't think Rachel and Ben have an open marriage, do you?"

Water spilled from the tub as Susan moved to the other side, where she could have a better view of her husband. He examined his half-naked reflection in the glow of an LED-framed vanity. The artificial halo made it difficult to parse his expression.

"No. I think Ben might have a bit of a roving eye when

it comes to attractive women," Susan said. "And Jenny is obviously a very attractive woman."

"As is Rachel," Nadal added.

Susan felt a stab of jealousy. Did he *have* to put such a sharp point on it?

"Sure. If you like short blondes." Susan rose from the water. She extended her arms behind her like Degas's dancer, showing off her chest in the soft spotlight from the overhead window. Nadal didn't appear to notice her dangling her nakedness in front of his face, fishing for a compliment. She sighed and stepped from the tub onto the cool tile floor. "Anyway, like any wife, Rachel is probably sensitive to Ben checking out other women, particularly given that phone call with her daughter." She lowered her voice, nervous to speak about people staying in the same house, even if they couldn't hear her. "It sounded like Chloe might have seen something inappropriate between Ben and a neighborhood mom."

Nadal reached for the razor glinting on the pedestal sink. "But Rachel said she was *already* seeing other people."

Susan grabbed a towel from a pewter bar behind him. "I'm sure she only said that to hurt Ben because she thinks he's been unfaithful. She's competitive and a litigator. She knows how to fight dirty."

Nadal stroked his jawline, already dark with stubble despite shaving that morning. Her husband grew facial hair so fast that he had noonday shadow. "She sure does," he said, still examining his reflection. "She fights filthy dirty."

Something about the wording unnerved Susan. Maybe

it was because *filthy dirty* wasn't a phrase anyone used. It sounded like something barrel-chested men said in pornos. "Why all this interest in Rachel and Ben's marriage?" She tried to sound teasing as she wrapped the towel around her body. "Are you intrigued?"

Rather than stare at Nadal as he responded, betraying the seriousness of her question, Susan strode over to the tub and released the stopper. Water drained in loud gulps.

"Come on, Susie. Of course not."

She looked back at her husband, hoping to see an earnest, honest expression accompanying his denial. Instead, Nadal painted a white foam on his cappuccino neck, indifferent to her need for reassurance. She watched him shave, his strong hand confidently scraping the blade against his angular jawline. Back home, on the West Coast, she'd always been able to admire him without any accompanying nervousness. But back then, she'd been more of a prize: an attractive, young lawyer at a thriving criminal defense practice, not to mention the woman who'd borne him two perfect boys, as far as they'd known.

She'd sacrificed her status to augment his, abandoning the career that had given her an identity so that Nadal could achieve his dream of ringing the opening bell on the New York Stock Exchange. And, Susan reminded herself, so he could earn so much money that they could send Jonah and Jamal—but especially Jonah—to schools where teachers tailored their lessons to individual children and didn't dismiss autistic kids. Even the school in Washington State hadn't done a good job bringing out Jonah's talents.

Though it had at least let him take classes with the "mainstream" students.

Happy sacrifices, Susan thought. Who wouldn't be happy to abandon her career for her husband and children? She walked up next to Nadal and draped an arm around his chest. It would all be worth it once Nadal succeeded. Her husband would be happy. Her boys would be happy. And that meant she'd have to be happy. They'd all be happy. Happy. Happy. Unless . . .

Rachel's flirty pout as she'd asked Nadal to help her choose the wine flashed in Susan's mind. Nadal was handsome, hardworking, and soon to be extremely well-heeled. Women would line up to steal him away. "Are you attracted to Rachel?"

He stopped shaving to roll his eyes at her reflection. "I was only asking about that crazy fight."

"You're avoiding the question."

He pulled from her grasp. "Because it's a land mine."

"Why is that?"

"If I say no, you're going to think I'm a liar because I just said she was an attractive woman." He wagged the razor like an index finger. "Though that doesn't mean I'm attracted *to* her." He resumed shaving. "And if I say yes, you're going to get all insecure and defensive."

"No I won't." Susan wrapped her arms tighter around herself, holding up the towel. "I want to know the truth. I'd understand if you found her appealing. I think Ben's handsome."

"But you wouldn't want him. He doesn't do anything."

Each sentence punctured Susan's ego. After all, like

fellow stay-at-home parent Ben, she didn't *do anything* either. Susan's anxieties reared up inside her like a poked python. "How could you say that? Watching the children is doing something, Nadal. It's doing a lot, in fact. You think I don't do anything all day?"

Nadal stopped splashing water on his freshly shaven face. His expression reminded her of the way he looked when he missed a highway exit. She could see him running alternative routes in his head, trying to find a U-turn. "Ben doesn't homeschool a special-needs kid."

"He writes books."

"It's not like they do well. All I'm saying is—"

"That an individual's value should be completely measured in dollars and cents." Her arms flung out in thrashing gestures. "Of course you think that. That's why my career wasn't important in relation to your company. And that's why I'm clearly not as desirable as you, or the hotshot lawyer next door."

The last part spilled out before Susan had a chance to consider the implications—or even if she actually meant it. She didn't really believe her husband had a thing for the married lawyer in the neighboring house, did she? He hadn't done anything to fuel her suspicions, after all, other than gossip about another couple's horrific public argument. If anything, he'd been avoiding Rachel all day.

Susan glimpsed her reflection in the vanity. Her towel had slipped off from all her gesturing. With her naked breasts, sopping hair, and dripping outstretched arms, she resembled some kind of mythological water monster, a shrieking harpy or murderous siren. Nadal, meanwhile, was dashing Odysseus, lashed to the mast.

"Honey." Nadal smiled at her reflection as though she were suffering from some unfortunate disease. "You don't need to be concerned about Rachel. She is *not* the kind of woman I'd want. Trust me." He faced her. "I'm sorry if I've been distracted recently. But you don't have to worry, okay? I love you. You're the rock of our family."

"Rock" was hardly a compliment, Susan thought. "Yup. I'm a rock. Hard and flinty."

Nadal approached her with his palms out, as though he literally held a peace offering on a platter. "Bad description." Again, he smiled at her. This time, the expression didn't seem as patronizing. He slipped his arms beneath her limp limbs. Susan didn't hug back, though she didn't move away, either. Instead, she let him press his hard chest against her own and smelled the lingering shaving cream scent on his neck.

"What can I say that would encapsulate how beautiful, wonderful, and perfect for me my wife is?"

He kissed her after each compliment, his lips traveling from her temple to right below her left ear. Susan's anger started to recede. Nadal couldn't help it if other women wanted his attention, she admitted to herself. What mattered was that he wanted hers, and he was here with *her*. Caressing her body. Becoming excited by the feel of her skin against his own. Susan tilted her head for a real kiss.

Nadal grinned. "I thought of rock earlier because you make me—"

A knock interrupted his analogy. They both froze, a pair of teenage lovers hearing the parents' car pulling into the driveway. The knock sounded again. Rachel? Susan thought. No, she wouldn't dare. Would she?

"Hey, Nadal, you in there?" Louis's baritone blasted through the door. Nadal lifted his chin to the ceiling and closed his eyes, pleading with someone above to bless their neighbor with a sense of decorum. Who knocked on another couple's closed bedroom door after ten o'clock?

"What does he want?" Susan whispered.

Nadal stepped back from her. The abrupt withdrawal of his body heat made her shiver. "I think I know." He walked around her into the bedroom. "Just a minute," he called.

Susan hastily grabbed for the towel on the floor and tied it around her torso. It barely covered the necessary private parts. A door creaked open. She hid behind the half wall, peering through the opening separating the master bath from the bedroom.

Gym shorts covered her husband's backside. Susan wished he'd simply left on his boxers. Louis needed to sense they'd been in the middle of something.

"Hey, hope I am not interrupting anything," Louis said.

"Um. No." Nadal rubbed the back of his neck. "Not really."

"I was hoping we could grab a scotch downstairs and chat for a few."

Nadal kept scratching at his hairline. "Um, sure. But if this is about the thing with—"

"It warrants discussion." The sharpness in Louis's tone

surprised Susan. What was he so worked up about? Ben and Rachel's fight? She stuck her head a bit farther into the doorway.

"Thing is," Nadal said, "I doubt I can be of any help, like I told—"

Louis cleared his throat loudly. He glared at Susan as though he'd caught her spying. She flushed with shame at being seen eavesdropping, and no small amount of anger. She'd been interrupted during foreplay and waited in the bathroom out of decency. Louis had no right to make her feel like an intruder.

Susan clutched the towel a bit tighter between her breasts. "I'd come out, but I'm not dressed."

Nadal looked back at her. He raised his eyebrows and smiled with half his mouth. Susan knew that expression. He was apologizing. "I'll be back in a minute. Louis needs my advice on something. Quick."

Before she could object, Nadal had closed the door behind him. Susan released her towel and ambled toward the narrow armoire across from the bed, disappointment seeping into her damp skin along with the room's cold air. How could Nadal simply abandon her, half-naked and aroused? Didn't he realize that their marriage needed quality time? When they were at home, work and the kids were always interrupting. Finally, she had wrested Nadal away from both, and he was going downstairs to commiserate with the neighbor.

Susan tried to imagine what Louis had wanted as she rifled through the wardrobe drawers into which she'd unpacked. Probably, he wanted to discuss contingencies if Rachel and Ben bailed on the vacation. Their two families couldn't afford the house alone, and they couldn't back out of the rental at this point. Rachel and Ben would either have to pay their share or find another family to take it over, which meant vacationing with someone they might not know at all.

Susan tried to push the unsettling thought from her mind as she jostled into a pair of boxer-style pajama shorts. She grabbed a baggy tank from her drawer, which was considerably more comfortable than the chemises she'd brought to entice her husband, though not as likely to return Nadal to the moment before Louis's knock. The borrowed-boyfriend look had been hot in college. But middle-aged married mothers had to aspire to higher standards.

For the past few weeks, Nadal had worked so late she'd been in button-down pajamas with her teeth brushed by the time he'd come home. They'd been sleeping next to one another like brothers on a hotel bed, squarely on their individual sides of the mattress, too wiped from their respective days to entertain cuddling, let alone what it might lead to.

Susan pulled the shirt over her head, telling herself she could wear the lingerie later in the week. There was little point donning uncomfortable lace just to wait, alone, in the room. Dressed, she slumped onto the white duvet covering the wooden bed like a mushroom cap. The filling puffed around her. She leaned into it, reaching for her husband's laptop charging atop the nightstand (much like her own forgotten computer in her bedroom back home). As long as

Nadal was busy, she might as well check her email. The boys might have sent her an "all's well" message, or at least notes confirming that they'd arrived safely at their camps.

The computer prompted her for a password as she pushed back the screen. She entered the twins' birth date followed by an *N*, a four, for the number of people in their family, and an exclamation point. Her techie husband was adamant about passwords having a requisite number of characters and symbols. He was less concerned about using the same code to unlock all of his personal electronics—or that she knew it. After all, she wouldn't try to hack into his company.

The computer screen flashed, revealing a white window packed with emails. Nadal's inbox. Apparently he hadn't bothered to log out of his last session. She pulled her finger over the touch pad, bringing the cursor up to the *X* in the right-hand corner. Before she clicked, an email caught her eye. It sat in a list, three down from the top. The sender was KLEIN, RACHEL.

For the second time in an hour, she recalled how Rachel had pouted at Nadal, batting her blue eyes like a butterfly flapping its scaly wings. She pulled the cursor to the message and paused atop the subject line: ABOUT THURSDAY NIGHT . . .

Last night. Susan's breaths shortened as she wracked her brain for Nadal's whereabouts the prior evening. He'd come home late, as usual, though not because of work. He'd gone to watch Jamal's final baseball game of the season. She'd gone too, but had left with Jonah during the fourth inning after he'd started to complain about the shouting. Afterward, Nadal had said, he'd taken Jamal out to a diner for hot dogs and ice cream. He'd acted as though they'd gone alone. Had Rachel and Will tagged along? Will was on the same team.

Susan tapped the track pad, not hard enough to open the message. She knew Nadal's passwords because he trusted her not to do any crazy spouse things like snoop through his emails, and she trusted him not to hide anything important from her. Reading the message would be a violation of their mutual trust. And she did trust him, didn't she? Nadal wasn't the one, after all, who had spent a year engaged in a flirtation with a slightly senior—and married—colleague. The relationship with Susan's "work husband" had ended the way all so-called "harmless" platonic relationships between people inclined to mutual sexual attraction did—spectacularly poorly. Her friend had been promoted, resulting in celebratory drinks that had culminated in an awkward shared cab ride to the train station during which he'd confessed his "complicated and undeniable" feelings. She'd awkwardly denied any similar emotions, embarrassing him and straining their working relationship to the point where basic civility had become difficult. When Nadal had suggested moving East to expand his business, Susan had willingly agreed, fearing what might happen if she and her new boss ever had another occasion to share drinks.

She was the (reformed) flirt, Susan reminded herself, not her husband. Surely whatever Rachel had written about concerned the boys' baseball game. Her neighbor probably would have sent the message to Susan had she stayed through the whole six innings. Unless, of course, Rachel was confessing her regrettably inappropriate yet unavoidable attraction to Nadal.

Susan double-clicked the message, ignoring the pinch of her conscience in favor of the queasiness in her gut.

Hi Nadal,
I saw you at Thursday's game, but you'd gone by the time I went over to say hello. I hope you don't feel like you have to avoid me. I know this is awkward, to say the least. I don't usually become involved like this with neighbors, let alone friends, but I can't walk away now. I think if we can keep this just between us, we should be able to come to an arrangement that works for everyone.
Looking forward to the vacation.
Rachel

The pain in Susan's stomach disappeared. She reread the message. Numb. *Involved like this. Can't walk away. Keep this between us. Come to an arrangement.* What other secret arrangement did unhappily married women come to with married men?

Susan's shock gave way to a heavy ache that started in her chest and spread to her limbs. Rachel's last words to them at dinner echoed in her memory. Ben had suggested that his wife sleep with other people, and Rachel had responded, *Maybe I already have.*

CHAPTER FIFTEEN

THE DAY AFTER

The home wasn't visible from the street. Gabby considered how convenient that would be for a serial rapist as she turned the Dodge onto the bleached pebble driveway. She parked behind a sky-blue Subaru, well away from the concrete building peeking from the trees ahead. Approaching the house on foot was preferable to driving right up to the front door. Andy didn't deserve advanced warning of her arrival.

The driveway branched out to a tiled path the same off-white color as the stones. She followed it to the beach house, immediately understanding why the home had been hidden in the forest. Save for the concrete shells of the structure's overlapping rectangles, the entire building was glass. Gabby could see straight through the front of the house to the pool and beach beyond—the same beach where Rachel had been murdered. If Ben had run about a mile east from Rachel's body, he would have seen the party.

A shirtless figure emerged from a portion of the house obscured by the concrete sides. He passed a dark wooden wall and pulled on a handle, revealing the interior door of a fridge. The man had brown hair, made darker by its wet state, and a muscular build. Strong thighs bulged from knee-length board shorts.

He, apparently, hadn't noticed her yet. She strode to the glass doors, looking for a bell but finding only a sleek metal handle. When the walls were all transparent, Gabby guessed, guests didn't need to announce themselves.

She tapped on a pane. The man withdrew his head from inside the fridge and faced her. His expression appeared mildly interested, and maybe also confused, though not evidently concerned. Perhaps he wondered whether she was someone from the prior night's party, returning for lost sunglasses. He shut the fridge and strode toward the glass wall.

Instead of opening the door, he paused by the handle and examined her face. No doubt, close up, he realized she couldn't have been a party guest. Gabby's thirty-seven years weren't painfully apparent from a distance. Anyone that got an HD view, however, could determine that she wasn't in her twenties.

"Hi, may I help you?" The voice penetrated the glass.

Gabby grabbed her badge from her belt buckle and pressed it to the pane. "I have some questions about last night."

The man's eyes widened, highlighting their river-green color. Gabby heard the click of a lock disengaging. She pocketed her badge as the wall of glass slid to the side, exposing half the house to the elements. "If this is about the underage drinking, it was all a misunderstanding." The man brushed his palm over his hair, shaking droplets from the clumped wet strands. "We'd had no idea that some of the girls were in high school until one of the dads showed up all crazy, throwing punches and shouting about sixteen-year-olds. My roommate Chris went out to apologize. He told all those girls to go home."

The man pinched the edge of his nose, wiping away some unseen mucus. "We don't even know how the high school kids heard about it, honestly. We'd invited a group of girls at this bar and told them to bring friends. Everyone there should have been twenty-one."

Gabby continued to stand and nod, letting the silence ask the questions that the man so clearly wanted to answer. Perhaps he'd keep talking about his innocence regarding underage girls until he made some sly admission about Mariel or a "strange man with a split lip."

"Anyway, since we didn't know, there wasn't anything intentional on our parts." He scratched the faint shadow on the edge of his chin. "We just wanted to have a party with some cute girls. We're not a bar. There's no one checking ID. And, even if we'd hired someone, we don't have the capability to determine what's fake or not. Most of these girls have international passports."

The man finally stopped talking. He stared at Gabby, no doubt waiting for her to say whether or not his excuse had satisfied the complaint she'd been called to investigate. She extended her hand through the open wall and stepped forward, throwing the guy off guard with the friendly greeting that she didn't really want to give. As he shook, she told herself the faux chumminess would be worth it once she got him in cuffs. "I'm Detective Gabriella Watkins. I understand the situation you were in, and I get that people sneak into parties. But we have to follow up on every call . . ."

She withdrew her notebook and pen from a jacket pocket with an apologetic smile, as though she were a census worker forced to complete a survey. He stepped back, allowing her into the house. Behind him, a mouthwash-colored pool sparkled in its toothpaste setting.

Gabby tapped her pen against the pad. "So, your name is . . ."

The man headed into the kitchen. "Andrew Baird." He crossed the gray hardwood floors to a white island that Gabby realized held all the necessary appliances, including a Keurig machine. He pointed to a wooden table surrounded by four white chairs. "You want a cup a coffee? I was about to make myself one. Up early surfing."

Gabby hovered by the kitchen island, refusing to sit in the spot Andy had designated—a subtle way of establishing her control in his space. "So, this sixteen-year-old. Did you get her name?"

Andy pulled the basin from the coffeemaker and placed it beneath the faucet. "No. I didn't even see her, really." He raised his voice over the running water. "I'm guessing she and her friends were out by the pool helping themselves to wine." Andy shut off the faucet and jostled the full reservoir back into the machine. "Chris talked to the dad, though. You can ask him."

Gabby glanced at the white staircase behind her, also encased in glass. She'd see anyone descending, but this Chris could still get the jump on her, given her position. "Is he here? Your roommate?"

Andy pointed to the glass wall facing the beach. "He's the dot on the water out there praying for a swell. He'll probably come in soon. Nothing's really breaking anymore."

Gabby couldn't see the human speck to whom Andy referred, though she asked for the full name and scribbled it down. As the guy who had gone out to talk to the infuriated father, Chris was the one who would have seen Ben—provided Ben had actually gone to the party. Andy would have been too busy trying to slip something into Mariel's drink.

Gabby followed up with a question about whether they were renting the home, even though she already knew the answer. When she asked about Mariel, Andy would invariably invent some things. She needed to gauge his reactions by forcing him to tell known truths and lies.

"We're subletting from a friend," Andy said. "It costs a fortune but, if you surf, what choice do you have? It's either rent a place here for the summer or fly halfway around the globe, praying you'll catch some waves before vacation's up. We're hoping our buddy will let us pop in on the weekends, too, since we sent a bit of extra cash his way."

Gabby wrote down *surfers*, even though the information

wasn't relevant to what had happened to Mariel. If she only noted the details that actually pertained to the rape or the murder, Andy would realize what she was here about and clam up. "What do you do besides surf?"

Andy shrugged, as though everything else wasn't interesting. "Banking." He gave a slight smile that Gabby guessed someone had told him was endearing, given the extra few seconds it remained on his face. "That's another reason we would never have brought underage girls here to drink. Too much liability."

Gabby wrote down the occupation as the Keurig machine began to hiss. "I'm not only here about the teenage drinking," Gabby said. "There was a young woman, Mariel Cruz, that came to the party last night. She has long black hair, tan skin. Filipina. Pretty. Do you remember her?"

Andy looked at the Keurig machine as if he suddenly needed to read the directions. He picked up the filled cup and stared at the liquid. Though pupil movements rarely revealed lying, avoiding eye contact entirely was often a tell.

"Do you remember her?" Gabby repeated.

He turned around, walking back to the wall of cabinetry. Again, he pulled open the door of the paneled fridge. This time he removed a carton of milk off a lower shelf, which he opened, poured into his mug, and returned to the fridge door. His movements were slow, the incidental activities of someone weighing the risks of denying having slept with the subject of a police investigation versus confessing to some sort of "voluntary" relationship. Gabby guessed he was replaying the prior night in his head, trying to establish the odds that his DNA had already put him with the girl.

"I do remember." The fridge shut with his final answer, cutting off the welcome blast of cold from the room. Though a breeze wafted from an opening in the east-facing wall, it wasn't strong enough to cool a glass oven. "She's beautiful," Andy continued. "We got to know one another last night."

Gabby jotted that down while maintaining eye contact. "Had you met her before?"

Andy leaned against the back cabinets, apparently forgetting that he'd promised to make a second cup of coffee. "No, but we really hit it off. I like her very much."

Gabby nodded. "I know what it's like to hit it off immediately with someone. My husband and I met in high school, and I knew from the first that he was the one. We had so much to talk and laugh about. I could have chatted with him for hours." Gabby continued smiling, tapping into her real feelings about Derrick to provide Andy with a false sense of ease. "What did you and Mariel talk about last night?"

Andy smacked his lips together. "You know, I'm not totally sure. To be honest, I'd had a bit too much to drink. Everything's a bit hazy. But I know we had fun." The lids drew down over the green eyes. "Why all the questions about Mariel?" His jaw dropped. "Wait, don't tell me she's in high school! She said she was an au pair. She said she was an adult."

Classic move, Gabby thought. Start discrediting the

victim by making it seem that she might have lied about something not even in dispute. "Nope. She's an au pair. Eighteen, but not in high school."

Andy grimaced. "I assumed she was at least twenty-one, like the other au pairs."

Gabby noted his tense facial expression. If Mariel was remembering the prior night's conversation about her age correctly, then Andy had just told his first lie. "I'm sorry if she had some alcohol here," he continued. "The bottles were lying around. Did she come home hungover and her house mom called you?"

Gabby ignored the question. "Did you sleep with her?"

Andy lowered his head over his cup, examining the liquid as though something floated in it. A smile stretched across his face. He extended his mug toward her in a kind of cheers. "A gentleman isn't supposed to tell." He punctuated the statement with another coy sip.

Then you should be blabbing, Gabby thought. She sighed, pretending to be particularly put upon by her duties. "Unfortunately, I have that report . . ."

The mention of a written document erased Andy's smirk. He lowered his cup and swirled the liquid. The Columbo act wouldn't work anymore, Gabby realized. The guy finally understood that she wasn't here to make him answer for some underage party crashers.

"Is she all right?" The concern on Andy's face was believable, though probably only because he actually felt the emotion for himself. If Mariel wasn't okay, then he was the obvious cause. "I invited her to have breakfast with me this morning, but she said she had to go. I sent her home in a car."

Gabby scratched at the sweat-curled hairs on the nape of her neck. Andy would use his ten-dollar car service receipt as evidence that everything had been consensual, and there'd be somebody on a twelve-person jury who would likely accept that argument.

Gabby looked to the water, centering herself before the most confrontational part of the interview. A figure moved up the beach, toward the lawn. The black wetsuit that he wore, despite the heat, reminded her of Batman. She hoped he wasn't action hero sized. Andy, though no more than five foot nine, was still significantly bigger than she was. Sometimes people forgot they were dealing with an armed law officer when reeling from an accusation that could land them in prison.

Gabby directed her attention back to Andy. He held his coffee cup between both hands, rotating it. Fidgeting. "Mariel came home with no memory of what happened before waking up next to you," she said. "Naked."

Andy raised his eyebrows, transforming them into accents that emphasized his surprise. The reaction was rather subdued for a rape accusation, Gabby thought.

"Well, maybe she didn't want anyone to know she'd slept with someone she'd just met." Andy walked over to the kitchen island and placed his cup in the sink. He turned on the faucet and reached for a bottle of blue dish soap, which he immediately squeezed into the mug. "It must be easier to say she doesn't remember."

He rubbed his thumb around the cup's lip, wiping away the DNA from his mouth. Gabby watched the nonchalant way he eliminated evidence, certain that he had nothing to worry about from Mariel's allegations. He'd spent time figuring out what to do if she went to the cops, Gabby figured. He'd say one thing. She'd say another. The case would go nowhere.

"Mariel went to the hospital for a rape kit." Gabby tried to keep her face slack, her voice light.

"Well, that's outrageous." Andy shut off the faucet. "Ask anyone at the party—she was all over me last night. We were having a good time. I'm sorry if she woke up and had buyer's remorse. God knows I'm having some now."

The far wall of the house suddenly retracted. Chris stood in the opening. He was significantly taller than his roommate, and he also looked significantly older, though Gabby guessed that might be due to the thinning blond hair set far back from his broad forehead and the silvery hairs between his pectorals.

"Chris, this detective here—Gabriella, was it?—she's looking into sexual-assault allegations against me." He gestured to his friend, becoming more animated given the presence of backup. "That girl from last night. The one that was making out with me in the kitchen. You saw her. She's now saying she didn't want to have—"

"She's claimed that she was too incapacitated to give consent," Gabby corrected.

"She wasn't too incapacitated to tell me all the crazy ways she wanted it," Andy said. "Isn't that consent?"

Chris looked stricken, though only for a moment. He held an open palm toward his friend. "She must have seen the house and smelled money. Andy doesn't have to drug women to get laid."

Gabby nodded, scrawling five words in her book. *Chris brought up the drugs.* She hadn't suggested to either man that Mariel was claiming she'd been slipped anything, only that she'd been incapacitated. The natural implication was that Mariel had been blackout drunk during intercourse, which wouldn't have actually made Andy guilty of anything aside from contributing to the delinquency of a minor. Rape in the second degree required that Mariel's incapacitation stem from being given a debilitating substance without her consent.

"Were there drugs at the party?"

Andy looked insulted. "No. Wine. Some beer. That's it. There weren't even shots." He shook his head. "If she was on anything, she must have brought it for personal use. We didn't see it."

With Chris and Andy backing each other up about Mariel's consent and Fiona claiming she'd believed her friend had feigned tipsiness, Mariel didn't have much chance of winning any case. A rape kit would only prove she'd had sex, and if drugs showed in Mariel's system, both Andy and Chris would say she'd willingly taken her own pills. Gabby had to hope that whatever substance had been stirred into Mariel's drink was something only two health-insured men could obtain with a prescription. Otherwise, the girl wouldn't have much of a chance at justice. She'd probably end up wishing she'd never told Dina what had happened and involved police in the first place.

Gabby closed her eyes for a moment longer than a blink, forcing her brain to switch gears from the rape investigation that was quickly going nowhere to her murder case. There were too many similarities between the party and the one Ben was claiming to have attended to doubt that he'd been at the house. However, his presence didn't mean he had an airtight alibi. He could have visited just long enough to create a semblance of having been somewhere else while his wife was being murdered. To rule out Ben, she needed to know *when* he'd been at the party.

Gabby approached the larger roommate. Chris had greenish eyes too, she realized, though a different color than Andy's. His were clearer and mixed with more blue, like sea glass rather than a graying river. "Andy said that a man came here to collect his underage daughter and that you went out to talk to him. Did you—"

"Yeah. We kicked those girls out as soon as—"

Gabby held up a hand. she'd already listened to Andy's defense for serving high schoolers. "This dad, I understand he got into an altercation with some guy that had been flirting with his kid."

Chris wiped sweat off his brow with the back of his hand. "I heard that, but the guy had taken off by the time I went outside."

"When was that?" Gabby pressed her pen to her notepad.

"I'm not sure." Chris wicked away the seawater clinging to his jawline with the heel of his hand. "Before two AM, probably. I went to bed around three, and it took a bit for everyone to leave—even after that crazed guy threatened to call the cops."

Gabby stared at the number two that she'd just scrawled onto the paper. Ben being gone from the party by that hour didn't make or break his defense. She needed to talk to someone who would have a more exact timeline. "Did you get the name of the dad and daughter?"

Chris scratched the scant hair above his ear. "Not really. I think the guy's name started with a D or E or something. I remember what they looked like, though."

Gabby nodded for him to continue, holding her pen at the ready.

"The girl was Black, very pretty. She had her hair slicked back in a ponytail and a lot of shimmery makeup on. Red lipstick."

As Gabby scrawled down the details, she couldn't help but think they all could have been used to describe Kayla. Teenagers, though, tended toward the same trends. A slick ponytail and shimmery makeup must have been whatever the magazines were plastering on their summer covers.

"The dad was also Black. He was bald and he had a goatee. I thought he might have been a body builder. He had huge guns and a big number two tattooed on his arm."

Gabby stopped writing. The chances of there being two bald, goateed Black men with number twos on their biceps in the area were next to nil. The man was Derrick—her husband. He'd grabbed Kayla from *this* party. An invisible hand squeezed her heart. Her prime murder suspect had been chatting up *her daughter.*

The notebook vibrated in Gabby's hand. She took down each man's contact information for her report and robotically warned them not to leave the area, her mind already on the phone call she needed to make.

"Do I need a lawyer?" Andy asked.

Gabby mumbled something about there not being any charges—yet—as she headed to the door. The glass walls seemed to aim the sun straight at her. She was sweating. Dripping. She needed to get out of this house. She had to see her daughter.

CHAPTER SIXTEEN

Jenny woke, surrounded by a dark, heavy damp. She thrashed against it, unsure of what it was or where she was. Oxygen streamed into her airways, bonded with the memory of her husband squeezing her neck until she'd passed out. She pushed herself upright under the sweat-drenched duvet and checked the moon's position through the balcony doors. It hung just above the horizon, a broken spotlight dangling far too low from the scaffolding. She hadn't been out long. Louis, however, was no longer in the room.

She lay there, forcing saliva down her raw throat, listening to the crashing waves still audible through the shut balcony door. A memory seeped into her swimming brain. She saw Louis, bent over scented candles in the small apartment they'd shared in med school. He lit them with short matches they'd confiscated weeks earlier from a corner bar. Each strike against the carbon strip illuminated, for a moment, the man she'd fallen for. The boyish face topped with ginger hair. The piercing blue-gray eyes beneath a preternaturally concerned brow.

Jenny remembered how Louis had cupped his hand around each flame, shielding it from the howling outside that had seemed to penetrate the thin walls of their highrise apartment. Growing up in landlocked West Virginia, she'd never seen a hurricane or a superstorm or whatever the meteorologists had named the vortex of clouds closing in on them. She'd watched the news, awed and horrified by footage of wind ripping willows from the ground and wielding them like battering rams against cars and streetlamps. When the power had gone out, she'd screamed, sure nature's strike force had finally arrived at their doorstep.

Louis's chivalry had gone into overdrive that weekend. He'd made certain she would want for nothing, loading the pantry days beforehand and clearing out the local liquor store of her favorite cabernet. He'd duct-taped the windows and filled the defunct fireplace with scented candles. He'd charged the electronics and rented her favorite films on DVD.

She remembered snuggling with him beneath musty extra blankets and munching on almond-butter sandwiches washed down with wine while the floodwaters blocked their building's egress. If she closed her eyes, she could almost feel the warmth of his skin, the way his body had radiated care and concern for her. The way it often still did.

She'd loved him then. Maybe she still loved him. But Louis had violated the unspoken rule that allowed their marriage to survive his "outbursts." If he hit her, he had to be flagrantly sorry for a very, very long time. Months, at least. Contrition and promises of reform had to follow his combustion, enabling Jenny to regain her power and remember the good times.

Their better days far outnumbered the bad. Louis had become abusive only in the past five years, since she'd taken the high-profile sports anchor position. A couple's therapist they'd seen briefly had suggested that Louis's anger stemmed from unresolved parental issues about money that made him feel threatened whenever it seemed like he was losing the traditional "male" provider role to Jenny. But she wouldn't relinquish her job and lose even more power to her unpredictable spouse. They'd reached an impasse. The only way through was for Jenny to run away.

She slid off the bed, searching the shadowed floor for her purse. She'd leave tonight. The quicker, the better. As soon as Louis realized that she intended to separate, he'd try to get to Ally and convince her that Jenny was making up the abuse for leverage in the coming custody hearing. There was no way she could allow Louis to take their daughter from her. Jenny knew the statistics. If she left Ally with Louis, chances were good he'd wind up hitting her, too.

Jenny grasped the corner of the bed and yanked herself upright. The room flashed dark and light as though the moon was set to strobe, an effect spurred by her brain's reaction to the prior trauma of having its main artery momentarily shut down. Her stomach lurched, threatening to send her dinner back up her inflamed esophagus. She stumbled to the balcony doors and flung them open. Breeze buffeted her face. She slumped into one of the Adirondack chairs and gulped salty air until her vision cleared.

Nadal's voice wafted from the yard below her. "As I said before, Louis, that's not our business. We're a technology platform."

"You're a medical group."

"A platform. A website open to anybody with a verifiable medical license and a smartphone. We can't provide insurance for the universe of—"

Jenny crawled from the chair back into the dark bedroom so that Louis wouldn't notice her presence. He might return to justify his anger, as he often did. She couldn't give him the opportunity to explain away his actions, again—to return to the room with a glass of water, a pain reliever, and a list of rationalizations peppered with apologies.

The voices rose, floating through the open balcony door like hot air. "That's not fair to doctors." Louis was near shouting, his blood still up from their fight. "It's abdicating responsibility."

"We'll have to agree to disagree, then." Nadal sounded calmer. "There's nothing left to say. We're not setting a precedent here."

Jenny heard the scrape of a chair across the deck. In a moment, her husband would barge back into the house, a heat-seeking missile looking for a warm target. The dim moonlight caught the pale color of her purse beneath the end table. She grabbed it, slipped out of the dark bedroom, and hurried to the ground floor. Louis and Nadal likely sat at the outdoor dining table. A glance over either man's shoulder would betray someone fleeing the house.

Jenny ran on tiptoe into the narrow entryway. Her rushing blood resounded in her ears like the soundtrack to a thriller movie. In those films, the abusive husband always caught the wife once or twice before she finally escaped. She glanced over her shoulder as she grasped the front doorknob. No sign of Louis.

Shells crunched under Jenny's feet as she sprinted down the driveway. She would run into town and then call a car service. Waiting outside the house was too risky. Louis could catch her before she had a chance to leave.

A large male figure stepped from the shadows beside a red car. The drumbeat in Jenny's head silenced. She froze, prey trapped in a hunter's scope. Excuses raced through her brain. She'd needed a sweater from the trunk. She'd wanted some air. She'd come out to apologize.

"Jenny?"

Her fear vanished. The voice was so different from the one that spiked the hairs on her neck. Ben walked toward her. The full moon cast him in a cobalt hue, the melancholy subject of a young Picasso. "Did he hurt you?"

The question made Jenny fully aware of her burning throat. She couldn't force an answer. Instead, she flung her arms around his firm torso and pressed herself to his chest, wanting to dissolve into the safety of his skin. "I can't take it anymore." Her words clawed and scratched their way out of her raw esophagus. "I'm leaving him. I'm doing it. I'm finally going to leave."

Ben angled his head down, enabling Jenny to meet his lips with her own. The kiss empowered her, just as it had the first time she'd experienced it, six months earlier.

She held his neck as she returned his caress, communicating *her* desire. Her approval. Her husband didn't deserve her fidelity. In the dark, encircled by Ben's strong arms, she didn't care what might happen. "I want you," she whispered. "I want you. I want you." With each repetition, her voice grew stronger. Louis couldn't control her. Louis didn't deserve her. Louis didn't know what she was capable of.

CHAPTER SEVENTEEN

THE DAY OF

"My husband cheated with the woman staying downstairs." Susan whispered the words in the silent bedroom, trying to compel her acceptance of the surreal situation by forcing herself to describe it. Nadal —the man who had pledged his enduring love and *fidelity* to her a dozen years ago, the partner with whom she raised their boys, the person for whom she'd left her job, her parents, her beloved West Coast, and moved clear across the country—he'd slept with Rachel. Rachel. The mother of their son's best friend. The damn neighbor!

Susan reread the email in front of her multiple times like it was a poem, trying to wedge different meanings into the words. Tears blurred the letters into a mess of black lines. She set the computer to the side, turned into the mattress, and thrust her face into a pillow. The fabric muffled her anguished screams. What was she supposed to do now?

She couldn't stay in the house with a home wrecker. But she couldn't simply return to Westchester either. The other woman lived next door.

She could *strangle* him! How could he have made such a stupid mistake?

Susan imagined how the affair would have started. Rachel, miserably married and looking for company, had probably run into Nadal in the city. No doubt she'd suggested a drink in some nearby hotel bar. Nadal would have agreed, finally heeding Susan's nagging to befriend the neighbors. One cocktail had turned into several. They'd begun flirting, much like Susan had with her ex–"work husband" after having one-too-many glasses of wine at the office Christmas party. Flirting could bloom into feeling so easily. Rachel had ultimately decided that she was attracted to Nadal—because what heterosexual woman wouldn't be? And Nadal, uninhibitedly drunk, and not needing to rush home to relieve the sitter as she'd always done, had checked into a room with the woman next door.

Afterward, Susan figured, he'd have returned home to his naïve wife dozing in bed. He'd likely mumbled something about working extra late, knowing she wouldn't question a longer-than-usual day. She'd most certainly kissed the lips that had been on Rachel's body minutes before and told him that she loved him. *Good-night, honey. Sorry work has been so rough.* Poor little trusting idiot.

Had the guilt sickened him? she wondered. Had he considered confessing but forced himself to keep the secret, believing they'd both be happier if she remained ignorant? Had he persuaded himself he could forget all about that night and move on?

Her husband didn't want to leave her for Rachel—at least not yet. The email made clear that he'd been avoiding her, and he'd been unwilling to go into the house with Rachel alone. Probably he felt guilty about what had happened. But Susan couldn't guarantee that would last—not if Rachel convinced him they could arrive at some *arrangement*.

The room suddenly felt like a sauna, its hot air saturated with too much emotion to inhale. She couldn't spend another moment under the same roof as that backstabbing bitch or her own lying spouse. Her black suitcase lay open beside the bed. Susan fell to her knees beside it and pulled at the zipper. She'd pack up and fly back to Washington for the week, forcing Nadal to consider his future without the wife who had stood by him, working and caring for the kids when he'd left his secure job to start a company in their unfinished basement. She'd give him a sample of solitary life as another middle-aged man pathetically preening for twenty-somethings. See how he'd fare.

Salty tears tumbled from her eyes into her trembling mouth. Who was she kidding? Nadal would do fine. He was a fit, handsome soon-to-be-multimillionaire. He'd have twenty-year-olds fluttering their eyelashes as soon as he entered a room. And, if he didn't, there was always Rachel, sitting somewhere on the beach, no doubt hoping Nadal might go out and check on her.

What if he was doing that right now?

Susan fled the bed as if the mattress had caught fire. She flung open the door and hurried into the hallway, hoping to hear Nadal and Louis's voices floating from the kitchen.

The mezzanine had the waiting air of a coffin. Someone had shut off the overhead lights, leaving the house illuminated solely by the full moon blasting through the wall of windows. The solitary light source transformed the empty great room into a chiaroscuro painting, casting a luminous halo on the white couch that contrasted with the charcoal shadows in every corner.

Footsteps echoed from the dark hallway that hid Rachel and Ben's bedroom. Susan shirked from the railing. She couldn't see Rachel like this, puffy from crying and in her we-don't-have-sex-anymore pajamas—the consummate sad little housewife. When she ultimately confronted Rachel, she'd be dressed and in full makeup, making clear to that tramp exactly whose husband she'd tried to steal. She'd be dressed to fucking kill.

A male figure emerged into the noir light, his body outlined by the moon even as his face remained in shadow. He turned toward the stairs. Susan recognized the shape of her husband. He'd come from the whore's bedroom.

Once, when Susan had been breaking down a roast chicken for her boys, she'd sliced near through her left index finger with a boning knife. The cut had been made with such precision, and with such a sharp tool, that she hadn't felt a thing. She'd watched the blood gush for a full second, staining half of the bird's breast a cardinal red before her adrenaline had kicked in, spurring her to wrap her wound in a paper towel and head to the hospital. Nadal's presence outside his lover's bedroom was that knife.

"Nadal?" She spoke his name as though it were a question. In some ways, she supposed, it was. The man she'd thought she knew would never have cheated on her, let alone been stupid enough to do it with a woman his wife risked seeing at every school event and sports game. Each time she walked out of their damn house.

"Hi, honey." His teeth shone in the darkness. "Sorry, that conversation took longer than I thought."

Susan examined his smile, searching for traces of his dishonesty. The moonlight worked like candles, obscuring the wrinkles and acne scars, the marks of poor living that nothing but darkness could mask. Nadal looked sincerely happy to see her, unconcerned that she'd almost caught him in the act.

"The conversation with Rachel, you mean."

"What? No. Louis." Nadal sounded genuinely confused. How could he lie so easily?

"You were coming from Rachel's room."

Nadal scratched at his jawline, reminding Susan that he'd shaved. He'd wanted to be nice and smooth for his girlfriend. "Louis had a question that I thought she might be able to answer."

"Then why didn't he ask?"

Nadal's head lowered as he stepped toward her. "Babe, are you all right? You sound—"

"Answer me. If Louis had a question, why didn't *he* ask?"

Nadal stood close enough for her to finally see his pinched brow. "She wasn't even there."

"Lucky me, I guess."

"Huh?"

"She was there the other night though, right?"

"What are you talking about?" Nadal's dark eyes betrayed him. Rather than narrowing with confusion, they opened wider. He knew what she was talking about.

"I saw the email!" Rage flooded her voice like sewer water from a released drain. "I opened your laptop to check for a message from the boys. Your email was on the screen. She sent you a message."

Nadal shut his eyes, blocking her from seeing the workings of his brain as he struggled to invent a believable excuse. "That was about work."

"Are you kidding me? I read it, Nadal. *I don't usually become involved like this with neighbors.* That's about work?"

"It was. She has a client that—"

"Stop." Susan's hands flew in the air, signing the disgust and disappointment she felt too deeply to verbally express. "Stop lying. I read it."

"What do you think you read?" Nadal lowered his voice to a seething whisper. "I am telling you that her email was about work. She has a malpractice case."

He thought her an imbecile! How else could he honestly expect she'd buy that he and Rachel had legitimate business together? Rachel was a glorified ambulance chaser and Nadal ran a tech company. Rachel wouldn't consult with him and he definitely wouldn't ask her any legal questions. He had a giant law firm on retainer. He was married to an attorney!

"You're unbelievable. You're standing there, lying straight to my face." Her hands shot out, as usual, to punctuate her statement. They landed full force on Nadal's chest.

Nadal's lips curled into a line. He shook his head as if she were Jonah in the midst of a fit. "There must have been some weird drug in one of those bottles of wine, because everyone here is going nuts. I told you the truth. Rachel emailed about work. And I'm not going to stand here while you create a scene."

She centered herself in the narrow hallway leading to their room. "I'm creating a scene? That's your tactic? Play the aggrieved spouse married to a crazy lady?"

Nadal raised an open palm. "It's been a long, stressful day. I'm going to bed. We'll talk about this in the morning when you're more rational."

"I'm completely—"

He grabbed her shoulder and pushed her to the side. The move was barely noticeable, more of a nudge than a blow. Still, she stumbled backward, reeling from his unexpected aggression. In twelve years of marriage and fourteen years together, her husband had never raised a finger to her in anger. Now he was shoving her out of the way.

She braced herself for a door slam as Nadal disappeared into the bedroom. But it didn't come. He passed through the jamb and flipped on a light inside, transforming the entrance into an invitation. Part of her—the part that still desperately loved her husband—urged her to accept. It begged her to follow him inside, close the door behind her, and keep posing questions until he broke down and apologized, enabling her to start forgiving him. A stronger part, however, kept her from moving, made her obey the hissing voice in her lizard brain warning her against trapping her husband in that room. She was too angry. Too capable of violence.

Susan turned away from the bedroom, toward the wall of windows. The moon dangled in the center of the top pane, an air freshener hung over a rearview mirror, driving out the dark and damp. Susan guessed the time was shortly before midnight. She'd have to find something to do with herself for the next hour until Nadal fell asleep. She couldn't trust herself to behave rationally around him—or Rachel.

Motion caught her eye. Louis sat at the outdoor table, pouring something from a glittering bottle. Scotch, probably. Maybe wine. Hopefully wine. She wiped her fingers beneath her eyes and nose, fixing herself as best she could without a mirror. Never before had she so badly needed a drink.

CHAPTER EIGHTEEN

THE DAY AFTER

Gabby's office door bounced against the wall, unable to absorb the fury with which she'd thrown it open. Her husband sat behind her desk, hands folded beside the placard with her new title. Kayla sat across from him. As Gabby stormed in, her daughter looked over her shoulder and pursed her painted lips as though watching someone behaving badly.

Their reserved demeanors poured salt on Gabby's raw anger. How could Derrick act so calm and collected when their daughter had sneaked into a party thrown by sexual predators to drink illegally, and he'd committed third-degree assault? Did he not realize what could have happened to them? Instead of investigating Mariel's date rape, she could be in a hospital, squeezing her teenager's hand as a forensic examiner roughly swabbed for a stranger's sperm, or perhaps wiping off vomit induced by some sickening cocktail of antiviral and anticonception drugs.

Derrick, meanwhile, would be in jail for sucker-punching a wealthy white tourist, praying that some prosecutor wouldn't look at his six-foot-three boxer body and dark Black skin and see a threat that needed to be locked up for the maximum year-long sentence. Worse, he could be in the hospital himself.

The thought of the alternative universe she'd come so close to entering made her vibrate like a high note. She stood in the doorjamb, shaking and staring at the irreplaceable pieces of her heart in the room, unable to release the scream in her chest. Tears blurred her vision of Kayla into another version, without the kohl emphasizing the upturned eyes and gloss slicking the pouty lips. She was her beach baby with golden-brown skin and braided pigtails, each tied with bright resin beads that clacked like castanets as she ran along the water's edge.

"I want the makeup off." The words exploded from Gabby's tight throat. She pointed to her husband. "There are tissues in the top drawer. Hand them to her. I want it off. All of it. Off."

Derrick opened the drawer, rolling his eyes toward their child as if to say *you did it now*. He passed the plastic tissue pack across the desk. Kayla peeled back the tab and withdrew a Kleenex. "I'm sorry, Mom." She wiped the napkin across her mouth, smearing the strawberry color rather than removing it. "I'd only heard it was a pool party. Alice—she's the au pair that watches Katie's little brother—was invited. She told her about it, and Katie said she was going. I thought the crowd would be younger."

Gabby swatted a tear and strode over to Derrick, passing a bookcase stacked with law manuals and mayoral commendations. She stood beside him and tried to glare through her tears at her kid. "You lied and you drank."

Kayla worried the tissue between her fingers. "I had a plastic cup with some rosé. It barely tasted like alcohol."

Gabby slammed her hand on the wooden desk, leaning over it so that her face was directly in front of her daughter's. "First off, Kayla, you shouldn't be familiar enough with alcohol to make that assessment. You will be spending the remainder of your summer either at work, studying, or on supervised outings with me and your father. No more going to the beach with your friends. No more sleepovers. No more, Kayla."

"But—"

Gabby shot her a silencing look. "You know what also doesn't taste like anything? Date-rape drugs. I spent the morning with a woman barely two years older than you that went to the same party and was slipped something. She woke up in bed next to a man old enough to be her father."

Derrick pointed a finger at Kayla's face. "Like that man you were talking to. Do you realize how fortunate you are that I came when I did, and even luckier that Zoe's mom peeked in on you all at midnight—after the woman finished a long shift at the restaurant and probably could have gone straight to bed." He shifted his attention to Gabby. "Violet called me frantic, asking if they were here. I didn't want to worry you at work, so I started calling all of Kayla's friends and driving around. At twelve thirty or so, I remembered that we have the Find My iPhone app and tracked her cell."

Derrick kept staring at her, awaiting praise for his detective work. Gabby didn't feel like applauding. He should have called her. If Kayla had thought to disable her location sharing, Gabby could have found the party in other ways: asking dispatch about noise complaints or directing the patrol officers to look out for a line of cars. She could have called all the taxi services in town and asked if there was a common address where many people were being dropped off.

"I'm sorry about that girl, Mom. It's awful." Kayla paused, letting the sentences resonate for a moment before following up with the inevitable *but*. "I know not to take drinks from—"

"Don't tell me what you think you know or don't know about people. The folks you know have been vetted by your father and I. You don't know anything about judging character and protecting yourself. All it takes is one guy that seems nice and helpful to bring you back a plastic cup of something that 'barely tastes alcoholic.' You know the man that you were talking to? The blond Tom Brady-looking one."

Kayla shot her father an annoyed, betrayed look, like he'd blabbed about the man's appearance. "I said Chris Hemswor—"

Gabby flung a hand toward the wall, beyond which lay Interrogation One. "He's a murder suspect."

Kayla shifted her full focus to her father, silently appealing for him to speak on her behalf. Derrick's tight jaw warned against pulling him into her defense. "I'm sure he's not a psycho killer," she mumbled.

Gabby straightened. "You think I'm joking? Why do you think I asked your father to bring you here to the station in the middle of a homicide investigation, huh? I need you both to look at that man and confirm he was the one you were speaking with last night." Gabby whirled on Derrick. "The one that you punched."

Her husband looked at her like a defense attorney surprised in court by an unknown witness. He pulled his bottom lip beneath his top teeth. "The man was chatting up our sixteen-year-old."

"No excuse," Gabby snapped. "You could have gotten her, Zoe, and Katie out of there without a fight. If it's this man, then he's a big guy, Derrick. He could have had a weapon. He could have had friends at the party. You didn't know."

Derrick rubbed his forehead. "I saw red, honey."

Gabby could sympathize, but being overcome with anger wasn't an assault defense. "We'll talk later." She gestured toward the door. "In the meantime, I need you two to look at this man and verify that he's the guy from last night. If he is, I'll need you both to give a statement to one of the officers on duty."

Kayla headed to the open door, trying to make amends for her disobedience by following directions without delay. Derrick pushed the chair back and stood, towering over

Gabby's slight form. The size difference didn't lessen her desire to sock him in the arm for putting himself at unnecessary risk and not calling her. It also didn't stop her from wrapping her arms around his hard torso and squeezing. He'd performed a parent's primary function, saving their baby from suffering the consequences of naïve stupidity.

He patted her head as she held on to his torso, burying her face in his ribs. "It's okay," he said. "It didn't happen."

She sniffed as she broke away. "When did you leave the party?"

Derrick pushed in her chair and rounded the desk. "A little after one. I was thinking of calling the cops, and the renter came over to talk me out of it."

"Near bald? Surfer? Green eyes?"

"Sounds right." Derrick held the top of the chair, leaning forward so that his height wasn't so intimidating. "The guy made an announcement that the cops were on the way. That seemed to shut everything down. Lots of people left around the same time we did."

"What about the man you hit?"

Derrick winced at the repeated mention of his assault. "He left right after the punch."

"What time?"

"Maybe ten minutes earlier, around one o'clock." Derrick scratched his bushy eyebrow. "I didn't really think about how large he was when I hit him. You're right that he could have gone a couple rounds with me. Guess it's good that he just put up his hands and started apologizing."

Gabby ushered them both into the hallway toward

Interrogation One. Instead of pulling back the door to where she'd left Ben to stew for the past ninety minutes, she opened the neighboring observation room. The closet-sized space wasn't big enough for the three of them, plus the uniformed officer sitting inside behind the computer screen, looking painfully young and even more painfully bored. Detective DeMarco would be finishing up his individual interviews. Officer Kelly was probably watching everyone else.

Gabby gave Patrolman Phillips the two-second explanation of why her husband and daughter needed to identify Ben through the one-way window without delving into the particulars of the fight. She waved Kayla in first, leaving Derrick outside so that his recollection wouldn't be influenced.

"Is this the man?"

Kayla craned her neck toward the window. Ben sat at the desk, staring at what would appear to be a mirror for him, without seeming to focus on anything reflected in it. His eyes were less red and the swelling on his lip had turned a dark purple. Gabby tried to see him not as a suspect but through the eyes of her teenage daughter. He had leading-man looks. Gabby could imagine a bunch of older girls at the party trying to talk to him. Her daughter was competitive. Even though Kayla couldn't have wanted anything to actually happen between her and a forty-year-old, she'd probably been flattered to have him flirting. His attention would have proved to any of the older girls present just how much Kayla could hold her own.

"That's him," Kayla said. "He told me that his name was Ben."

"How long were you talking to him?"

Kayla gave her a guilty look. "A while. Maybe thirty minutes."

Gabby cleared her throat. "And what time did he leave?"

"As soon as Dad . . ." Kayla glanced at the uniformed officer.

Gabby circled her hand, urging Kayla to spit it out. "It'll all end up on the record."

Kayla's shoulders rounded. The prospect of causing legal trouble for her father had finally made her appreciate the seriousness of her actions. "As soon as Dad hit him. We got home at twenty-five after one, and he'd left earlier. So maybe one o'clock or one ten?"

"And his clothes?"

Kayla's unlined brow raised in confusion. "Huh?"

"Were his clothes dry?"

"Yeah. Why does that—"

Gabby cut off her question with an instruction to wait outside and bring in her dad. Derrick's large body overwhelmed the small room. The temperature ticked up a couple degrees as he examined the man through the glass. "It's him." He looked down at Gabby, an unreadable mix of emotion in his brown eyes. "He killed his wife?"

Gabby stopped herself from responding—even though she knew the answer was no. Susan had seen Rachel, alive, on the jetty around 12 AM, after witnessing Ben's return from the beach. There wouldn't have been time for him to kill his wife, change into dry clothing, find the party, and then casually chat up her teenage daughter before getting into a fight with her husband. And the forensic expert was sure Rachel had died before one AM.

She gestured with her chin to the uniformed officer behind her husband, signaling that she couldn't tell Derrick anything official about the case, especially now that he'd become a part of it. A skilled defense attorney could use any information Derrick possessed against her, arguing that she'd wanted to avoid an assault charge against her husband, leading her to pin the murder on Ben. From this point forward, she'd have to be careful not to share any details of the murder investigation.

She told the patrolman to take Kayla's and Derrick's statements, a job that visibly brightened the young man's blank expression. No one liked staring at a suspect in an empty room for hours. "Thanks for everything, honey." She hugged her husband. "I'll see you whenever I can get out of here."

The end of her day couldn't come soon enough. Gabby was acutely aware of her exhaustion. She'd run out at eleven the prior night to investigate the DUI and had been working on adrenaline and indignation for the fifteen hours since—and she was no closer to solving either case. Ben, her prime suspect in Rachel's murder, had a solid alibi. And Mariel's rapist had multiple people attesting to her apparent consent.

Gabby leaned against the door to Interrogation One as she watched Officer Phillips lead her husband and daughter toward a private area where they could provide official statements. She stifled a face-swallowing yawn as they exited the room of cubicles and then turned around to face her next task: letting Ben go.

She opened the door and called his name from the jamb, prevented from entering by regret. She'd treated him like the murder suspect that his injuries and actions had suggested. He hadn't deserved any of it. "Your alibi checked out," she said. "You're free to go."

Ben rose from the table. His beaten posture as he shuffled toward the exit negated his handsomeness. He looked ill and aging, an "after" picture of a washed-up celebrity.

"I'm sorry for your loss." Gabby's sympathy had the opposite effect of what she'd desired. Ben's face twisted in pain.

"I have to tell my kids now," he said. "I need to head to their camps."

The tears from Gabby's earlier encounter with Kayla returned. She'd been trained not to touch suspects. But her human instincts had existed before the academy. She patted Ben's arm. "Can you think of anyone that would have wanted to hurt your wife?"

Ben sucked in air, suppressing his sobs. "I've been thinking about nothing else the entire time I've been in here. All I can come up with is this case that Rachel was working on. It was big, involving the death of a young boy. I could tell that it was worrying her, but she wouldn't divulge any details beyond what I just told you." He rubbed the corner of his right eye. "Not talking about work was unusual for her. Rachel always felt like attorney–client privilege didn't extend to telling significant others. She'd usually talk my ear off about whatever she'd been working on." Ben chuckled, the laughter sounded like crying. "Maybe someone was angry about the case. I know her personal Gmail account and password, though not her work one. You can go through it, maybe?"

Gabby didn't know if the information would prove helpful, but she lacked any other leads. She pulled out her notepad and took down Rachel's login and password information. Afterward, she escorted Ben to the station exit, wishing him luck with his children.

Each step back to her office felt heavier than the last. By the time she reached the door, her legs were wobbling beneath her weight. She slumped into her chair, pulled up a Gmail page, and logged into Rachel's private account.

The first three emails were all unread direct mailers for online stores that Rachel must have frequented. 10% OFF THE SUMMER'S HOTTEST DRESSES. SHOES. SHOES. SHOES! DON'T MISS THIS SALE! Gabby was about to close the page when she recognized a name in the list of unread messages. Susan Ahmadi had sent her friend something at 12:15 AM. In the subject line were three words: ABOUT THURSDAY NIGHT . . .

Gabby clicked on the message, expecting to see photos of Susan and Rachel socializing. One line of bolded, all-caps text dominated the screen.

STAY AWAY FROM MY HUSBAND.

CHAPTER NINETEEN

THE DAY OF

Jenny's tailbone throbbed atop the thin carpet in the back of the SUV. She peeled her spine from the hard surface, propped herself up on her elbows, and surveyed her surroundings: tan leather walls, gray tinted windows, a low dome ceiling. The Suburban's third row had folded flat with the press of a button, creating a bed long and wide enough for her and Ben to lie beside one another, albeit with Ben's head poking between the second-row bucket seats. She grimaced as she pictured William and Chloe in the car, their camp suitcases piled where she reclined. She'd slept with their dad. And she'd done it before.

The first time had been in more respectable surroundings, though only slightly. Jenny could still remember Ben's home office that day six months earlier. He'd converted a screened porch off his kitchen into a permanent writer's room, complete with a desk, a couch, and books piled in every possible cranny. The room overlooked the backyard.

That afternoon, it had been flooded with white light reflecting off the recent snow. The glow had intoxicated her as she'd knelt beside Ben's bare legs, rubbing his knee with antiseptic.

She'd decided to give him a cortisone injection, free of charge—a thank-you for letting Ally sleep over the prior night, despite Rachel being away at a conference. Louis had been growing increasingly testy, and Jenny had asked Ben to watch Ally, hoping that a kid-free evening would dial down the building pressure.

Instead, it had pulled the lid off. She and Louis had experienced their worst fight in over a year. Louis had accused her of ignoring him in favor of gallivanting among her admirers, and when she'd countered that she'd been *working off their mortgage*, he'd cracked the back of her head against a wall. She'd locked herself in the guest room for the remainder of that night, ignoring Louis's sporadic apologies and pleas to talk things out "rationally," reemerging only when she'd been sure he'd left for his hospital rounds. All the usual day-after emotions had filled her heart: rage, betrayal, hurt, fear. But she'd felt something new that morning, too—a burning desire to get even.

Given Louis's dislike of *the boy toy next door*, lavishing attention on Ben had seemed the perfect act of passive aggression. She'd stopped at the pharmacy and then gone to the house armed with a syringe, iodine, a tube of lidocaine, and a bottle filled with a gummy white corticosteroid solution. Ben had answered the door, looking ruggedly handsome in a T-shirt and jeans, the silver-flecked scruff of a shaveless week shining on his jaw. Seeing him, Jenny had felt a queasy mix of attraction poisoned with her latent fury. It had bubbled in her gut and blurted from her mouth in the form of gross flirtation. "I brought a thank-you present," she'd said, shaking a clear plastic bag containing the medications and all- too-obvious inch-and-a-half-long needle. "So, drop your pants."

Ben had suggested they move to his office, and Jenny had trailed him through the kitchen, still messed with syrup-streaked plates and an unplugged, unwashed waffle iron. He'd entered the office and then stood in the center with his hands shoved in his pockets, rocking back on his heels. "So, um, do you want any water or anything first? I guess I probably should have offered when we were in the kitchen."

Jenny had interpreted the jittery body language and hesitant speech as nervousness about the injection. "I know it looks big. But, I swear, it's just a little prick. You'll barely feel a thing."

Ben had responded with the same awkward sexual humor she'd displayed at the door. "I said something like that to Rachel once. Now we have two kids."

The resulting laughter had shattered some of the tension in the chilly room. He'd gone to the couch, unbuttoned his pants, and shimmied them down to his ankles, exposing his knees and blue boxer briefs. Jenny had instructed him to sit and then knelt between his legs to rub iodine over the arthritic knee. She'd told him to relax, pulled out the needle, filled it with the necessary mix of painkiller and joint filler, and then inserted its long nose into the thin space behind his patella. "In a few days," she'd said, popping her equipment back into the plastic bag, "that knee should feel all better."

"Thanks." Ben had winced, as though the shot had hurt more than she'd said. "And how about your head?"

She'd responded as if he'd revealed psychic powers, shooting upright and backing away.

"There's a little blood in your hair." Ben had given her a guilty smile. "I saw when you were kneeling."

A pat to the back of her head had confirmed the bump and crusted hair. The prior night's blow had hurt, but she hadn't thought it bad enough to leave a visible injury. "I banged it on the . . ." She'd trailed off, unable to think of any piece of furniture high enough to be casually slammed by a skull.

"You don't have to protect him," Ben had said.

A better woman, Jenny thought, would have balked at the suggestion that anything was wrong with her husband or her marriage. She'd have feigned shock and stuttered something about Ben speaking out of turn. But she hadn't felt up to playing the part of a good wife. Someone had finally spotted the suffering beneath her smiling mask.

Instead, she'd told him everything: how Louis's jealousy over her success and notoriety led to arguments that occasionally became violent; how they'd unsuccessfully tried therapy several times; how she'd considered leaving but feared destroying Ally's stable life and Louis using their daughter as a foot soldier in the resulting divorce battle.

Ben had listened to it all like a best friend, refusing to

let her share the blame when she admitted to hitting Louis back, or sometimes baiting him so that she could get the violence over with on her terms. As she'd looked into Ben's kind eyes, their blue so much deeper than Louis's, she'd thought that Rachel must be the stupidest woman in the world not to realize how lucky she was to have him. Why couldn't she have a man like this one? Jenny had asked herself as Ben thumbed a tear from her cheek and stroked her hair. Why, in fact, didn't she?

And now, like that first time, Jenny's sense of self-righteous satisfaction had lasted only until the moment of Ben's shuddering orgasm. Lying on the Suburban's lowered back seat, her underwear tossed near her head, she felt only a deep disappointment. She'd cheated on her husband with Ben, a guy skeevy enough to sleep with his neighbor in the family car while his unsuspecting wife moped outside. In doing so, she'd become the kind of woman mothers warned their newly married daughters to watch out for, the one wives monitored at work functions, tracking their unnecessarily seductive movements as they worked the room in business-inappropriate attire. The woman pathetic enough to be the *other* woman.

Jenny rolled into a sitting position. "Are my clothes behind you?"

Ben sat up, rounding his stomach over his bent knees to keep his head from hitting the ceiling. He picked up the pile of crumpled fabric on his left side and passed it to her. "Do you want to go home? I can drive us home right now. At this hour, we can probably get back by three AM."

Jenny slipped her feet into her shorts and pulled them on, feeling her way in the near dark. "You've been drinking for hours. You can't drive right now."

"You take the keys for the first hour. I'll grab a black coffee on the road. We can switch once I sober up."

Despite the night's charcoal filter, Jenny could discern the intensity of Ben's gaze. She looked away. "I can't leave with you."

"Okay. You'll take a car service, then? Or the train? I'll drive and meet you back home."

The urgency to escape that she'd felt thirty minutes earlier suddenly seemed unnecessary. Foolish, even. Louis had choked her for betraying his trust and sharing their private marital shame. In actuality, she was guilty of far worse.

Ben cupped the back of her neck. She winced as the tips of his fingers grazed the bruised skin on her throat. "Jenny. You can't stay."

Not forever, Jenny knew. Not if things didn't change. She understood that a marriage where neither party consistently loved, honored, or cherished the other wasn't sustainable. But she no longer felt that she *had* to leave as soon as possible.

The physicality of the past twenty-four hours had drained her energy. She couldn't imagine doing everything that needed to be done in her current state: moving financial assets, grabbing her clothing from the house, renting an apartment, hiring a divorce attorney. Telling Louis and Ally. She couldn't have all those conversations. She could barely swallow.

She pulled her blouse over her head and reached for her purse. The pills inside it would make her feel better. She could figure out her next move once her throat stopped burning and her head stopped pounding.

She unzipped her bag and plunged her hand inside. She felt the rough canvas of her makeup bag. The smooth leather of her wallet. Her nails didn't hit the plastic cylinders containing her self-prescribed abusive-husband treatment: Oxys and Ambiens. She had a vision of fixing her makeup in the bathroom. Her pain pills and sleep aids were on the bathroom sink.

"I have to go back inside. My throat hurts."

"What?" Moonlight glinted in the center of Ben's navy eyes. "You're not going back to him. You said you were done."

"I need my pain medication." Her voice cracked. "My throat is burning. My arms are bruised. And I'm so tired. I want to get some sleep and then—"

"Sleep? Next to that asshole? Jenny. I am here and I can help. I can take you someplace safe. I can get you home."

Jenny felt a surge of anger at Ben's misguided chivalry. The last thing she needed was another man forcing her to do something she didn't want to do. They were sleeping together. That was it. She was Ben's way of getting back at Rachel for treating him like a servant. And he'd never given her anything more than a temporary reprieve from her life with Louis.

"You'll take me home, huh? We'll have sex again, maybe." Bitterness sharpened her tone. "And then what?"

Ben grasped her biceps. He didn't dig his fingers into

her flesh like Louis had earlier, but he held her firmly. "He'll kill you one day. You know that, don't you?"

"He's not a murderer, Ben."

"Not yet. You told me that after he gets rough with you, he's on his best behavior for months." He released her arms and raised his index finger to his face, indicating her bruise on his own cheek. "He gave you that shiner what, last week? It's Friday and he choked you in a house filled with your friends. What do you really think he'd do if he found out about us?"

Fear filled the hollows inside Jenny. Ben had never gotten this passionate with her before. Was he threatening to tell Louis if she didn't leave with him? Would he betray her like that, knowing the consequences she could face?

"A lot of men would do horrible things if they discovered their wife sleeping with their neighbor." She spoke carefully, watching Ben's face for signs of a threat. "That's why we can't ever let Louis know. It would be terrible for both of us."

"He'll kill you even if he never knows, Jenny. He'll kill you because you keep giving him another chance. He'll kill you because you'll let him."

Jenny closed her eyes, locking the building tears beneath her lids. In the darkness, she saw Louis's hateful stare as he squeezed her neck. He'd looked at her like he'd wanted her to stop talking. To stop existing. She lifted the hem of her blouse and brought it to her wet cheeks. "I have Ally. What am I supposed to do?"

Ben grasped her hand. "Ally needs her mother alive and

well. You have to leave. Go home. Call a lawyer. File for divorce. You have your own money. You'll get the house. You'll have Ally. I'll testify that I saw the bruises. Take photos of your neck. You can use them. No judge in the world will award custody to an abuser."

Ben made it sound so easy. Natural, even. But his fantasy didn't feature Louis. She hadn't married a man who accepted defeat.

"Please." Ben's eyes shimmered. "Please leave him. Please. I love you."

Jenny averted her gaze, unable to see him lie to her face. He didn't really love her. Ben enjoyed sex with her. He found her attractive. He liked talking sports with her, laughing at their awkward, self-deprecating jokes and discussing school activities. But love required more than some common interests and sexual compatibility. It demanded a willingness to sacrifice for the other person, to subordinate your own needs and desires. Jenny wasn't sure Ben really loved anyone besides his children.

"Please, Jenny. I'll file for divorce, too. No one will know we were together beforehand. Louis will think he finally crossed the line and Rachel will think our fight was the final straw. After we're both officially separated, we can start seeing each other again."

Jenny scoffed. "Think of what you're saying. Rachel won't let you keep that house, and she'll fight you on alimony. You'll have to stop writing and get a . . ." She trailed off rather than saying the offensive phrase on the tip of her tongue. *Real job.*

"I don't care. I'll do anything to know you're safe. I can get a sales job somewhere." He chuckled. "Can't you see me hawking vacuum cleaners door to door? 'Excuse me, miss. Have you heard about the life-changing cleaning power of the Dyson ball?'"

Jenny laughed in spite of herself. "I think that profession died with Willy Loman."

Ben's strong arms wrapped around her torso. "I'm not worried about work. I can get a job. I am worried about you. I love you, and I believe that you love me too, Jen. Please."

Jenny wanted to return the sentiment, but she couldn't—at least, not yet. She'd never let herself think of Ben as a truly romantic option. She *did* love being in his arms. She loved feeling protected and cared for and wanted by a desirable man; it temporarily erased the pain of being beaten by her husband and lessened the humiliation she felt about everything she'd allowed to happen. Ben even suppressed the gut-roiling, bone-shaking fear of everything that would come if she dared change the status quo. But Jenny knew Ben's arms could hold her pain at bay for only a little while. The chalky pills in her bedroom would keep it away for far longer. If she was going to do it—if she was going to really leave Louis—she'd need all the chemical courage she could get. "Give me ten minutes, okay? I need to get my meds."

CHAPTER TWENTY

THE DAY OF

Underwater lights turned the pool ominous. The supernatural glow spilled out onto the lawn, imbuing the whole scene with an otherworldliness befitting a sci-fi horror flick. Louis hunched over the table, one hand supporting his head and the other his drink. He looked like he might want to be alone, but Susan couldn't respect that desire. Misery needed company, or at least alcohol. Louis could provide both.

"Make it a double." She pointed to the scotch on the table. "It's been that kind of night, right?"

He lifted his head from his hand and exhaled. Grabbing the bottle, he gestured to one of the half-dozen used glasses. "Nadal was drinking out of that one."

Susan pushed her husband's empty tumbler toward her neighbor. He poured like an inebriated bartender, filling the wide glass to the halfway line rather than splashing in two shots. "The ice out here is all melted." He stood to pass the drink to her as she sat on the bench across from him.

Susan shrugged as though the lack of any water to cut the brown liquor wasn't a big deal, even though she never drank whiskey, let alone straight up. As she brought the alcohol to her lips and inhaled its sharp aromas of burnt sugar and hair spray, she felt transported to her teenage years when she'd pretended to enjoy the cheap beers older kids smuggled into parties. *I'm cool. I like this liquid that tastes like leftover pasta water and expired spices.* She'd thought that, at thirty-seven, her days of feigning interests for friendships would be behind her.

But she'd thought a lot of things that life was proving false, Susan reminded herself. Better not to think at all.

She gulped from the glass. The liquid seared her throat, stripping away her senses of smell and taste. She chased the swallow with her own saliva to stave off a cough, telling herself that the taste was necessary for numbness. Enough of it and she would no longer feel like a car with a busted transmission, uncontrollably slamming into new emotional gears. Racing panic. Halting depression. Speeding anger. Stopping disappointment. She'd be able to lie beside her husband and, just for tonight, shut down.

Nadal was probably already asleep. The man could pass out anywhere. A coach airline seat. A twin bed with a kid kicking him in the chest. Once, she'd watched him nod off in the corner at a bounce-house birthday party. The first year of the twins' lives—when he'd needed to wake up early for work and help with tandem nighttime feeds—had trained them differently. She'd become conditioned to snooze rather than sleep, always ready to jump up in response to some cry from the kids. Nadal, conversely, had learned to drop into REM wherever and whenever he could.

She could picture him exactly as he'd been all those years ago. His olive complexion, lined only at the corner of his eyes back then, and only because he'd been sleeping so little. They'd both been tired all the time. Each working all day and then coming home to play with the kids until the wee hours of the morning. They'd selfishly let the boys keep night and day confused. Better that they sleep with the sitter and really know their parents, they'd said. Every night, she and Nadal had stayed up with their babies, musing about what they would do with them when they got older. *Rest is for the dead*, they used to say, rolling around in their bed, with its smell of baby powder and Johnson & Johnson's shampoo. They'd been so happy, then. Overworked. Overtired. And unbelievably, sickeningly happy.

Susan's eyes began to burn worse than her throat. She braced herself and swallowed a third of her drink. It went down easier this time. She could detect something like butterscotch mixed in with all the bitterness. People liked whiskey because it was a metaphor for life, she decided. A whole lot of shit with the occasional taste of sweet.

"You're quiet." Louis considered her over the top of his glass. He raised his drink. "Eighty proof for your thoughts."

The alcohol had already worked its magic on her neighbor. Gone was the aggressive man who had knocked on her door an hour earlier and demanded that her husband share a scotch with him. In his place was the semi-charming, awkwardly inappropriate guy from dinner. Susan liked the latter Louis much better than the former, though she couldn't say she really relished either version. Out of all the people in the house, she and Louis had the least in common. Most of what he discussed involved work, a subject she couldn't weigh in on anymore, at least not in any way Louis would take seriously. With Jenny, Rachel, and Ben, she could commiserate about the kids or the school or town activities. But doctor Louis wouldn't relate to her as a fellow parent.

"Nice moon tonight," she said.

Louis looked over his shoulder toward the beach, perhaps just noticing the champagne-colored orb sparkling over the bubbling sea. Susan smirked at her mental association. Her analogies were already under the influence. Good. She sipped her whiskey again. It was opening up. She could taste an almost fruity flavor. Her sense of smell had returned, too. She inhaled the sea air perfumed with salt, the dusky scent of sand, and the green odors of the surrounding grass and scraggly trees. The mix reminded her of a men's cologne. Something fresh and beachy—the kind her husband never wore.

Louis stood from the bench, apparently sick of his near-silent company. The sight shifted Susan back into panic gear. Drinking with acquaintances was socially acceptable. Downing whiskey alone in an empty backyard was the mark of a problem. She struggled to think of some witticism or anecdote that might amuse Louis enough to remain with her until she finished her liquor. But her brain was too clouded with scotch and her memories of Nadal to invent anything original.

Louis grasped the base of his shirt and pulled it over his head. "I'm going for a swim."

Susan leaned back onto the table edge, a druggy relief replacing her adrenaline. She found herself like the main character in *A Clockwork Orange*, stuck to the chair with her eyes unable to close, forced to stare at Louis's long-legged stride over to the pool, to watch his skinny yet defined torso elongate as he curled his toes around the edge of the coping, swept his arms over his head, and dove into the water.

He entered the pool with barely a ripple. Watching his smooth form, Susan could almost understand why Jenny had thought him a catch. Louis wasn't handsome like Ben or sexy like Nadal, but he had a kind of boyish appeal coupled with brains and an arrogance that amplified his talents. People who truly believed they were great had a way of converting those around them.

Susan suddenly felt like swimming alongside him. Not, she told herself, because she was anything like her weak-willed husband or the traitorous siren perched atop the jetty beyond, posed to wreck happy marriages. She wanted to swim because Louis made it look like it felt good. And, darn it, she wanted to feel better.

Rustling snapped Susan's attention to the side yard. A large figure moved along the scrub brush in the shadowed part of the property, beyond the reach of the pool's underwater light.

She sprang from her seat, ready to scamper into the house or scream. "Hello?" Though she felt sharp, the greeting came out slurred. "Hello?"

A man stepped from the bushes—not into the illuminated circle around the pool, exactly, but at least into the moonlit area where she could better discern his outline. "Sorry to startle you. I'm heading down to the beach to talk with Rachel."

Only Ben. Susan stifled a relieved giggle. "Good luck!"

She immediately regretted her response. *Good luck* was for business meetings and charity races. No one wanted to hear something so flip in response to a marriage falling apart. It sounded absurd. Moreover, she didn't want to wish Ben *luck* making up with his whore wife. Rachel didn't deserve to have Ben groveling for forgiveness when she'd slept with Nadal. She deserved to be shoved in the fucking ocean.

"Thanks." Ben resumed his shuffling march toward the path. "I'll need it."

"Wait!"

Ben stopped. *Your wife is sleeping with my husband.* The words stuck in Susan's throat, trapped by some self-preservation instinct preventing her from blurting out life-altering statements under the influence. She forced herself to envision how she'd follow up the accusation. There'd be a trip upstairs for Nadal's computer in order to show Ben the evidence. Nadal might wake and want to know what everything was about, forcing her to confront him, again, in an emotional state—this time with Ben raging downstairs.

Even worse, Ben might go after Nadal. What man wouldn't get physical with the guy who had made him a cuckold? Oddsmakers would favor Ben in any fight against her husband two to one, easy. Ben had been a linebacker, whereas Nadal was a fit dad. She wanted her husband sorry and humiliated, not permanently brain damaged. Nadal was her partner and co-parent. She loved him, damn it. A one-night stand didn't change that for her.

Susan slapped the top of her head as though she'd forgotten what she'd wanted to say. "Nothing. Never mind."

Ben's shadow turned back toward the path. Susan watched him jog down the sandy strip between the dune grasses out to the beach. He turned toward the jetty. In the moonlight, she could make out the shape of a person atop the rocks. Fabric flapped behind the figure. God, how she wished that Rachel would become stuck on that jetty, Prometheus lashed to the rock for stealing what didn't belong to him. Forgiving Nadal would be so much easier if she never had to see Rachel again.

Susan returned her attention to the backyard. Louis had ceased swimming to stare at her, probably ready to recommend some doctor hangover remedy. She looked away from him to the table. Greasy paper plates topped with uneaten bits of food invited vermin to a dinner party. She stacked them on her bare forearm and strode over to the outdoor bin, balancing the mess with all the confidence of a former waitress. They all had their secret skills, she thought. Some people dove into the water like gannets. Some people efficiently dispatched messes, despite being drunk. Some people expertly lied to their significant others. They were all so fucking talented.

She dumped the lot and then went back for the glasses. Before she reached the table, she was stopped by a sharp pain in her left foot, like she'd stepped on a crab hidden in the grass. Yelping, she hobbled to the bench on her good foot and the side of the injured one.

"Are you all right?" Louis stood in the water, arms draped over the edge of the pool.

Susan slumped onto the seat and pulled her right heel over her left knee. In the pool lights, she could just make out the inch-long shard embedded inside. "I think I stepped on Rachel's broken wine bottle."

Louis pulled himself from the pool. In seconds he was kneeling beside her, cupping her heel in his palm. "It's big, but it doesn't look too deep." He gently released her foot and then reached for the whiskey bottle. A shot went into Nadal's tumbler. He passed her the glass with one hand and grasped the bottle with the other. "Drink that."

"What?"

A searing pain answered her question. Louis knelt by her heel with the whiskey tilted over her foot. "Scottish disinfectant," he joked. He gestured with his chin. "Really, drink that."

Susan threw back the shot as Louis squeezed her heel. With a surgeon's steadiness, he pinched the glass between his fingers and plucked it from the wound. She felt the pressure release as the shiv came out, followed by a dribble of blood. Louis tilted the bottle over the gash a second time and then reached back into the grass for his discarded shirt. He pressed the fabric against the wound. "It's not deep. A few minutes of pressure should do it."

The shot, mixed with the shock of what had happened, made Susan feel sloshed again. She stammered and slurred a string of thank-yous punctuated with compliments on Louis's medical ability and excuses as to why she hadn't seen such a large piece of glass shining in the lawn. "I completely forgot she'd dropped that wine earlier."

Louis pressed his hand harder into Susan's foot. "Well, that's Rachel for you. She makes a mess and doesn't care if her friends are hurt in the process. I know you don't know her well, but you're going to find that woman cares about one thing—money."

Susan nodded her agreement. Perhaps Rachel had made a play for Nadal because she'd heard he would be very wealthy once his company went public. "There's a special place in hell for people that don't know the importance of family," she quipped.

"Or friends." Louis grinned up at her, continuing to apply pressure. "I bet she'd sue the homeowner's insurance on your behalf for hurting yourself on the bottle that she broke, though—as long as she could get her cut. She'd argue that it was the homeowner's responsibility to provide renters with decanters that wouldn't break from a fall of four feet. They should have known better than to assume adults would behave responsibly."

Susan snorted. "I think the rental agreement included a pledge to behave responsibly."

"Oh well. Rachel will have to sue the glass manufacturer, then. Imagine, glass being breakable!"

Louis laughed, a little too loudly for the lame joke. Susan was tempted to ask why he, too, disliked Rachel. But she feared doing so would only raise the question of why she was so comfortable with making fun of a so-called friend. Drunk or not drunk, she couldn't get into that without first really having it out with Nadal.

Susan felt a surge of disgust at how her husband had callously involved Louis in his cover-up, claiming he'd been outside Rachel's room to ask a question on Louis's behalf. "Hey, when Nadal was down here, he said he was looking for Rachel to ask a question for you."

Louis's smile faded at the corners. "Oh, he told you about that?"

"Well, not much. What—"

Scratching footsteps interrupted her question. Simultaneously, Susan and Louis turned their attention to the beach path. Ben strode toward the house, his back hunched in defeat. No one followed him into the yard.

"Ben," Susan called.

He looked up for a moment, long enough for her to see his shamed expression in the pool lights. Susan scooted back on the bench, concerned that Ben hadn't seen the reason Louis knelt beside her, grasping her foot. "I cut my—"

Ben jogged past them into the side yard, toward the cars. Susan looked down at her doctor, seeking direction as to whether they should try to clarify things. Louis slowly withdrew his T-shirt from her heel. "Rachel probably threatened to sue him for emotional damages," he said, shaking out his shirt. Susan's blood had left a large dark mark in the center of the light fabric, a bull's-eye for a marksman.

"Give that to me. I'll wash it."

He balled it up. "Don't worry about it. It's a shirt." He gestured to her heel. "Bleeding stopped. But you should put a Band-Aid on it."

Susan did her best to compensate Louis for the medical care with compliments as she hobbled around the table, collecting glasses. She turned the wine goblets upside down and slid the stems between her fingers, enabling her to carry four in one hand. Louis grabbed the remaining wine glass, promising to return for the scotch tumblers. "You're injured," he said sternly as she started to protest. "We can't have you hoofing around like a pack mule, and I don't want you to reopen your heel."

She took the long way around the pool to get back to the house, avoiding the entire area where Rachel had dropped the bottle. When she approached the edge of the lawn, she turned toward the beach and the jetty. Perhaps Rachel, humiliated by her public argument and unable to reconcile with Ben, had decided to go home. Her spirits lifted at the thought, though only for the moment it took to see Rachel's outline standing atop the jetty, her kimono waving behind her like a cape. *Super bitch*, Susan mumbled under her breath.

Louis stood holding back the door, despite having to wait for Susan's lame walk around the lawn. She thanked him for the umpteenth time and walked through to the sucking sound of the front door popping open. The hallway was too dark to see who had gone out. Whoever it was, though, closed the door behind him or her with barely a click.

Susan glanced behind her to see if Louis had registered the noise. He smiled with half his mouth, a kind of smirk that Susan now read as more satisfied than sarcastic. Probably just Ben coming in through the front, she decided, seeking to avoid them all until morning.

She limped over to the kitchen sink and placed the glasses in a line. Louis added his lot and then headed back to the door for the final collection. Water squealed through the pipes as she turned on the faucet and began rinsing everything with the half-full bottle of Dawn left on the counter. Just as she finished with the last one, Louis returned with the four scotch glasses. He grabbed a paper towel and began drying as she rinsed. A doctor that does the dishes, she thought. She could definitely understand what Jenny had seen in him.

After everything was dried and put back into the appropriate cabinet, Louis announced that he would head upstairs to shower. Susan thanked him again for fixing her foot and waved good-night, feeling a smidge better that she'd made a friend of one couple during the trip. Rachel and Ben were no longer an option, though she supposed feigning friendliness would be unavoidable. Their boys were very close. She couldn't ask Jamal to abandon a pal because she found it painful to see the kid's unscrupulous mother, especially when she'd have to see her over the fence, anyway—all the time.

The thought sickened Susan. She hobbled over to her purse, left in the kitchen, and withdrew her cell. She hit the email application, scrolling down to a message from Rachel discussing her wish list for the rental. *A hot tub*, Rachel had said. She'd probably wanted to cozy up to Nadal inside it. Susan hit reply and changed the subject line to the one imprinted in her memory. She typed the five words that she wanted to scream in Rachel's lying face and hit send.

The email failed to make her feel much better. There would be no way she and Nadal could stay away from the hussy next door. The only way they'd never see Rachel again was if that bitch disappeared.

CHAPTER TWENTY-ONE

THE DAY AFTER

Gabby placed the emptied garbage pail beside her new prime suspect's elbow. Susan sat behind the table with one arm resting on the surface and the other propped up on the joint, forming a bracket support for her forehead. At the sight of the bin, she lifted her head to face Gabby, displaying the sallow complexion that had prompted the emergency barf bucket. "I don't think I'll vomit again," Susan said, her breathy voice belying the statement. "I got it all out at the beach. I'm just tired."

Murdering someone takes a lot of energy, Gabby thought. She pulled out her chair. "I understand Detective DeMarco informed you of your Miranda rights."

Susan squeezed her eyes shut and rubbed her left temple with the heel of her hand. "I've told you both everything I know about last night."

"What about Thursday night?"

Susan's eyes snapped open. Gabby pulled her notebook

from her jacket pocket and flipped through a couple of pages, pretending to search for something said during another interview. "You sent an email to Rachel shortly before her murder demanding that she stay away from your husband." Gabby eyed Susan for new fidgets. "They were having an affair."

The look on Susan's face encouraged Gabby to push the garbage pail a centimeter closer. "No." Susan took a shallow breath. "It was nothing like that."

Gabby tilted her head. "Well, it must have been something like that for you to tell a friend to stay away from your husband."

Susan dropped her forehead into her hands. The act could be read as exhaustion or regret. Gabby could definitely sympathize with the exhaustion. She could also understand—if not fully empathize with—how the anxious and seemingly sensitive woman in front of her had been thrown into a murderous rage. "I get how you must have felt," she said to Susan. "I'm married, and I can't imagine what I'd do if one of my neighbors—a woman I'd considered a friend, no less—went after my husband." Gabby ducked her head, trying to look Susan in the eye. "I'd do more than tell her to back off in an email, that's for sure. I'd confront her face-to-face, make sure she knew how serious I was about protecting my family."

Susan drove her fingers into her hair, pulling back the pieces that had dried stringy from a hasty rinse, likely in one of the station bathrooms. "I wish I hadn't sent that stupid message. I was being overly sensitive. Rachel wasn't after Nadal."

"Did she tell you that when you confronted her?"

Susan dropped her arms and straightened her neck. The eyes that met Gabby's were hard as marbles. "I didn't confront her."

"Come on, Susan. Do you really think anyone will believe that? She was after your husband."

Susan rolled her eyes. "Nope. I had a few scotches with Louis in the backyard. Afterward, I sent that email and then passed out on the couch."

"The couch?" Gabby had expected Susan to claim to have slept beside her husband, thereby establishing an alibi. Instead, her suspect had confessed to sleeping alone. Susan had either slipped up, or she'd consciously come clean because she knew Nadal wouldn't lie for her. Or, perhaps, she suspected that someone—likely Ben—had seen her on the couch. Whatever her reason, though, she'd just admitted to lacking a verifiable alibi for the time of Rachel's murder.

Gabby softened her tone, aiming for a kind of sisterly sympathy that might stoke a confession. "I understand that you now think you overreacted. At twelve fifteen AM, though, you thought Rachel was after your husband—a man you've been married to for over a decade, right? With whom you have two children. You'd have been understandably upset. I would have been. Any woman would have been. You would have wanted to tell her to back off in person. And I can understand how things would go awry. Rachel was argumentative, clearly. She'd already had a huge public fight with her husband. I can imagine her getting defensive instead of apologizing like a decent person. What did she do on that jetty?" Gabby lowered her voice to a conspiratorial level. "Scream at you? Push you? That's really how you cut your foot, isn't it?"

Susan's lips were pressed together like a stamp on an ink pad. Gabby read the strained body language as a desperate effort to contain the truth. The confession was at the tip of Susan's tongue, fighting to be freed.

"I'd understand if you pushed her into the water. I really would. If it were me, I'd have wanted to knock her off her perch, too." Gabby searched Susan's eyes for confirmation but saw only the same flinty stare. "Or maybe, even worse, she shoved you and you pulled her down with you. You had to defend yourself. She'd screwed up her own marriage and now she wanted yours. She was threatening to steal your husband, destroy your family, take your boys' father . . ."

Gabby trailed off, giving Susan a chance to fill in the ellipses. The woman inhaled until her chest threatened to tear her tank top. Gabby suppressed a smile. *Here we go.*

"Thank-you for outlining the prosecution's case against me." Susan sat back in her chair. The distressed demeanor Gabby had witnessed since that morning vanished. "Now I understand what I'll be dealing with if this nonsense ever makes it to court, which I very much doubt." She folded her arms across her chest. "I'm invoking my right to remain silent and my right to an attorney. This interrogation is over, as is my stay here, unless you arrest me. As I believe that is your intention, I request to speak to my husband. Since he is here, as a voluntary witness, I ask that you send him in so that I may inform him of my whereabouts and have him contact an attorney. I'm certain one of my former colleagues at Jungblut, Abramson, and Dershowitz will take the case. No doubt Jungblut herself."

The name of the famous defense attorney was a slap across the face. Thanks to several high-profile celebrity cases, Jungblut was known nationwide, not just for winning cases at trial but for getting charges dismissed before the court even convened. She'd become famous for getting cases thrown out for violations of the right to a speedy trial, insufficient evidence, and questionable handling of evidence.

Gabby gawked at the former emotional wreck before her. She'd made a grave mistake, she realized. When Detective DeMarco had asked Susan's profession, she'd said only that she homeschooled her autistic son. Gabby hadn't given much thought to what the woman had done for a living prior to becoming a stay-at-home mom. If anything, she'd assumed she'd probably been a teacher or a child psychologist. She certainly hadn't thought *lawyer*.

Attorneys couldn't be handled like average suspects. The typical guilty person could be cowed by a good story or cajoled into a confession simply by an authority figure showing some sympathy for a violent reaction. But lawyers knew that whatever story the police and prosecution crafted—no matter how compelling and logical—was no more than a fairy tale unless backed by facts. Gabby had unwittingly revealed that all she had against Susan was a motive theory, a nasty email, some blood in the backyard, and a lack of an alibi witness. Without a confession, the circumstantial case would barely be sufficient to press charges, let alone win a jury trial—especially if Jungblut was the attorney.

Gabby slammed the door behind her as she exited the room, furious with herself for misjudging the fellow mom. She stormed past the cubicles and into the corridor, heading to the soft interrogation room where Detective DeMarco was no doubt grilling Nadal about his "relationship with the deceased."

Before throwing the door back, she peered through its transom window. Nadal sat on the couch with his hands in his lap while DeMarco glared at him from a corner of the room. Given that Nadal's wife had been a criminal defense attorney, Gabby suspected he'd demanded a lawyer as soon as DeMarco had finished Mirandizing him.

Gabby flung open the door. "Interview over?"

DeMarco shot Nadal a sideways glance. "He exercised his right to silence before saying hello. He's demanding his attorney."

"Well, she's in Interrogation One," Gabby quipped.

DeMarco's expression cursed for him. "That's convenient."

Nadal didn't react to the conversation being conducted in front of him. He sat on the couch like he was waiting outside a hospital room, hands folded, head bowed.

"If you would come with me," Gabby said, "your wife would like to speak with you. We intend to arrest her for the murder of Rachel Klein."

Nadal shot up. "That's insane."

The uncontrolled emotion evident in the abrupt movement gave Gabby an idea. An incensed non-lawyer might not be careful with his words, particularly if he thought he was defending his wife or his honor. Since he'd asked for a lawyer, Gabby couldn't ask him any questions related to the case. However, there was no law stating that Gabby couldn't inform him of his wife's situation, encouraging him to let slip whatever had led Susan to discover the affair, or mistakenly believe there'd been one.

"Well, her motive's not so crazy. She thought you were sleeping with Rachel." Gabby kept her voice level, as though she had the evidence to back it up. "That would be a lot for any wife to handle, especially given that the other woman had pretended to be her friend, and lived next door."

Nadal shook his head like an obstinate child. "Susan knows that's not true."

Gabby smirked. "We have that email, and she's not denying it."

"Because she's protecting me." Nadal threw his hands out, too upset to rein in his gestures. "The email wasn't about an affair."

"I don't believe that." Gabby raised her voice, turning up the room temperature. "I read it. Anyone that reads it—"

"It was about work!" Nadal stood like an evangelical preacher appealing to the crowd, both palms out to invoke the Good Lord. "Work. The whole thing was concerning a case. I can show you the damn document."

CHAPTER TWENTY-TWO

THE DAY OF

Jenny opened the front door barely wide enough to slip through sideways. She rushed through the hallway, compensating for the squeak of her sneakers on the concrete floor with speed. When she reached the end of the corridor, she hovered there and squinted at the far wall of windows. If Louis wasn't outside, she'd have to forgo her medications. She'd couldn't risk another fight in a locked bedroom.

Susan sat at the outdoor dining table, clearly exposed by the moonlight and glow from the pool. She watched someone swimming. Jenny recognized the arms breaking above the water. Louis was doing laps, releasing his anger with a new exercise given that he'd knocked out his sparring partner.

He wouldn't see her while facedown in the water. Still, Jenny stuck to the shadowed area under the second-floor loft, emerging into the light only to race up the open staircase. She turned down the hallway to the master suite and rushed to the bedroom. It appeared as she'd left it: lit by moonlight, the bed mussed but made. She could discern the impression of her prone body in the duvet, an inverted chalk outline in the puffy ground. Deep divots flanked the concave center where Louis had placed his knees.

The sight increased her determination to get her medications and get out of there. She ran to the bathroom, her heartbeat throbbing in her inflamed throat. The bottles were visible where she'd left them on the wide rim of the pedestal sink. Their labels, however, were not.

She pressed down one of the bottle's childproof caps with the heel of her hand and twisted it off. It was too risky to turn on a light, so, like a blind woman, she confirmed the nature of the pill by touch, tracing her finger on the round face to feel the letters *OP* stamped on the surface. The acronym stood for OxyContin Purdue, the brand manufacturer. She thought of it as an abbreviation for *opiate*, or a cipher for what it could accomplish in sufficient quantities: Obliterate Pain.

She chewed the pill, grinding up the time-release coating between her back teeth to hasten the effects. The medicine coated her tongue, a bitter paste that might have made her retch if the taste hadn't been so familiar. Given the tolerance she'd built up over the past five years, one pill wouldn't do much more than soothe her neck and perhaps file down the edges of her anxiety. If she really wanted to feel nothing, she'd need far more.

Later, she promised herself. Ben still had another hour

or so before he could pass a Breathalyzer test, and she wasn't the best night driver. She needed to remain alert until she could hand over the wheel. After that, she could take another couple of pills to really take the edge off. Once at Ben's house, she could swallow an Ambien, too, enabling her to get a head-clearing sleep and wake up refreshed for all the daunting tasks ahead: moving her money into a private account, securing an apartment somewhere that Louis wouldn't immediately suspect, finding a divorce lawyer, and confessing the abuse to Ally.

The thought of her daughter delivered a harsh dose of reality. Jenny couldn't go to Ben's house for a good night's sleep. She needed him to take her to the airport. If Jenny knew her husband—and after fifteen years together, she did—he'd be heading to Ally's camp within thirty-six hours, as soon as he realized she'd taken off. She couldn't let him get to their daughter first.

Jenny raced to the stairs, gripping the railing as she sprinted down the steps. Within minutes, she was out the front door, shells crunching beneath her feet. She expected to hear the beep of doors unlocking as she reached the Suburban. When she didn't, she knocked on the side panel and then rounded the vehicle, pressing her face to the driver's-side window so that Ben could see she'd arrived.

The doors still didn't unlock. Through the tinted glass, she saw a vacant driver's seat and no one in the shotgun position. Her panic swelled like an incoming tide, rising with every second she remained exposed and alone on the driveway. Jenny tried forcing it back with excuses. Ben must have gone to grab some things from his own room. She'd run through the first-floor hallway so quickly that he didn't realize she was waiting outside. If she took a deep breath, he'd be there.

But her chest felt too constricted to breathe. Jenny slunk to the opposite side of the car, the one that would be less visible should Louis—not Ben—exit the front door looking for her. The moon shone like a searchlight. She pulled her phone from her purse and began checking flights to Maine from the East Hampton airport. The earliest one was at six AM and had a stop, making it take five hours. JFK International was an hour's drive and a much larger airport.

Shells cracked to her left as she typed in the new search. Jenny whirled toward the sound, flinging her heart into her esophagus. Ben, she thought. Please be Ben.

The sight of the massive shadow blurred her vision. She launched herself toward it, throwing her arms around his waist and pressing her lips to the neck level with her face. "I wasn't sure if you changed your mind."

He pushed against her shoulders. Her sneakers skidded back over the shells. "Why did you do it?"

Jenny caught the shimmer of Ben's teeth between his lips. The grin didn't match the harsh tone of his question. He wasn't smiling, Jenny realized. He was sneering.

"Do what?" She reached for him a second time, grabbing the side of his shirt before he could wrest himself away. "I don't know what you're talking about."

He yanked the fabric from her fist. "Don't, Jen. I talked

to Rachel. I wanted to tell her I was leaving. I owed her that. She told me that she knew I was cheating."

"Well, you told her to sleep with other people. She probably guessed. I—"

"She knew every excruciating detail of our first time. Except, conveniently, for your name." Ben backed away, extending his arm from his body like a running back trying to block a tackle. Jenny heard a crack as shells crunched beneath his feet. "It makes sense, now, why she was livid at dinner. You'd told her. You'd emailed or texted that you'd seen me with someone and she got the message when she went inside. Of course, you didn't say with who—"

"No, Ben, I—"

"Against the window in my office!" Ben's voice was so loud it seemed to echo in the open air. "I'm trying to understand why you'd be so brutal, Jen. The only reason I can come up with is that you'd had enough of Louis and wanted to make sure that Rachel left me too so that I'd be waiting for you."

Jenny pressed a finger to her lips, silently begging him to lower his voice before Louis heard. Ben ignored her plea, nearly shouting her name. "But it backfired, Jen. Rachel is on the warpath. She's going to argue against joint custody. She plans to say that I exposed myself to the kids by having sex in the house while they were home, in full view of the windows. She's going to paint me as a sexual deviant." The moonlight transformed Ben's handsome face into a tragedy mask. "I knew she'd want the house and to fight alimony. I was prepared for that. But not my kids. Not my kids, Jen!"

Ben's volume added a physical force to his speech, turning every sentence into a blow. Jenny's legs shook from absorbing the impact, threatening to give way at any moment.

"I didn't do it." The denial burned through her inflamed throat, emerging like a soft puff of smoke. "Please believe me. Please."

Again she flung herself toward him, praying that he'd catch her and remember the love he'd professed less than fifteen minutes earlier, that the feel of her shivering body would convince him she was innocent. Ben jumped back. She stumbled into the empty space he'd occupied.

"I would have given up everything for you, Jen. Everything but my kids. I'm a father first." He pointed at her chest. "Rachel said the only way she'd consider not fighting joint custody was if I told her who I'd slept with." He sniffed. "You didn't leave me any choice."

Her legs finally buckled. Shards of shells stabbed Jenny's knees, but the pain was nothing compared to what would come. If Rachel knew, it was only a matter of time before Louis did, too.

"I love you, Ben. Please." Jenny's kneeling position emphasized her begging. She needed Ben's strength to help her do what was required to escape from Louis. "You have to take us away from here. I have to get to an airport, to Maine. I have to tell Ally before he—"

"I can't. I can't lose my kids." Ben retreated to the Suburban's driver's-side door. "I can't be here right now, Jen."

Jenny watched him slide into the cab. She heard the engine rumble. The tires crunch against the crushed-shell drive. Her mind didn't really register any of it, though. Instead it pulsed with a looping logic: *If Rachel tells Louis, then Louis will kill me. He'll kill me. He'll kill me.*

Fear forced her upright. She took off at full speed through the scrub forest, not stopping to swipe at the shell splinters digging into her knees. Sand exploded beneath her feet. Bushes cut into her bare legs. She fought through it all, refusing to let anything in the rough terrain slow her down. Ally needed her mother, and Jenny was running for her life.

CHAPTER TWENTY-THREE

THE MORNING OF

The rising sun shattered Susan's alcohol-induced coma. Her eyes fluttered open to the unfamiliar sight of a white coffee table. Susan recalled that her last conscious act had been to slump on the great room couch, the firm cushion of which pressed against her cramped thighs.

She shoved her hands into the scratchy woven fabric and pushed herself upright. Sitting swirled the poisons in her stomach. Panting breaths failed to quell her nausea. Why had she drunk so much?

She leaned back into the couch. She knew why she'd drunk so much.

A glance through the glass wall revealed that it was too early to rise on vacation. The sun was merely a suggestion on the horizon, little more than a peach haze evaporating into violet clouds—a pastel promise of a pleasant beach day. Susan cursed the fair weather. She had to confront her husband of twelve years about his affair. A swirling hurricane would have been a better backdrop. The current view simply mocked her.

Her head pounded with the demand for more alcohol to dull her headache. She knew better than to listen to it. Water was the only liquid capable of flushing the toxins from her system.

The whine of her belly begged her to reconsider as she grasped the sofa arm and hoisted herself into a standing position. Vomit lurched into the base of her throat. She slapped her palm over her mouth and sprinted to the sink, holding in the contents long enough to hurl them into the metal basin.

By the time she stopped vomiting, all the liquid seemed wrung out of her system. With the last of her energy, she turned the faucet full blast until every chunk and trace was forced down into the pipes. She tilted her head beneath the spigot, filled her mouth with water, spat, and filled it again. The third time, she swallowed, despite the lingering flavor of last night's refuse. The liquid hit her stomach like a rock dropped in a full puddle, threatening to splash vomit back into her mouth. She kept everything down by guzzling the water until the nausea was replaced with the uncomfortable pressure of bloat.

After splashing cool water on her face, she turned off the faucet, took a deep breath, and started toward the stairs. Her injured foot throbbed as she walked, reminding her of the physical wound Rachel had inflicted in addition to the psychic ones. She mumbled epithets as she ascended the stairs, compensating for the tenderness in her heel by leaning heavily on the banister.

Nadal's snore greeted her as she slipped into the room. He lay atop the sheets on one side of the bed, preserving her rightful place beside him. Boxer shorts covered his backside. A latte-colored arm spilled slightly into her space, as though waiting for the body that it usually snuggled in the mornings. Or, perhaps, any warm body. As the email proved, Nadal wasn't choosy.

Part of Susan wanted to grab her unused pillow and beat him awake. The more vain, if not rational, part of her refused to confront him looking like a dishrag. When they argued, she wanted him to see her as the desirable woman he loved, not an alcoholic wreck who deserved to be walked out on.

She tiptoed past Nadal and into the bathroom, leaving the door open a crack to avoid the click of the lock engaging. She didn't hear the creak of mattress springs as she began to run a bath, but still she didn't wait for the tub to fill for fear that he'd soon stumble in. She sat in an inch of cold water and soaped, rinsing off with the handheld attachment.

Susan brushed her teeth and washed her face as the drain slurped down the bathwater. With the same towel around her from the night before, she stole back into the room for her makeup bag. Nadal still snored. He was programmed, she realized, to wake to the sound of her voice or his internal seven AM alarm clock. All other noises could be relegated to the part of his brain titled *Things My Wife Will Handle*.

That part of his brain was about to get a lot smaller, she decided, stepping back into the bathroom. Nadal would have to earn her forgiveness by playing a much larger role in their family. Susan considered all her demands as she applied the necessary lip gloss, blush, and concealer to mask her hangover. He would have to come home regularly for family dinners. One night per week, perhaps Tuesdays, he would take over teaching Jonah or ferrying Jamal to a late activity, giving her a chance to take a Pilates class or have coffee with Jenny. She wanted a weekly date night, too, to help rebuild their connection. Maybe she'd even sign them up for dance lessons.

A smile wriggled from her mouth as she remembered the rumba classes they'd taken before their wedding. Nadal had possessed admirable rhythm in his hips. More than she'd had, according to the sixty-year-old former flamenco dancer who had taught the lessons. Susan recalled teasing that she might lose her thirty-one-year-old fiancé to a flexible sexagenarian—emphasis on the *sex*. Nadal had in turn joked about his pelvic prowess, rotating his hips like he was twirling a Hula-Hoop and claiming that the blood of famous Egyptian belly dancers ran through his veins.

Her smile faded. They'd kidded about infidelity once, as though it were a genetic disease from which they'd been spared instead of a wild virus. She still couldn't believe that the man slumbering in the neighboring room had been infected.

A stinging behind her eyes warned her against applying mascara. She examined her dour expression in the mirror, emphasized by the damp, dark hair hanging to her shoulders. *It's not going to get any better than this*, she told herself.

She steeled herself with a minty breath as she reentered the bedroom. "Nadal, wake up."

At the sound of her voice, he murmured something and reached further into her space on the bed.

"We have to talk."

He pawed the air beside him and then, feeling nothing, finally rotated toward the sound of her voice. His eyes opened like blinds, pulling back in segments until she could see his dark pupils expanding in the dim light. "Good morning." He yawned and stretched as he sat up on the mattress. "I didn't sleep well. What time is it?"

"Time to talk about that email."

Nadal dragged his fingers down his nightly beard. He let his hands fall to his thighs and slowly got to his feet. "It's work, honey." He lumbered toward her. As he passed, he patted her on the shoulder. "I'd rather not ruin the vacation over it."

She watched him clomp over to the sink and splash some water on his face.

"You already ruined it when you slept with Rachel!"

Nadal turned around like he'd been backhanded. "What?"

"She wrote about how she doesn't get involved with neighbors. She thinks you both can come to an arrangement as long as you don't tell your spouses. You've been avoiding her since it happened."

Nadal blinked at her. "It's about a lawsuit."

How could he continue to lie? Her empty stomach churned with emotion and the prior night's poisons. She could be sick again.

"I'll show you," he said. He hustled into the bedroom, adjusting his boxer shorts with one hand as he flipped back the laptop screen with the other. The screen flashed its demand for a password.

"I already read the email, Nadal."

Typing responded. He carried the device over to her, supporting it with his left palm while tracing his right index finger over the track pad. She leaned back against the wall, needing support to continue standing in her dehydrated state.

"She's suing me. Look." He rotated the laptop screen to face her. Instead of an email, she saw a PDF of a formal legal document. Centered at the top of the letter was THE LAW OFFICES OF RACHEL KLEIN along with her business address, email, and phone. Beneath the header was a list of the other parties that had received the mailing, along with their respective contact numbers. Susan recognized the style of the form before even reading the bolded REGARD-ING line. It was a notice of intent to sue.

"But . . . but that email," Susan stammered, her mind too busy reconciling Rachel's words with the new information to properly articulate. Could Rachel have meant that she typically didn't sue her neighbors and that she wanted to keep the case from their spouses so as not to ruin the trip? Or had Nadal met her to discuss the issue and one thing had led to another?

"But you've been acting cagey around her."

Nadal snorted. "Yeah. She's targeting my company—that's not something *friends* do, as far as I'm concerned. And she's been trying to corner me to discuss a settlement this whole trip."

He released the laptop into Susan's waiting hands. "Read it. You'll see."

The relieved tears clouding her vision wouldn't let her make sense of the screen. Susan looked above it to see her husband's sheepish smile. He was embarrassed for her. She'd gone crazy over a questionably worded email, shouting at Nadal and making him shut down rather than explain the whole story. She was all the bad words that she'd thought about Rachel and worse.

Susan winced at the memory of her drunken email. She owed Rachel an apology, though not as big a mea culpa as she owed her husband. "I'm so sorry. I'm such an idiot." She stared at the wavy letters on the screen instead of facing Nadal. If he'd accused her of cheating, she'd have been full of righteous anger and indignation. But he stood in front of her, looking sad for both of them.

"God, I'm the worst. I'm the absolute worst." Shame mixed with the relief and unspent anger in her bubbling stomach, giving her new reason to be sick. "I've been drinking too much, clearly. That's no excuse. But I'm going to cut way back on the alcohol."

"Well, that might be good," Nadal said. The quick agreement suggested to Susan that he had considered talking to her about her wine consumption before. "Better to stop a problem before one really takes hold."

Nadal ran a hand through his dark curls. "It's not all your fault, though. I've been working so much and then acting secretive on top of it. I can see how you'd be concerned." He sighed. "I should have told you right away. Rachel got this personal-injury case a month or two ago, I guess, but she only recently realized that she could rope in Doc2Go. She met with me about it Tuesday afternoon. Completely blindsided me. I thought she was coming to offer her legal services or to consult, since everybody I say hello to in our new town tells me I need to put them on the payroll in some capacity." He shook his head. "You'd think people didn't have jobs before I showed up."

Susan felt even worse. She'd been nagging her husband to befriend the neighbors, and they'd all been trying to shake him down for money. "I'm so sorry."

Nadal shrugged, as if to say he'd expected as much once his firm began doing well. He started back toward the bed. "I'm sorry you worked so hard planning this vacation and she would do this right before we left." He plopped atop the mattress. "It didn't even occur to me how her email could be read because I knew what it was about. But, in hindsight, she really does have a messed-up way with words. *I can't walk away now. Keep this just between us.*" He rubbed a palm over his face and then held it out toward her. "I get why your first thought wouldn't be that the neighbor was taking us to court."

Susan dropped onto the duvet beside her husband and leaned miserably into his side. "But it shouldn't have been cheating." She fell backward onto the mattress, letting the fluffy fabric envelop her, wishing she could sink into it and disappear. "I suppose I've been feeling self-conscious since leaving my job. More of my self-worth was tied up in my paycheck than I realized. I'm just . . . ugh."

Nadal laid down beside her and slipped his arm beneath her neck. He pulled her into him, letting her nuzzle into his chest. "You're not ugh. I'm to blame also. I shouldn't have kept this from you."

"I understand why you did, though. You thought you were helping me have a nice vacation." She groaned. "I am so sorry."

He kissed the top of her head. "You said that already."

She pressed her face between his pectorals, letting his chest hair tickle her nose. "How can I make it up to you?"

Nadal's fingers pulled through her wet hair. "I don't know. Sex?"

Susan pressed tighter into her husband, letting the towel slip below her breasts so that her bare skin touched his naked torso, hoping it would be enough for the moment. The emotional roller coaster she'd been riding was poor medicine for a hangover. Her stomach still debated whether it wanted to keep down the water from earlier. "I drank myself into a stupor last night," she mumbled. "I can't bounce around too much right now."

Nadal's chest shook as he laughed. "Oh, babe." Another kiss landed on her forehead. He rolled over and got up from the mattress, leaving her half naked on the bed. "Actually, I could use your help with the case, when you feel up to it. We have our team looking at it, of course. But they're all Valley lawyers used to thinking that everyone plays by Facebook rules: think fast and break things. We're in New York now, and I think a criminal defense attorney might be more accustomed to critically examining culpability."

The request reinflated some of her self-esteem, enabling her to sit up and take a deep breath—which she immediately regretted. It threatened to make her retch again. "Fresh air might do me some good. Talk me through it on the beach? We can watch the sunrise."

Nadal grimaced. "It's that early?"

"There's no sleeping beside a wall of east-facing windows."

"Is it a nude beach?"

"No."

Nadal kissed her shoulder. "Then I guess we should both get dressed."

* * *

Susan sucked in salt air and stepped onto the sand. The aroma coupled with the cool breeze eased her nausea. Holding her husband's hand also helped settle her churning stomach. The pressure of his fingers between her knuckles made her feel less sick with herself for her terrible mistake. He was a good man and he loved her. She could take confidence from that.

They walked slowly, pacing themselves to the sunrise.

During the time she'd taken to get ready, a golden circle had peeked above the horizon line. To Susan, the sun's face resembled a godly child peering above a rippling navy blanket. She missed her kids.

"The case involves a nine-year-old boy." Nadal looked straight ahead at the jetty looming in the distance. That was a difference between her and her husband, Susan thought. He was always focused on a goal while she got enveloped by the atmosphere.

"The same age as our twins, as Rachel has reminded me countless times in an effort to horrify me into forking over money. Remember when she dragged me into the house for wine?"

Susan stroked the back of Nadal's hand, an insufficient gesture of affection for all the trouble she'd caused.

"Anyway, the boy had strep throat." Nadal cleared his throat, as if for emphasis. "He suffered a fatal allergic reaction after being treated at his home by a doctor contacted through Doc2Go. Apparently the kid was allergic to penicillin. And the doctor prescribed amoxicillin, which is basically the same fucking thing."

The epithet drew Susan's attention from the scenery back to her husband. When they'd met, Nadal had cursed often, a consequence, he'd claimed, of his upbringing on the outskirts of Boston and his teenage rebellion against his strict Muslim parents. But he'd reined himself in since having the boys. For Nadal to drop an f-bomb, he had to be pretty upset.

"So, okay," he continued. "The doctor screws up, says he

wasn't informed about the allergy. Fine. Usually there's a second line of defense—the pharmacy. Unfortunately, this boy's parents can't go to their usual place, which has the allergy on record, because it's closed. So they visit a new convenience store to fill the prescription and forget to tell the pharmacist that their son is allergic to the most commonly prescribed antibiotic." Nadal's stride lengthened. "I mean, what happened to these parents is horrible, and I don't want to vilify them. I really don't. But how do you have a kid with a penicillin allergy and not realize that's what you're giving him? How do you not check?"

Susan thought of all the sick visits with their boys over the years. Often she'd been so exhausted from the night of soothing, cleaning up vomit, and forcing down unwanted medicines that, by the time she'd reached the urgent care, she'd forget to tell the doctor anything beyond the past twenty-four hours. Of course, she hadn't had a kid with a deadly allergy. Still, she could sympathize. For someone with an ill child and no medical training, doctors were akin to gods. The assumption was that they knew everything already.

"And the boy died?"

"I guess the parents gave him the medicine and put him to bed." Nadal's walk slowed. "The boy's throat closed up and he couldn't alert them. They woke to find him on his bedroom floor, unresponsive." Nadal stopped to examine the sand creeping up the sides of his sneakers. "It's all so fucked."

As his wife, Susan wanted to come to his defense.

Doc2Go hadn't made the diagnosis. It was the physician's job to ask the family for allergy information and the pharmacist's job to explain the risks of the medication before filling a prescription. Her internal lawyer, however, made her consider the other side. Nadal's company had provided the family with the doctor's information and, by allowing him to use the site, certified his qualifications for the job.

"The site asks for allergy information, right? I remember a long questionnaire."

Nadal nodded vigorously. "Of course. The patients have to supply it, just like they would at a hospital."

"Did the parents neglect to include the allergy information?"

Nadal's hands went to his hips. He shook his head. "Damn doctor didn't read it."

"Isn't there a check box that doctors are supposed to tick, saying they read it?"

"It's on the site . . ."

Nadal's lack of eye contact told Susan to probe. "But?"

He kicked the sand. "Doctors can see the patient's location and agree to take the case without checking the box first. It's a stupid glitch. We already fixed it."

Susan sucked air through her teeth. "You fixed it?"

"Yeah. It was a fucking glitch. That's all. We fixed it."

The swear betrayed that Nadal suspected—and didn't want to hear—what she would say next. Susan looked out over the water, taking a moment to judiciously select her words. The sun's glowing face had moved an inch higher and light stretched toward the shore, indicating that the day was finally serious about starting.

"Fixing things could be an admission of guilt, honey." Susan kept her gaze trained on the horizon. "You wouldn't have changed anything if there wasn't something wrong."

Nadal tossed his hand, dismissing her argument. "Someone pointed out a user experience issue and we fixed it. That's what we do. It's not because we think we're responsible for every doctor that uses the site."

She understood why her husband felt that way. Technologists were, at heart, scientists. They operated according to the same method: see a problem, develop a hypothesis to fix said problem, test it, note the relative success and complications of the solution, improve the methodology, repeat. Mistakes were part of the process. They didn't fear them as much as they should.

"How much do they want?"

Nadal picked up his pace toward the jetty, his frustration fueling his speed. "They sued the doctor's insurance for a million six weeks ago. He apparently responded by putting all the blame on the site, claiming he'd never been alerted to the allergy information, didn't know it was on the application, and hadn't been informed by the parents. Rachel hinted to me that she could make it go away for double that without needing to go to court." Nadal scoffed. "Two million dollars! That's two years' salary for five senior developers. Do you know how much that will slow progress and the profitability timetable? And the payout alone will enrage the investors. The VCs will probably want to move up the IPO so they can cash out before anything else happens, but we'll be less equipped to do that because we'll have spent the new-hire budget on legal fees."

Nadal's nostrils flared like an enraged bull as he charged toward the rocks. "I'm sure Rachel told the family that the company doesn't want any bad press before the big dog-and-pony IPO show, so they feel well positioned to fight. And, unfortunately, she's right."

Susan put an arm around Nadal's side and pulled herself close, offering her physical support since she couldn't promise to make anything better. Negative headlines would erase much of the work Nadal had done building up the company's presence and brand on the East Coast. He'd have no choice but to give Rachel what she and her clients demanded.

She focused on the water, not wanting Nadal to get worked up from her lack of fight. The pale-blue sky was streaked with gold and grayish green. Cirrus clouds swirled high above, adding white wisps to the beautiful painting. "I'm sorry that you've been dealing with all of this."

"It's not your fault. It's Rachel. She's fucking shameless." He snorted. "Do you know she told me that she was helping me out with the suit?"

"How's that?"

"According to her, another lawyer, one not tied to our family, would try the case in the court of public opinion. They'd shame the company into a massive settlement for God only knows how much. However, because she knows us and knows how *reasonable* and, her words, 'forward thinking,' I am, she's certain we can come up with a number that compensates her client for their unimaginable loss without making a big scene."

Susan's inner lawyer couldn't help but feel a bit impressed by Rachel's argument—the way she'd delivered the threat under the guise of friendship. *I'll play nice, but only if you play ball.* Susan looked up at Nadal and rolled her eyes, trying to make light of the solid intimidation tactic. "Remind me to thank her."

"Yeah. What a bitch, right?"

Susan resumed walking, feeling more guilty with each step. She'd mentally called Rachel that word a thousand times in her mind the prior night. But the truth was, the woman really hadn't deserved it. She hadn't been a husband stealer, and she also wasn't a greedy monster who had sought out a suit to screw her neighbors. She'd taken the case before she'd known it involved Nadal. Dropping it simply because she had a burgeoning friendship with one of the named parties could be considered unethical. And, if Susan were honest with herself, Rachel probably was doing Nadal a favor not involving the press and dampening enthusiasm for his IPO. He couldn't expect her not to seek a multimillion-dollar settlement. Two parents had lost their little boy. Rachel's job was to ease their pain and suffering with as big a payout as possible.

"I wouldn't be too harsh on her, honey. Rachel can't simply drop a case that she's already been working on. And two million, for the death of a child, isn't exorbitant. Another lawyer might just have read the hype-heavy business articles and asked for an amount that you'd never be able to absorb with your current resources."

They reached the jetty as Susan finished her defense. The wall of rocks pierced the water like an arrowhead. The ocean slapped against it, creating little white crests that rippled toward a female figure reclining against the rocks.

Susan startled at the realization that they weren't alone. From the forward tilt of the stranger's head, Susan guessed that she was napping, though she couldn't imagine trying to tan or sleep at such an early hour, and certainly not with the tide creeping in.

"Lawyers." Nadal named the career with more venom than he'd injected into countless four-letter words. "You always take each other's side."

"Don't be silly. I'm only saying to give her the benefit of the doubt." Susan shielded her eyes from the sunlight to better see the sunbather. Without the glare, more details became visible. Wrinkled heels. White legs. Hair, darkened with seawater, pasted to a pale neck. A white bathing suit.

She recognized the suit. She'd thought about it more than once the prior night on the couch, torturing herself by imagining it pooled on the floor beside a floral kimono while the pale body it had covered draped itself across her husband's torso.

"You really don't see the immorality of—"

She nudged Nadal with her elbow. "Hi, Rachel," she shouted.

"Speak of the devil," he muttered.

He turned back toward the house. Susan braced herself to apologize. With luck, Rachel hadn't yet read her email and therefore hadn't been stewing about it. Susan decided she'd be humble and self-deprecating, taking responsibility while also explaining the mitigating factors of her drunkenness and exhaustion. She might apologize on Nadal's behalf as well, explaining how hard he'd worked for years to bring Doc2Go to fruition and how unnerving it was for him to see his "baby" sued for the first time.

"Rachel?" Susan called out.

A wave crashed against the jetty, spitting water toward her friend. Susan forced her legs forward despite a deepening sense of foreboding. "Rachel?" she shouted again.

The lack of any response stopped her from saying the name a third time. She dropped to her knees beside the mannequin form. Rachel's chest wasn't moving. Susan knew CPR, but she was in no position to perform it. Already she felt bile building at the base of her throat.

She screamed for Nadal. Footsteps beat toward her. Moments later, he was kneeling by her side, pressing two fingers into the skin below Rachel's jaw, shifting her bent head to reveal the paisley print of bruises spread across Rachel's neck. After ten seconds, he dropped his hand to his lap.

"Try again," Susan insisted. "Maybe it's faint."

Nadal pressed his fingers into another spot. He counted only five seconds this time. Each one felt like an eternity. "There's no pulse. Her skin is cold."

Susan suddenly became aware of a smell wafting from

Rachel, a funky odor, like brackish water without as much sulfur. Sour liquid reared into Susan's throat. She scrambled from Rachel's body on all fours, a crab scuttling toward a hole. Her ears filled with the sound of rushing blood. Susan heaved. Frothy yellow bile poured onto the glistening sand.

This was her fault, she thought. She'd fallen asleep wishing the worst things upon Rachel, praying for the woman to disappear, permanently, from her life. Such entreaties were never answered by God. And the devil never did anything for free.

PART III

CHAPTER TWENTY-FOUR

THE DAY AFTER

Gabby observed Nadal through the one-way-mirror, scanning for signs of the murderous rage required to hold a struggling woman underwater for a full five minutes. He didn't exhibit the behaviors that she'd come to associate with violent men caged in small spaces. He didn't pace like a tiger, or compulsively fidget, rubbing his hands over his arms, drumming his fingers on the desk, or jiggling his knees. He didn't close his eyes, retreating to some place in his mind where he was still free. He also didn't cry, as so many did upon realizing that one act of extreme selfishness or explosive anger was about to cost them everything.

Instead, Nadal sat at the desk, actively waiting. His eyes, which were alternatively trained on the mirror or his hands, were focused and alert. His palms lay atop the desk in a relaxed position. His feet rested flat on the floor. He didn't appear comfortable—the stark room was designed to make sure he couldn't be. But he didn't seem itching to shed his skin, either.

Gabby wished she could talk to him. On the advice of his wife, Nadal had declared he would not utter another word without his attorney present. Furthermore, Susan had laid into her husband about revealing the lawsuit, shouting in front of Gabby and DeMarco that he'd made a terrible mistake conversing with the *enemy*.

"The detectives here are not on the side of truth, honey," she'd said. "They're on the side of keeping their community calm and the tourist dollars coming in. They'd prefer, I'm sure, to arrest someone that Rachel knew, because then her killing becomes an isolated incident rather than what it is: a predator roaming the area. And, since they lack any evidence to suggest that her murder was at all personal, they're keeping all of her friends in here, hoping to shake us up."

Though Gabby had thought Susan's characterization grossly unfair, she hadn't objected to her speech. The woman was entitled to hurl a few unfounded accusations at her—after all, she'd suggested that Susan had killed her neighbor for cheating with her husband. Besides, arguing with Susan would have only riled her up more, and the woman was already strutting around like a rooster in a cockpit. She'd stormed out of the station, swearing at the top of her voice to call Nadal's lawyer and personally sue the East Hampton police for *all kinds of damages* should they dare arrest her husband on *baseless allegations* or release *one iota of info* concerning a *yet-to-be-filed* lawsuit against a *privately held* business, *not at all relevant* to their investigation.

Gabby had read enough of Rachel's intent letter to realize that much of Susan's ranting had been little more than posturing. The lawsuit was definitely *not* irrelevant to the murder. If a two-million-dollar suit wasn't enough to make friends mortal enemies, Gabby didn't know what was. Her new theory was that Nadal had approached Rachel on the jetty to negotiate a settlement favorable to his company. Rachel had refused, and he'd lost it. Although Gabby had to admit: the self-possessed man in Interrogation One didn't seem like the kind of guy to lose it.

A copy of Rachel's letter lay in her lap, printed from a PDF in Nadal's email. Gabby read the argument set forth in the document a second time, seeking a better reason for Nadal to want Rachel dead. Gabby couldn't imagine he would have killed Rachel in blind hope of making the case go away. He was too smart for that. Nadal had to have been so angry that he'd lost the ability to see things rationally, she decided. But why become so enraged that night? He'd known about the lawsuit for days. What had changed?

Gabby rubbed her eyes and opened her mouth in another face-swallowing yawn. She'd reached the portion of her sixteen-hour workday when even a third cup of coffee couldn't keep her alert and focused. She transferred the letter from her lap to the desktop, stood up, and jogged in place, trying to jolt her brain with a little exercise. *Think, Gabriella. Think!*

She stared at the stoic figure in the one-way window as she shifted her weight from the ball of one foot to the other. An hour earlier, she'd accused Nadal's wife of murdering

Rachel over a betrayal. The same motive, she supposed, could apply to Nadal. He'd likely thought Rachel had wronged him, using their friendship to target his life's work. Perhaps Rachel had admitted as much during the vacation, thus justifying his growing fury—or she'd been pestering him about the suit, stoking his rage.

Gabby tried to imagine Nadal livid. But the image didn't materialize.

A knock pulled her attention from the screen. Gabby stopped her Richard Simmons impression before the door opened. She stood in the center of the cramped space, no doubt looking guilty and embarrassed for having nearly been caught running in place. DeMarco hovered inside the doorjamb. He held a manila folder between both of his hands, an altar boy with a prayer book. "Sorry for interrupting. The coroner's report came back. They rushed it given the nature of the crime."

Gabby stretched her arms over her head. She felt less tired, though her second wind had more to do with her hope for what lay inside the envelope than her brief exercise session. "Tell me we have some hard evidence."

DeMarco passed her the folder. "She was killed between twelve thirty and one AM. If there was any DNA from her killer, the water destroyed it. But there were fingerprints on the neck belonging to Nadal Ahmadi."

Gabby opened the file and scanned the first page of the near dozen inside. "I don't know that the fingerprints mean much. He said he checked her pulse."

DeMarco scratched his chin. His usually shorn jaw

showed a significant shadow. "Well, that might be a reason for the prints. Or maybe he only did that to cover up strangling her. There were a couple sets of his index and middle fingers on her neck. And a partial palm print near the center of her throat."

Gabby looked back through the window. Nadal stared at the mirror as though trying to see through to the detectives he knew were in the neighboring room. His brown eyes seemed to be appealing to her. *Don't do it. Don't.*

Gabby didn't feel great about her next move, but she had to make it. Nadal's prints were on the body. He'd been embroiled in a two-million-dollar lawsuit with the deceased. He was refusing to answer questions. And, given that his wife had been passed out after a night of heavy drinking, he lacked an alibi witness for the time frame of Rachel's murder. She couldn't let the man hightail it back to Westchester. With his money, it might be the last time she saw him.

"Let's do this, then."

Detective DeMarco fished a pair of metal cuffs from a pouch on the utility belt securing his dress slacks. Gabby followed him into the hallway and then pulled back the door to Interrogation One. DeMarco went in first, dangling the bracelets.

"Nadal Ahmadi," she said. "You are under arrest for the murder of Rachel Klein."

CHAPTER TWENTY-FIVE

THE DAY AFTER

Cicadas were screaming. Their stuttering mechanical screech struck Susan as she exited the police station, barreling over her like a broken lawn mower. She hadn't noticed the insects at the beach. Though, she supposed, that wasn't surprising. She'd been so concentrated on setting up her family in their new town this past year, and distracted by her own identity crisis (not to mention her nightly glasses of wine), that she hadn't critically examined her surroundings—or whom she'd been surrounding herself with.

But now, her focus had returned. A dozen years as a criminal defense attorney had equipped Susan with a psychic X-ray, enabling her to see her opponents' internal strategies. That detective was going to arrest her husband. Rachel's submersion had surely corrupted most, if not all, of the physical evidence, leaving the police with little choice but to build a case based on the trio of means, motive, and opportunity. Nadal easily possessed the strength to strangle or drown Rachel, and two million dollars, while not a devastating amount to Nadal's company, was a sufficiently damaging sum to appear a compelling motive. Her hungover, thoughtless admission that she'd slept on the couch had provided the cops with the final piece of their circumstantial case, depriving her husband of an alibi.

Susan cursed herself as she hurried down the street, rushing to escape the locusts' deafening crescendo from the tree-lined properties beside the station. She pulled her phone from her purse and began scrolling through her contacts. She needed to get her former boss on Nadal's team. But first, she needed to call Greg Travers, Doc2Go's general counsel and chief business officer, not to mention Nadal's dear friend, back in Seattle. He'd be the one answering calls about the arrest of the firm's CEO on murder charges related to a lawsuit against the company. She couldn't have Greg surprised and revealing anything to police or the press that would unintentionally exacerbate Nadal's already bad situation.

The lack of a news van parked on the street was a fortunate surprise. Susan attributed it to the police's desire to keep the murder quiet until they were ready to announce an arrest. The East Hampton department was small enough that they could control the flow of information. It also helped that Rachel had been killed on a private beach and discovered before the people with access had set up their sun umbrellas.

The cicadas' screech faded as Susan reached the town's

main street, identifiable by the two lanes of traffic in each direction and the wide sidewalks, lined with restaurants. She crossed in the middle of the street, heading toward a white public bench in front of a juice bar. Greg's line was ringing before she sat down.

"Hello? Susan?" Gregory said her name like his caller ID had made a mistake. She'd never phoned him before.

"Yes. I'm calling about Nadal. He's been arrested on murder charges, or is about to be." Had Susan been thinking like Nadal's wife, saying the statement aloud would have sent her into hysterics. But her shift into defense-attorney mode had given her a preternatural calm.

"Our neighbor, Rachel Klein, was found dead on the beach, either strangled or drowned," Susan continued. "We were vacationing with her. And as I'm sure you are aware, she was representing the family suing the company for negligence."

Susan paused, giving her points time to find their mark, the way she would have if Greg had been a jury member. When she heard Greg's breathing quicken on the other end of the line, she resumed her opening statement. "To my knowledge, there isn't any hard evidence connecting Nadal to the crime. The cops just saw the two-million-dollar suit and thought *motive*."

Susan stopped a second time, hoping Greg would fill the silence with facts helpful to Nadal's defense. *The suit is in the process of being settled*, maybe. Or, *Nadal was under strict instructions not to talk to Rachel about the case, making it unlikely that he would have gotten into any kind of altercation with her about it.* Susan would even have taken an assurance that Nadal had looked forward to arguing the case in court, even though any eagerness to fight the grieving family of a dead child would have made him look like a combative jerk. Her husband would need to come off as likeable to combat any negative biases that "a jury of his peers" might harbor against people of his Middle Eastern background, wealth, or occupation. Still, better a jerk than a murderer.

"Shit. Shit. Shit. Shit. Shit." Greg whispered the swear over and over, a train chugging toward a cliff. "Shit. Okay. Shit."

Susan had expected Greg's shock. But the string of epithets rang with a hopelessness she hadn't anticipated. She wiped the sweat from her brow, brought on by the bench's position in the sun rather than fear. She had too much to accomplish in the next few hours to allow herself to feel afraid. "He obviously didn't do it, Greg. I'm not certain that a prosecutor will even take the case with the circumstantial nonsense they have. But I need you to be ready for the press with something better than a *no comment.*"

A child shouted in the background on Greg's end. "Not now. Daddy's on the phone." Susan heard the twitter of birds and then the slam of the door. She forced a swallow. Greg had been enjoying the day with his kids, she told herself. He needed a minute to switch into emergency mode.

"Okay. We'll start working on a statement: 'Rachel Klein was a dear friend of Nadal Ahmadi and his family. They are saddened by her loss and flabbergasted'—no, not that—'deeply hurt and shocked that the police would arrest

Nadal without any evidence. The lawsuit was a business matter that was already being handled through the proper channels.'"

The ease with which the statement rolled off Greg's tongue relieved Susan. This was the ally she needed. "Yes, stress those last two points."

"What about his alibi?"

Susan gripped the phone tighter, tempted to smack the side of her head with it. "He'd gone to bed upstairs. I drank too much and passed out downstairs. I'll say that I would have heard him if he'd left the house, but they'll argue that I was too inebriated to wake up. I apparently didn't hear another friend come in."

Greg cursed again. "The press isn't going to like that. They'll think that if his own wife can't back him, then—"

"I know." Susan nearly groaned, responding like herself rather than her professional alter ego. She curled her free hand into a fist, fighting the return to the insecure, anxious woman she'd been earlier. "I'll send you some pictures of him smiling. The business shot on the web page is too stoic."

"Good idea." Greg coughed. "It'd be even better, though, to send the media hunting in another direction. Are there any other possible suspects? The victim's husband, maybe? Or that ER doc? He was at the house with you guys, right?"

Susan took a breath. This was what defense attorneys did in emergencies—they created reasonable doubt even if it meant casting the blame on someone who likely didn't deserve it. "Rachel's husband had argued with her right before her murder, but I wouldn't focus on him. The cops wouldn't have let him go unless he had a pretty airtight alibi. And, unfortunately, I don't see how Louis was involved at all. My guess is that someone saw Rachel—"

"Not involved?" Greg said, incredulous. "Rachel was suing Louis's malpractice insurer for a million dollars. He's the doctor in the case, the one accused of prescribing without getting a complete medical history."

The new information blasted through Susan's brain, shattering the picture of the prior night that she'd formed in her head. Louis hadn't asked about Nadal's company out of personal curiosity. He'd wanted to get a sense of how Nadal intended to respond to the lawsuit. He'd demanded the drink with Nadal to pressure him into settling the case quickly, perhaps hoping that two million would sufficiently entice Rachel's clients to accept his insurer's initial offer.

Greg was still talking, arranging the pieces of the puzzle as Susan was putting them together herself. "My guess is that Louis had more to lose from the case than us. Insurers drop physicians for stupid mistakes like that, or they hike the premiums to something unsustainable. And good luck continuing to work without coverage."

Susan remembered Louis's hard words about Rachel the prior night. He'd characterized her as greedy and implied that she brought frivolous suits to make money. He'd been angry. More than angry. Her case could have cost him his career—the very thing that defined him. Susan hadn't realized, but Louis must have been murderous.

"Does he have an alibi?" Greg asked.

"My guess is only his wife, but you know that prosecutors don't give a spouse's word much weight. I doubt that the police even know about Louis's involvement. I didn't even know."

Susan recalled how Nadal had consistently referred to the doctor in the case by his profession or pronoun. She hadn't given it much thought, figuring that he wasn't mentioning the name since she didn't know the man or had been bound by a confidentiality agreement. But he'd been protecting Louis.

The cicadas' softer chirp swelled behind her. Nadal had been trying to keep the lawsuit hush-hush so as not to ruin the vacation. Perhaps Louis had done the same as well, withholding the news from Jenny to avoid causing a rift between her and Rachel. Or, maybe, Louis had simply been too embarrassed to tell his wife. Louis prided himself on being a superb doctor. He wouldn't have wanted to reveal to anyone that his prescription error had resulted in a child's death.

But, regardless of Louis's reasons for keeping the suit quiet, Nadal needed to tell everyone about his involvement. Now.

"I've got to go, Greg," she said. "I've made a mistake."

Susan hung up before he could respond and sprinted toward the police station. She shouldn't have instructed Nadal to remain silent. They both had to tell the cops everything they knew about Louis Murray.

CHAPTER TWENTY-SIX

THE DAY AFTER

Jenny knew what she had to do. The plan had come to her the prior night as she'd run from the house, emerging fully developed like some parasite she'd unwittingly nurtured for years. Its existence had horrified and disgusted her, at first. Still, Jenny had known that she couldn't kill it. She needed it.

She ran it over in her mind, again, as her body slid on the plastic bench in the back of the police car, threatening to send her careening into Louis. He was sitting too close to her, continuing to play the loving, protective spouse as he had the entire time in the police station. The over-the-top affection was a transparent plea for her silence, fueled by Louis's fear that she might suddenly unwrap the scarf from her neck and explain the welts all over it. He'd been asleep by the time she'd finally sneaked into the bedroom the prior night, and they'd both woken to the thuds of police boots downstairs. Having not had a chance to apologize and contextualize his actions, Louis didn't know whether she'd forgiven him or if he was one wrong word away from her pressing charges.

Louis's concern about the cops was unwarranted, though. Jenny's plan didn't involve the police arresting her husband and handing her a restraining order, which Louis would respect about as much as her personal space. There was only one way to keep Louis from murdering her someday—like Rachel had been. She had to kill him herself.

Jenny gripped the handle of the police door as the car swung a right onto the block of beach houses, refusing to let gravity pull her back into her husband's embrace. She might latch on to a hug as evidence that Louis loved her enough to change. When the truth was that, though he loved her, he wasn't strong enough to change.

The cruiser stopped in front of the house. She robotically thanked Officer Phillips through the glass divider. The young cop released the locks on the back doors. "You're lucky the place wasn't designated a secondary crime scene." Phillips leaned his head out the open driver's-side window as Jenny passed. "You wouldn't have been able to collect your suitcases. Fortunately for you both, the woman that owns the place has some pull. I guess the department didn't want to risk paying her the fifty thousand she'd lose canceling a month's worth of renters."

Louis rounded the car and reached for her hand. Jenny quickly raised it instead, waving good-bye to the patrolman before her husband could grab her fingers. She could feel

Louis waiting at her side, his energy tugging at her like a current.

She broke free of it, jogging past him to the glass front door, framed by the already parted barn doors. Inputting the unlock code took a moment, enabling Louis to slide an arm beneath her dangling purse and grab her waist. He pressed his lips to her temple, inches above the bruise still healing from the prior week. "I love you," he said.

Jenny controlled her shudder, murmuring something that he could interpret as her returning the sentiment. Behind them, shells rattled beneath the cruiser's chassis like change in a dryer. Jenny opened the door, looking over her shoulder to watch the marked car turn onto the main road before entering the house.

The place felt searched, even though it hadn't been ransacked. Sand, likely jostled from police boots, littered the cement floor in the great room. One of the couch cushions had been tilted forward. The recycling bin had been pulled from its former spot and the plastic bag with the empty wine bottles removed.

The scotch, however, still occupied its last known location on the kitchen counter. Jenny wrested free of Louis's groping presence for the second time and headed toward the near-empty bottle. "I need a drink." She pointed to the whiskey. "Grab you one for the road, too?"

Louis hovered by the couch, pulling at his bottom lip as he often did when he wanted to discuss something uncomfortable. Jenny warned him off without words, looking him in the eye and unwrapping the red scarf coiled around her slender neck. She balled the fabric in her fist and tilted her head back, displaying the potato-shaped swellings in purple, yellow, and red. "My throat is killing me. All those questions." She groaned and picked up the bottle. "I need to steady my nerves. Would you get the bags?"

Jenny knew that Louis would never refuse a "man's job" like carrying heavy luggage. He dutifully turned around to the steps and headed to the second floor. She watched him climb. He held the banister as he ascended, releasing it for only a moment at the top step. A buzzing called his attention to his back pocket.

He answered after he was securely on the landing. "Hello? Hi, Ally!"

Jenny tried to ignore the stabbing pain in her chest at hearing her daughter's name. Ally was a daddy's girl. She'd missed him enough after twenty-four hours to check in. She hadn't called Jenny at all.

Jenny opened the dishwasher drawer and withdrew two of the tumblers from the prior night. As she placed their wide, hexagonal bottoms on the counter, she tried to think only of their heft and not what she planned to do with them, of how losing Louis would rip through her daughter's heart.

Jenny grabbed the whiskey and filled one glass. She cursed under her breath, pretending to have spilled some in case Louis watched, and then peeled three sheets of paper towels from a roll beside the sink. The bedroom door shut as Louis went to get the bags. Jenny started to work faster, smoothing the paper towels into a pad atop the counter, telling herself all the while that Ally would recover from what she was about to do. A torn muscle, as excruciating as it was, could be repaired. Jenny knew how. And the heart was just a muscle. She'd devote herself to replacing the love and affection Ally missed from her dad, again becoming her daughter's friend and confidant. And Ally, whether she knew it or not, would grow up healthier and happier without an abusive man in the house.

Jenny dropped the purse hanging off her shoulder onto the counter. She sifted through it for her prescription bottles and then dug both hands inside to open the sleep aids, afraid that if she put the bottle on the counter, Louis might pop out of the room unexpectedly and see it. As fast as she could, she plucked five from the container, placed them on the paper towels, and then folded the sheets over the white, oblong pills, creating a zolpidem sandwich. A ten-milligram Ambien was enough to put a grown man to sleep for hours. Fifty milligrams wouldn't kill Louis, but it would make sure he was conked out when she drove him to a deserted beach later, filled his pockets with stones, and dumped him in the water. She'd report him missing after a few hours, saying he'd taken the car after claiming to not be able to live with himself for what he'd done to Rachel. Unlike her, the police didn't know that Louis could live with himself no matter what.

Jenny picked up an empty tumbler and brought the heavy base down hard against the bump in the paper towels. She slammed it down a second time, twisting afterward to really crush the pills into a powder. Using the paper towel like a funnel, she poured the flecks into the glass and then tossed the sheets into the sink's garbage disposal drain. She poured water on the paper and then flicked the switch affixed to the backsplash, grinding up the evidence that wouldn't be dissolved by liquor. Finally, she poured three inches of whiskey over the powdered pills.

The liquid's alcohol content was sufficiently high that she didn't even need a spoon to dissolve the pieces. Swirling the glass for a few seconds did the trick. The resulting amber mixture reminded her of Louis's hair in the sunlight.

Jenny ignored the emotional cramp that accompanied the observation. Pain didn't matter. She needed to get to the end of this.

Jenny downed her unadulterated shot for courage and then gingerly climbed the stairs, holding Louis's tumbler tight to her chest. The drugs would take about ten minutes to hit his system. After that, he'd become sluggish and sloppy. His speech would slur. His eyes would glaze. He'd say things that only made sense to his subconscious.

"Louis." Jenny called to him through the master bedroom door as she ascended to the second floor. "Honey, are you ready?" She knocked. "Are you still talking to Ally?"

The door flung back. Louis barreled from the room like a beast under attack—nostrils flared, eyes wild with fury. He charged at Jenny, driving her back toward the floating staircase. She struggled to find the root of his anger. Had he told Ally about Rachel and she'd become upset? Had he accused Ben and Ally had refused to believe it? Why was he looking at her like that?

Jenny extended the glass in her hand. "I poured you that whiskey."

Louis grabbed the drink and threw it back like a shot of tequila. He smacked his lips together and then brought the crystal up to his face. For a moment, he seemed to admire its craftsmanship, checking out the angles of the thick walls, weighing its solid base. "You fucked him, didn't you?"

The question registered just before Louis smashed the glass into the side of her head.

"She saw the whole thing, you whore." The words wafted over to Jenny, cushioned in white noise. A fizzing rushed through her ear canal. She saw shoes: leather moccasins dyed a deep indigo that she'd bought Louis specifically for the vacation. He loomed over her. He was saying something. Yelling something.

"Chloe and Ally were in the fucking backyard. They saw everything. You and him. Right there in the window."

The right shoe lifted and pulled back. Instinctively, Jenny wrapped her arms over her bleeding head and brought her knees to cover her vital organs. She screamed, a reflex to the pain that she knew was imminent. The foot swung down, slamming into her shins with a fury.

"Right there in the fucking window."

Jenny heard the snap of her splintering fibula. Her body reacted to the break as though it had plunged underwater. Instinct took over, trapping the air in her lungs. Blood rushed to her head with all the pain of a brain freeze.

"Chloe wanted to wait to tell her mom until they'd gone to camp, apparently, so she wouldn't be around them fighting. Ally didn't even want me to know at all. She had to beg Chloe not to tell Rachel it was you." A second kick landed in the center of her solar plexus. Pain burned the air in Jenny's lungs. She gasped and coughed as she curled into a tighter ball. "But when Chloe told her that Rachel was dead, Ally was afraid you were running off with her best friend's dad."

Needles stabbed into Jenny's bare skin. As she brought her arms to cover her face, her skin seemed to shimmer with glitter. No. Not glitter. Glass. The tumbler had shattered. Louis had drunk before it had broken, hadn't he? She couldn't think straight with the throbbing in her rib cage and the pounding in her head. Either way, the pills would take time. And she wouldn't survive ten minutes of this.

She pressed her left hand into the shrapnel-covered ground and twisted her knees under her, trying to stand on her good leg. Before she could rise, Louis grabbed her hair, yanking her back onto her haunches. He crouched in front of her, his features twisted into a gargoyle's expression. "You must think you're really special, huh? You can have any man you want. Is that it? Even the married playboy next door."

A stinging slap on her mouth sharpened her understanding. Chloe and Ally had known about the affair. The call had been Ally telling Louis. And Louis was going to kill her.

Jenny didn't waste her energy on excuses. Nothing she said would matter. Her only hope was to wrestle free of her husband's grasp and somehow escape down the stairs before he could shove her, headfirst, onto the concrete floor below. Though she thrashed in his grasp, he managed to hold on, despite the drugs coursing through his system.

"How many times did you go over there for a lay, Jen?" Louis brought his face closer to hers. Jenny wrenched herself back in one final attempt to break free. Louis held on and screamed in her face. "How many fucking times?"

He'd beaten her so many times. She needed it to end.

"Well?" Hair ripped from her scalp as Louis yanked her upright. Her broken leg buckled, bringing her back down to her knees despite Louis's grip on her hair. "You don't deny it?"

He dragged her toward the stairs. Tears spilled down her cheeks. She remembered her husband as he'd been once. The young doctor who, after nights of interrupted sleep and sewing people back together, had come home to stroke her pregnant belly and assuage her nerves. The father who had built dollhouses, sat for tea parties, and taught Ally to ride a pink bike with a Hello Kitty bell. The husband who had carried her over the threshold of their home, caressed her, taken care of her. She'd loved that Louis. But he'd died long ago. And now he wanted to take her with him.

CHAPTER TWENTY-SEVEN

THE DAY AFTER

Susan talked with her hands when excited. Gabby sat in her office chair, trying to maintain a concrete expression as she watched Susan's emphatic air chops. A petty part of her hoped to end the conversation in the same abrupt way of their earlier interview—this time with Gabby thanking Susan for outlining the opposition's "ridiculous" case. A larger part of her wanted to usher the woman from her room, drive with the sirens blaring to the bed she'd abandoned eighteen hours earlier, and collapse atop the mattress.

Trumping all those selfish desires, however, was an ache to arrest the right person. Though Gabby's head told her that the businessman in lockup was the most likely culprit, her soul lacked faith that she'd put away the right man. Slapping cuffs on Nadal should have felt righteous. Instead, she'd felt wrong—not to mention worried that the prosecutors' office would agree.

She didn't know whether arresting Louis would feel any

different. At the house, the redhead had been true to stereo-type, hot-tempered and quick to hurl accusations. It was possible he'd killed Rachel in a rage about the lawsuit, had his wife cover for him, and then fingered Ben to deflect blame. But since Gabby hadn't personally interviewed him, her sixth sense was silent on the matter.

"Louis's whole ego is wrapped up in being this great doctor," Susan continued. "The prospect of losing his license would have driven him crazy. Believe me. He killed Rachel. You can't charge Nadal."

Gabby rotated her chair a couple of centimeters to either side, using activity to fight off the sleep she desperately needed. "Reasonable doubt is for trials, Mrs. Ahmadi. We have a case against your husband."

"No, you don't."

Gabby stood, signaling the end to Susan's audience. "I'll talk to Louis first before filing my report on Nadal's arrest. That's the best I can offer."

Susan's arm flung toward Gabby's bookcase. A clock sat on the indicated shelf. "You better hurry. One of your offi-cers already drove him and Jenny to their car."

"What?" Gabby rounded the desk. She'd told Detective DeMarco *not* to let anyone leave. He must have thought Nadal's arrest had changed things. "I'm on it." Gabby opened the door, letting Susan out first. "I'll let you know."

With the siren wailing, Gabby reached the house in five minutes. Two vehicles sat outside the rental. Gabby exited her cruiser and approached the entrance. The late-afternoon sun reflected in the house's windows, preventing her from seeing inside. She pressed the bell on the electronic lock. Through the door, she heard the buzzer and what sounded like a man shouting. Pressing her face to its tinted glass panels revealed nothing save for a darkened view of the empty foyer and tunnel-like hallway. She heard the sound again. A man was definitely yelling.

She hustled around the side of the house and into the backyard, keeping her right arm bent by her holster, hand angled in the ready position. The glare that had blinded her in the front now illuminated the view through the glass wall. Gabby saw the white couch, its pillows askew, and a whiskey bottle atop the kitchen counter. The male roar was louder, though its source remained hidden.

A female scream drew Gabby's attention to the second floor. Louis stood on the mezzanine level, his right leg bent behind him as though he were about to kick a soccer ball. By his feet, Jenny lay curled in an armadillo defense—bony arms covering her face, hands spread over the top of her head, knees tucked to her chest.

"Stop! Police!"

Gabby's command went unheeded. Louis's foot slammed into Jenny's leg, sending her rounded form several inches closer to the open stairwell. Gabby watched through the windows as though she'd stumbled upon a drive-in theater showing a horror flick. Louis crouched beside his wife and wrapped his fist in her hair. He began yanking her upright, pushing her toward the open stairs.

He's going to toss her over. A surge of adrenaline overcame Gabby's paralyzing shock. She ran to the door and its electronic lock. Four numbers, she remembered. A date in history. One of them had been a nine, she thought.

Her overwhelmed and exhausted brain would never deliver the correct digits. Louis's curses pierced the windows. He was dragging Jenny by her hair toward the staircase, screaming epithets and questions.

"How many times, Jen? How many fucking times?"

Gabby grabbed her gun, aimed the muzzle at the glass, and pulled the trigger. The explosion was followed by a sharp crack. A perfect circle punctured the tempered glass. An alarm screamed to life, alternating tones like an ambulance siren between blaring robotic warnings. "Attention. Glass break detected. The police have been called. Attention . . ."

Gabby wrapped the hem of her jacket around the Glock's hot barrel, holding the pistol like a tomahawk. She rammed the grip against the bullet hole. This time, glass sprayed. She switched her weapon into her left hand and stuck her right through the opening she'd created. Shards scratched white lines into her brown knuckles and tore at her sleeve as she stretched down to the handle.

The door lock released. Inside the house, the alarm was as loud as if Gabby had been outside her cruiser with the siren blaring. She rushed into the great room, added her right hand to the left already gripping the Glock. Her index finger found the trigger. "Police. Step away," Gabby screamed, loud and shrill as the alarm. "Step away or I'll shoot."

Louis released his wife's hair but remained standing over her, positioned to send Jenny hurtling down the staircase with a hard kick to her side.

"Step away!" Gabby brought the gun up higher and gazed down the barrel, signaling to Louis that he was in her sights.

"She did it!" He pointed to the mangled person at his feet. "She killed Rachel."

Jenny appeared incapable of hurting anyone. Her arms wrapped around her torso as though holding her ribs together. Blood matted her dark hair and dribbled down the right side of her face. Deep purple welts encircled her bare neck.

"I was trying to protect her," Louis shouted, ignoring the contrary evidence in front of him. "I lied and said she was with me last night. But she was out there." The finger accusing Jenny flung toward the wall of windows. "I saw her fighting Rachel from the balcony. She tossed her into the water."

Jenny pressed a hand to the floor, pushing herself up on her side. She tried to say something, but all that emerged were a series of sputtering coughs. Gabby didn't need the woman to defend herself. From Gabby's vantage point, it was clear who was the killer.

Louis grasped the railing atop the mezzanine's glass wall. "I thought she'd found out about the suit and confronted Rachel. I thought I had to cover for her. I thought she'd done it for me. For us." Louis's shoulders shook. For a moment, he looked as broken as his battered wife.

"Come down." Gabby gestured with her weapon to the open staircase. "Come down and we can talk about it."

He took a step toward the landing, keeping his hands glued to the banister. Gabby lowered her gun to her chest, ready to aim again should his anger return. Tears squeezed from Louis's squinted eyes. "She was sleeping with Ben!" His voice rose another impossible decibel. "She did it. But she didn't do it for me."

Gabby again shouted for him to come down, adding noise to the cacophony. The alarm, the mechanical alerts, the anguished shouts—it all condensed in the room's double-height ceilings before pouring on top of her.

Louis turned toward Jenny. As he'd accused her, she'd managed to inch backward from the landing and grasp the top of the glass knee wall. "You're lying." She pulled herself upright, leaning heavily against the partition. "You did it. You! I was afraid of you!"

"Liar." Spittle gathered in the corners of Louis's mouth.

"Look at me!" Jenny shouted. "Look what you've done to me. You killed her!"

Louis released the banister and stepped onto the stair landing, toward his wife. His legs vibrated. "I hate you, Sabrina. You emasculating witch. I see your broom."

"Do not come any closer to her!" Gabby looked down her gun slide, targeting right below Louis's shoulder, the widest part of him as he stood with his side facing her. If she shot too low, the bullet could hit the glass, breaking the wall that kept Jenny from falling twenty feet onto the concrete floor below.

"I see you flying like my mother." Louis took a stumbling step toward his accuser. "Above us all. You have her powers."

"Stay back or I'll shoot." Gabby changed her position as

she shouted, assuming a better spot to put a bullet into Louis before he could lay another hand on his wife—before he could murder another woman.

"I always knew what you were!" Louis pointed a shaking finger at Jenny. "You won't hurt me. You'll fly to hell."

Louis lunged at his wife. Gabby pulled the trigger.

For a moment, the shot's explosion hushed everyone and everything in the room. It seemed to compress the sound waves, enabling Gabby to hear the bullet's whizz through the air toward where Louis had stood moments before. Jenny broke the relative silence with a scream so loud it hushed the alarm. The wail had one word: *Louis*.

He fell forward as the shot still rang out. Jenny extended her arms, as if to save him from going over the balcony. Instead of grasping his shirt, however, Jenny's palms landed flat on his stomach.

Louis stumbled backward. Gabby watched, helpless, as his heel slipped over the lip of the top step. Suddenly, he was falling off the stair, limbs flailing, desperately swimming in the air. Gabby looked away before he hit the ground. Still, she heard the crack of his head against the concrete, a hammer splitting a melon. It resounded louder than the blaring alarm, Jenny's sobs, the glass-break announcements, and Gabby's own panting breaths. She heard it on replay as she approached Louis's body.

She let her eyes travel from his twisted limbs up his torso. Gabby didn't see a bullet wound. But blood and brain matter was seeping from Louis's broken skull. The man was dead. And she'd helped kill him.

PART IV

CHAPTER TWENTY-EIGHT

THE WEEK AFTER

When it came time for her own funeral, Susan wanted a closed casket. She made the decision as she examined Rachel's waxen face in the open coffin, her pale skin unnaturally tanned with layers of beige makeup, her thin lips sewn into a disapproving line. Rachel didn't look at peace. She looked pissed.

Susan placed a hand over Rachel's cold fingers and mumbled a Hail Mary. The prayer was one of the few she remembered from her Catholic upbringing and seemed fitting coming from one mother to another. "I'm sorry," she whispered, swapping an apology for the amen. "I was so upset about what I thought you'd done, I didn't realize you were in danger."

Susan took a breath, rose from the kneeler, and retreated to a small section of unadorned wall. Lilies and white roses overwhelmed the room, springing from baskets and snaking around mounted wreaths the size of small

271

Christmas trees. Their heavy perfume clouded the air like spring pollen.

There were more bouquets than people, Susan thought. Not that the crowd was small. A mix of Rachel's relatives, coworkers, and real friends filled the room. Many parents in town had shown as well, though not as many as Susan had expected for an involved PTA mom with two kids in the local schools. Summer vacations had likely kept many away. Few could afford to cancel a trip because of the death of an acquaintance.

Nadal sat across the room beside both Jonah and Jamal, whom they'd pulled from camp to support Rachel's son Will. Jonah looked intently at his hands, hidden by the rows of chairs, likely worrying the silent balls and buttons of the fidget cube in his lap. Jamal stared at the front of the room, studying the adults in line to pay their respects. Both her boys wore charcoal suits, as they likely would have at a trial.

The tears Susan couldn't shed for the wax figure in the coffin flooded her eyes. A false accusation had come so close to tearing apart her family. Even if Nadal had ultimately prevailed in court, the seriousness of the charges would have kept him in jail until the jury verdict, depriving her sons of a father and her of a husband. And the allegations alone would have inflicted irreparable damage to Nadal's reputation, undoubtedly forcing his removal as CEO of the company he'd founded and ruining its chances of ever going public, possibly even rendering him permanently unemployable.

Moreover, a not-guilty verdict had never been guaranteed, despite Susan's posturing to the contrary in front of the detectives. Court cases, she knew, were about making juries want to believe in a defendant's innocence as much as they were about facts. Her husband was a wealthy man of visible Middle Eastern descent, with Muslim parents, who worked for an industry reviled for taking jobs from "average Americans," and he was being sued by the parents of a deceased nine-year-old boy. He was a good man. But the wrong twelve people might not have been able to see that. For a moment at the beach house, Susan herself hadn't.

She swiped at the drop streaking her cheek and then scanned the crowd for the families that had not been as fortunate as her own. Ben stood at the open entrance to the private room, the somber head of a heart-wrenching receiving line that included his son and a younger woman Susan assumed was Rachel's sister. His daughter, Chloe, sat with Rachel's parents across from the coffin, their pale figures like wilting jasmine in a stark black vase.

Susan wanted to say something to them, to beg forgiveness for all the ways she'd failed their mother. She'd been in the backyard with Louis and had watched him go upstairs. Had she not gotten so drunk (she wasn't drinking nowadays), perhaps she would have heard him leaving the house and asked what he'd been up to. Being seen might have made Louis rethink his plans.

But she couldn't explain all that. The respectful thing,

Susan decided, was to abstain from the receiving line and *not* remind Chloe of her mother's final day. Her family would sign the book on their way out, which would be soon. Jonah couldn't take this many strangers for much longer.

Susan weaved through the crowd and then shimmied past seated guests to the open chair beside her husband. Nadal patted her side as she sat, acknowledging her return. She leaned into him, her chest tight with emotion, and mouthed a thank-you to God for sparing her family the grief that had befallen the others. They'd dodged enough bullets to suggest divine intervention.

Susan followed up her silent thank-you with a whispered plea to help Rachel's children. She couldn't say why God hadn't intervened for Will and Chloe. They were truly the innocent ones in all of this.

A commotion by the door interrupted Susan's prayers. Ben and Will stood side by side in front of the entrance, barricading the viewing area rather than welcoming people inside. The already quiet room hushed. Susan rose to better see over the turned heads of Rachel's family members.

Jenny stood in the arched entrance to the room, hunched like a much older woman. A silver cuff shone on each arm, connected to the crutches that supported Jenny's hands and, judging from her stance, the majority of her weight. She wore a knee-length black dress. A plaster cast protruded below it, covering the length of her right calf.

Susan had heard of Jenny's injuries through the police. She'd been waiting at the station for Detective Watkins's return when the desk officer had suddenly begun dispatching units to the beach house's address, shouting about a man beating his wife half to death.

Hearing of Louis's brutality, however, had not prepared Susan for the evidence. Jenny's bottom lip was scabbed and swollen. A jam-colored stain spread beside her mouth. Yellow and green bruises encircled her neck. Her black eye had finally healed, though, allowing an undistracted look into her sad, doe eyes.

"Ally wanted to pay her respects," Jenny said.

Susan had missed the presence of Jenny's daughter. She squinted at the entrance, noticing the young woman partially shielded by Jenny's frail figure. The girl had ash-blonde curls and an incongruous tan. It was Ally, Susan realized with a start. Jenny's daughter had bleached the auburn hair she'd inherited from her father.

Ben looked over his shoulder at his own daughter—her face hidden in her grandmother's chest—and then back at Jenny. His expression befitted a man lashed to the rack. "Chloe knows." He dropped his head. "Maybe just Ally."

Susan couldn't make sense of Ben's words, though Jenny's lack of movement while Ally went inside made their meaning clear enough. Jenny wasn't allowed in. Ben couldn't welcome the spouse of his wife's murderer.

Ally approached the coffin, head down to avoid the crowd gawking as though she'd been a coconspirator in her father's crime. Her frail shoulders shook with sobs. The line waiting to have a look at the mortician's work retreated, allowing her to cut in front. Ally dropped to the kneeler with a choked groan.

Jenny looked on, her bruised mouth wrenched in pain, unable to soothe her daughter without causing Ben's suffering family more grief.

Ally bawled as though her own parent lay in the casket. A murmur rippled through the seats. Female voices mumbled about appropriateness and decorum. *Imagine how hard it is for Chloe, seeing her. It was her father.*

Susan shuffled from her row and then walked around the viewing line. Gingerly, she placed a hand on Ally's shoulder. She wanted to tell her she wasn't responsible for her father's actions and that she didn't need to feel ashamed. But she also didn't want to presume to know how Ally was feeling. Sometimes, silent support was the best kind.

"I'm so sorry, Mrs. Hansen. I'm so sorry. I'm so sorry." Ally's apologies dribbled out between sobs. Susan helped her stand, wrapping an arm around her side. She guided her back to where her mother had stood moments before, beside a frightened-looking Ben.

Jenny had already left the room. Susan spied her hobbled form over Ben's shoulder, heading toward the exit. She released Ally to follow. Before the girl could hurry toward her mom, Ben stopped her with a pat on the arm. "Hey, Ally." A smile materialized on his strained face. "No one blames you, kiddo. I hope you know that. What happened is not your fault."

Ally lifted her head for the first time since arriving, looking directly into Ben's dark-blue eyes. "I know, Mr. Hansen. I know it's not my fault." She pointed in Jenny's direction. "But what happened to my mom is yours."

CHAPTER TWENTY-NINE

THE WEEK AFTER

Gabby leaned against a column supporting the covered entrance to Dina Collette's home, the lab report rolled in her right hand like a riot stick. Mariel's urine had tested positive for the prescription sedative zolpidem. The technician with whom Gabby had spoken that morning had insisted that the levels he'd detected were typical of drug abusers, or those who had developed such a tolerance to the medication that they required multiple pills to sleep. Mariel hadn't struck Gabby as either an addict or an insomniac.

Dina emerged from the front door, her long legs extending from the white skirt of a tennis dress. The day was right for the sport. Bright, sunny, with little humidity and a firm breeze off the water. For once, Gabby wasn't sweating in her suit jacket as she waited outside. Annoyance, however, had prickled the hairs on her neck. She hadn't asked the housekeeper for Dina—she'd asked for Mariel.

"Detective Watkins. Good to see you again." Dina

extended her hand for a shake, forcing Gabby to shift the paper baton to her nondominant side. "I read that you saved a woman from being murdered by her husband after he'd killed their neighbor. Kudos to you. You're a real hero."

Gabby's neck grew hot. The h-word had been bandied about to the point where it had become embarrassing. As far as Gabby was concerned, a hero would have brought Louis in to answer for his crime, not watched him fall fifteen feet, headfirst, onto concrete. The other detectives in the department, however, didn't have as high a standard. When DeMarco and her colleagues called her "sergeant," they no longer sounded snarky.

"I was fortunate that I got there in time," Gabby demurred. "I'd hoped to speak with Miss Cruz. The toxicology reports came back, and it's looking like she was drugged, as you believed. There was zolpidem in her system."

Recognition flashed in Dina's eyes. "Zolpidem. That's Ambien, right? I have a prescription for that to help me sleep. Ever since having the twins, the slightest creak wakes me."

Gabby tried to keep the disappointment from her face. Though she highly doubted that Mariel would have known the contents of Dina's medicine cabinet—much less have stolen from it—any access she'd had to the drug would be a boon to the defense. Andy Baird's attorney would argue that his accuser had sneaked one or two before coming to his party.

"You're not missing any pills, are you?"

A pink flush crept up Dina's slender neck. "Oh, I wouldn't know unless the whole bottle was gone. I don't take it every night, only when I really need a solid eight hours. You can't drink on them."

Gabby imagined Dina repeating the same damning sentence to the county prosecutor. The drugs were the only evidence keeping Mariel's case from being he-said/she-said. Dina suggesting that her pills could have disappeared without her knowledge might make the county pass on the case altogether.

"I didn't realize they could be used as a date-rape drug," Dina continued. She shook her head in disgust. "Those bastards."

Bastards with money for a good lawyer that will probably get away with it, Gabby thought. The eagerness to speak with Mariel that Gabby had felt minutes earlier started souring, a fruit going bad after one day too long in the basket. She needed to salvage it. If Mariel sensed that the detective on her case didn't have hope for getting her justice, the girl would just give up. "I should speak with Mariel. Is she in her room?"

Dina brushed her palm over a sleek side of her blonde ponytail. "I'm sorry. I thought my housekeeper would have told you. She's not here anymore. She went back to the Philippines on Wednesday, four days ago. With everything that happened, she really wanted to be with her mother, which I could understand. I wanted her to fight, but she was going to have her mother send money to bring her home and they don't have much. I bought her the first ticket I could."

Dina's hand went to her clavicle, worrying the prominent bones like invisible pearls. "I feel so bad about what happened. I know she's eighteen, but you and I both know how young that really is. Maybe I should have warned her about the kind of things that can happen to girls here. I didn't want to scare her. In retrospect, I should have prepared her better."

"Is she coming back?" Gabby asked even though the emptiness in her gut had already told her the answer.

"No. She's staying with her family. Before she left, I explained that the police might need her if they press charges." Dina sniffed. "She didn't seem at all excited about that. I got the sense that she'd prefer never to see that man again and forget about it. You remember? She didn't even really want to discuss what had happened with you."

Gabby looked down at the rolled report that she knew wouldn't ever be labeled an exhibit. She sighed and asked Dina for a telephone number to contact Mariel, just in case. Dina had only an email address connected with Mariel's au pair account. "I think she's taken her profile down, though," Dina said. "I've been scouring the site these past few days for replacement childcare, and I haven't seen her on there."

Gabby swallowed the swear rising in her throat. She asked Dina for the au pair service's name and scribbled it in her notepad, aware that the chances of the business tracking Mariel down if she didn't want to be contacted were slim to none. Disappointment slowed her stride as she walked back to her car. Gabby stopped and closed her eyes, picturing Mariel's tearful reunion with her mother. She imagined herself as that mother, and Kayla as the girl.

Rage obliterated all her other feelings. Andy and his friends could not get away with drugging and raping young women. She couldn't let it end like this.

She slid into the unmarked Dodge's driver's seat, turned the ignition, and flipped on the hidden siren and flashing lights. Andy had claimed to be subletting from a friend that let him use the place some weekends. The weather was perfect for surfing—and for putting a couple of smug assholes on notice.

*   *   *

Different cars were parked on the shell driveway than before: a gray Subaru along with a long blue Volvo topped with a roof rack. The SUV's Maine plates and barcode on the window kept Gabby from giving up on finding Andy. He'd probably rented the same model in blue the prior week.

She checked the time on her phone as she slipped between the brush barricading the beach house. It was midday, aka surfer nap time. Low tide to midtide was when the water was glassy and the swells were biggest. The water level at the moment would be too high for big waves.

Gabby charged up the path to the glass house. Inside, four men gathered around a kitchen table, their wet suits unzipped and pulled down to their waists. Gabby banged her badge against the glass, causing a commotion inside. She watched it like a sitcom: the guys rising all at once, the quizzical looks on the new faces, Andy's gesturing explanation followed by Chris's nervous scratching of his sunburned scalp. One of the new guys, possibly the actual summer renter, headed to the door.

As soon as the glass wall retracted a few inches, Gabby barged through the opening, taking advantage of the ease with which her small frame could slip through cracks. She ignored the man shouting about warrants and calling the "real" cops, storming instead toward the sandy-haired, green-eyed man in the kitchen. Andy's bare stomach was braced for a hit.

"The rape kit came back." Gabby slammed the paper onto the kitchen counter, where everyone could see it. "The girl that woke up beside you, not remembering you two having sex. Her system had been flooded with Ambien and very little alcohol. She was drugged."

Andy's eyes darted to his mates. "I didn't do it. I don't even know where she got that stuff. Like I told you, she seemed fine to me and all about it. Maybe she took something to be less inhibited."

Gabby placed her right hand in her pants pocket, pushing back the jacket to flash her gun. "Or you spiked her punch with sedatives to make sure she'd be out of it, willing to do whatever you suggested."

Chris stepped toward her, hands up in mock surrender. "Let's not get hysterical. Look, I was at the party, as you know. I saw that girl. She didn't seem high on anything, let alone Ambien. I've seen people on that drug. It makes them all loopy, gets them saying things that don't make sense.

I'm a fish torpedo. Your head's a candied yam and I'm going to eat it."

The fourth man laughed as though he knew the story from which Chris had taken his examples. Gabby glared at the guy like she'd caught him cursing in church. "You have a lot of experience with seeing girls high on Ambien, then."

Chris's hands went to his bare sides, swelling from the tight polyurethane pants covering his lower body. "I'm not saying that. But I've seen it." He pointed to his friend. "And Andy here couldn't have known anything about that girl other than that she was eighteen and raring to go."

There were a couple more chuckles. Apparently, Chris was the comedian of the group. "I mean, people on that drug are walking around in a dream state," he continued. "Half the time, they're hallucinating. They don't remember their own name, not to mention the name of the person they're talking to."

I hate you, Sabrina. You emasculating witch. Louis's strange screams resounded in Gabby's head. He'd called his wife, Jenny, by another name. He'd accused her of flying on a broom. At the time, Gabby had thought he'd been speaking in metaphors. Could he have been high?

Chris clapped Andy on the back. "I know you think this guy's some man-whore, or a sexual predator. But until two weeks ago, when his girlfriend broke up with him, pretty boy was a one-woman guy." Chris shrugged. "My guess is this girl was afraid of getting canned for sneaking her boss's pills, so she made up a story that a mom would be sympathetic to. That's all this is." A proud smile stretched across Chris's face, as though he'd settled a disagreement between friends and come out the good guy.

Gabby wanted to slap that smile off his face. Instead, she snatched the lab report. "This report also says she had alcohol in her system." She looked at Andy as she dipped her hand into her back pocket and pulled out a pair of black zip-tie cuffs. "And you clearly told all your friends she was eighteen. So, Andy Baird, put out your hands. You're under arrest for furnishing alcohol to a minor."

Chris's smile vanished, and Andy, for an instant, looked like he might cry. "But I didn't know—"

"Mariel told you her age before you gave her the punch." Gabby grabbed Andy's wrists and put them in front of him. She slipped the nylon restraints over his hands and pulled them tight. "You have the right to remain—"

"I want to remain silent and I want a lawyer," Andy said.

The other two men had shifted their weight, subtly distancing themselves from their arrested friend. Chris, however, was clenching and unclenching his fists. "You're going to cuff him? For what? A couple-hundred-buck fine?"

Gabby nearly winced at the dollar amount. It wasn't enough punishment, and it wouldn't hurt Chris. For all she knew, Chris—not Andy—was the one who had dissolved the Ambien in the punch. He was the guy that seemed to know all about the drugs effects. "The police are aware of this house and all of you in it," she shouted. "One more party with underage drinking, one more call from a crying girl saying that she felt coerced, and I'll haul you all in for sexual assault and conspiracy to commit rape. And if you're here thinking, *So what; it'll be our word against some humiliated young woman*, know that I will tip off the papers as to exactly what went on here. How do you think your employers will feel about that? I'm sure the *New York Post* will think of something perfect to plaster on the front page above your preppy mug shots."

The man who had answered the door raised his hands in surrender. He strode back toward the retracted wall where Gabby led a silent Andy. "There won't be any more parties, Officer."

"Detective Sergeant," Gabby sneered. "And there better not be."

She took her time crossing to the exit with her suspect, emphasizing her lack of intimidation despite being out-numbered four to one by men twice her size. Without a cooperating victim, scaring them was her only means of deterrence.

The breeze buffeted her back as she led Andy to the car. True to his word, he was taking his right to remain silent dead seriously. She opened the door and ordered him inside, certain that her charge of serving minors would stick, even though she'd never get him for spiking the punch without Mariel's testimony. She slammed the door thinking about what Chris had said about an Ambien high. Even if Andy hadn't been the one to slip Mariel the drugs, he had to have known she was too out of it to con-sent. She'd have been stumbling, as Chris had said. Spew-ing nonsense.

Again, she thought of Louis's last confusing words. He'd called Jenny a witch with magic powers. And, right before he'd started speaking gibberish, he'd accused her of murder. Gabby pulled her cell from her jacket pocket and dialed DeMarco.

"Sergeant Watkins," he answered. His tone sounded respectful, ready for instructions.

She stepped away from the car, out of earshot of Andy in the back seat. "I need you to go down to the coroner before he releases Louis Murray's body. Tell him to run Louis's fluids for psychotropic drugs, especially zolpidem, also known as Ambien. And then start the paperwork for a prescription drug–monitoring request for Jenny Murray."

DeMarco cleared his throat. "Sergeant, that case is all wrapped up, though, isn't it? The guy was going to lose his medical license. His livelihood. He was violent. He would have killed his wife if you hadn't stopped—"

"Louis Murray wasn't a good man, detective." Gabby cleared her throat. "But I need to be certain that Rachel's murderer isn't still out there."

CHAPTER THIRTY

TWO WEEKS AFTER

Jenny picked the doll from the top shelf of Ally's closet, where it had no doubt lain, unnoticed and unloved, for the last five years. It still smelled of cherries from when Ally had added auburn highlights to its nylon hair. Though American Girl made dolls with Ally's olive complexion and curly wigs, finding one with reddish hair and honey-brown eyes had proven impossible. Jenny had opted for medium-brown hair and hazel eyes, turning her biracial daughter vaguely Latina. Ally had then "fixed" her hundred-dollar-plus doll with a pack of two-dollar scented markers.

The dye job was streaky and strange, though not as alarming as the one Jenny had bought for Ally at the salon. She had understood her daughter wanting to erase Louis's most obvious contribution from her reflection. Still, she'd begged her not to go through with it. The red curls had been Ally, just like the yellow-toned complexion that browned in the summer and the soft bridge of her nose passed down from Jenny's mother. Ally, however, had threatened to do it herself, forcing Jenny to book the appointment or risk her daughter ruining her hair.

She'd been shocked when Ally had emerged a blonde. They'd agreed she would go brunette, perhaps a similar shade to Jenny's rich brown color. But Ally must have always had other ideas. Jenny had left, unable to watch the stylist obliterate one of her daughter's most recognizable traits. As soon as she'd gone, Ally had told the hairdresser to bleach it. When Ally looked in the mirror, she evidently hadn't wanted to see her mother, either.

Jenny stuffed the doll into the crook of her arm, her hands occupied with the crutches she required to hobble toward the large cardboard boxes labeled ALLY'S BEDROOM, DONATE, and TRASH. Few would want a doll with marker-colored hair, but maybe a mom somewhere would see it in a consignment store and figure out how to swap out the wig for a style that more closely matched her own kid's locks. As she dangled the doll over the box destined for Goodwill, she glimpsed one of the red streaks framing the round face. The doll landed in the box of items destined for their new home—wherever that would be.

Jenny limped back to the closet. She leaned on her good left leg and the crutch beside it, freeing her other arm to pull out a folded pile of last season's sweaters. She was examining the loud Christmas pattern at the top of the stack when she heard the doorbell.

She stood stock-still for a moment and closed her eyes, trying to decipher whether the tone was really someone at her door or the intensifying of the white noise and high-pitched tone she had heard constantly since Louis had bashed the glass into the side of her head, permanently damaging her hearing.

The bell sounded again, clearer this time. She didn't move toward the hallway. It was either another delivery of moving boxes or a reporter late to the party. There was no one to visit her. The "friends" she'd had in town were staying away, *giving her time to heal* and no doubt avoiding the awkwardness of seeing her shattered leg or asking about next steps. And Ally's pals all knew Ally had gone to stay with Jenny's parents in West Virginia until her mother figured out their next move.

The house was already on the market. Remaining in the home they'd all shared since Ally had turned two was not an option. It held too many memories—good for Ally, bad for her, and painful for the both of them. Jenny was considering an apartment in the city. A kid could disappear among 1.6 million people, enabling Ally to avoid being gawked at by locals who knew her story.

Given her job on television, Jenny couldn't vanish anywhere. She wouldn't quit, though. Money had to come from somewhere. Louis's life insurance policy had been two million dollars, or two years of their combined income, and Ally would need a good chunk of that for college. Jenny couldn't complain about the sum, though. She was lucky to have any of it. Had the detective actually killed Louis rather than startled him, leading to the fall, the insurance company wouldn't have paid a dime.

The bell rang a third time, stoking Jenny's curiosity. She avoided the windows as she headed into the laundry room angled to overlook the L-shaped driveway in front of the house. Ben stood on her stoop, several feet in front of the FOR SALE sign hammered into the lawn. He reached out to hit the buzzer a fourth time and then seemed to think better of it, turning from the door.

The sight of him leaving her, again, shortened her breath. She dropped one crutch and hobbled toward the stairs. The banister served as her second limb. She leaned most of her weight on it as she carefully descended.

By the time she opened the door, Ben was at the curb. She called out to him, wincing at the desperation in her reedy voice. He turned back and hustled up the walk, realizing, perhaps, the effort it took to hold open the door when she couldn't stand straight.

"I had to see how you were doing." He rubbed the back of his neck, seemingly embarrassed by the admission, as though she'd dumped him and he'd shown up on her doorstep. "Can I come in?"

Jenny knew she should say no. He'd sold her out, after all, revealing her name to Rachel despite knowing what Louis might do to her once Rachel told him. In some ways, Ben was as responsible for everything that had happened as she and Louis were. But he was standing in front of her, the handsome man who had professed to love her once. She wanted to forgive him, to believe he'd been put in a desperate situation and would never hurt her like that again.

Before she could, though, she needed him to honestly answer one lingering question.

Jenny backed into the foyer, allowing Ben inside. As soon as the door slammed, his arms were around her, lifting her up, taking the pressure off her broken leg. In spite of herself, she leaned into his embrace.

"I'm sorry. I'm so sorry," he whispered into her ear, a spoken-word lullaby that she knew by heart. "I thought you'd told her. I never imagined that the girls had come into the backyard that day and seen us. I couldn't think of any other way that Rachel would have found out. I thought only we knew. I'm so sorry. Please, forgive me. Let me make it up to you."

The begging reminded Jenny of Louis. As Ben led her toward the sitting-room sofa, she wondered if his contrition was any more real than her husband's had been. After five years cycling through apologies and anger, Jenny doubted she could tell the difference between a genuine "sorry" and one meant solely to stave off consequences.

Ben helped her sit on the couch and then joined her on the neighboring cushion, angling his body to face her. The light from the side windows highlighted the gold and silver in his hair. He was still movie-star handsome, Jenny thought, but the pain of the past few weeks had aged him, adding deep lines between his brows and across his forehead that Jenny would have sworn hadn't existed two weeks earlier.

He brushed her hair back from her face, examining her healed skin. None of the scrapes and bruises had left visible scars, though her shattered leg would take six months to fully repair itself and her hearing would never be the same.

"You look beautiful." He gave her a wine-glass smile, easily broken. She couldn't relax into it until she knew the truth.

"Did she tell you?"

His eyebrows tried to unite in confusion. "Chloe? Yes, she said that she told—"

Jenny placed a hand on his thigh. "Did Rachel tell you that Louis hit me? Did you know before I came to your house that day when you saw the blood on the back of my head?"

Though Ben's lips parted, no sound emerged. His chest pulsed with quicker breaths.

"You acted as though you hadn't known Louis had hurt me until then. You saw my head, and I always believed you'd guessed how I'd gotten it from my cagey behavior. But did you know before? Had you seen me with sunglasses on and realized, or noticed a scratch? Did you know?"

Ben rubbed the back of his neck. "I don't know. I might have suspected things weren't good. But . . . but I didn't exactly know."

The words were the right ones, but Jenny could see in Ben's eyes that he didn't believe them. He wasn't a good liar—that was one of the traits that had made her feel most safe with him.

Since Louis's fall off the balcony, Jenny had learned to be much better with her own performances. She nodded solemnly and wrapped her arms around him, soaking in what she knew would be a final good-bye. He pulled her tight to his chest, whispering thank-yous for taking him back, telling her how much better things would be in the future.

A ring interrupted his plans. Ben bolted upright, clarifying that the sound hadn't been in her head. "Are you expecting anyone?"

"I thought the press was done trying for an interview after I gave my station that exclusive. But maybe not."

For a moment, Ben looked like he wanted to bolt through the house and out the back door. He could cut through their adjoining yards before the press saw him. A look back at her, reaching for her crutch, appeared to change his mind. He stood straighter. "I'll get rid of them. There's nothing wrong with me checking on your recovery."

Ben crossed into the foyer and opened the door. "Hello?"

"Mr. Hansen."

She recognized the voice. The woman's screams often echoed in Jenny's dreams. "Detective Watkins?"

Ben stood to the side, allowing the officer into the foyer. She looked as Jenny remembered her, dark hair pulled back in a low ponytail, her small frame covered in a fitted gray pantsuit. Jenny's heart dropped into her stomach. She could think of only one reason for Gabby Watkins to drive the two hours—perhaps four in traffic—to see her in person.

"We need you to come with us," Gabby said. A uniformed officer with the badge of the local police entered behind her. Jenny wondered how many more officers were outside. The more cars there were, the greater the likelihood that the cops suspected what she'd done.

Jenny grabbed her crutch and then shimmied to the edge of the couch. She pressed her hand into the armrest, using it to launch herself into a standing position. "I need my other crutch. It's upstairs."

Ben moved into the room, his hands folded across his chest in delayed defiance. "What is this about? She's still recovering."

Gabby looked at Jenny like she knew. "We want to clear something up. We found high levels of Ambien in Mr. Murray's blood. Mrs. Murray has a prescription."

Jenny had a visceral reaction to hearing her name united with Louis. She'd permanently severed that connection. "Please don't call me that. My maiden name is Reid. Jenny Reid."

Gabby nodded to the officer. The cuffs in his right hand caught the sunlight through the windows behind him. Ben seemed to notice the glint at the same time Jenny did. "Who cares if he took a bunch of pills? He was trying to kill her. He murdered my wife. He should rot in hell."

Jenny knew Ben's tirade wouldn't make a difference. She stepped forward, resigned to what was coming. Part of her was almost grateful for it. She no longer had to worry about being arrested someday, in front of her daughter. "Ben, would you get my crutch from Ally's room?"

Ben looked from the officers and back to her, breathing through his open mouth. "Louis murdered my wife!"

Detective Watkins looked at him like he was a child insisting upon the existence of Santa Claus. Jenny couldn't have her say anything more in front of him. Whatever happened, she needed Ally to believe the story she'd told, and that couldn't happen if Ben knew the truth.

"Ben, please, my crutch."

He muttered about the insanity of the police as he headed up the stairs, glancing back every few steps to make sure she was okay, as though he could somehow prevent the inevitable. The detective watched him disappear down the second-floor hallway, a gift, Jenny knew, that the police weren't obligated to give her.

"Okay, Ms. Reid." Detective Watkins made eye contact with the local officer. He moved forward, the cuffs dangling from his palm.

"You have the right to remain silent. Anything you say can and will be used against you in a court of law. You have the right to an attorney . . ."

EPILOGUE

THE YEAR AFTER

Mother's Day didn't exist inside the Rose M. Singer Center, though nearly all the women housed there had children. Some of the inmates even had their babies with them. Rosie's had a nursery for newborns whose first screams had echoed in Rikers Island's hospitals. Citing studies showing that infants with stronger maternal bonds developed healthier, researchers had insisted that the prison's postpartum population be able to keep their newborns nearby. A relationship with even a violent mother, they maintained, was preferable than no exposure at all.

Jenny prayed the social scientists were right as she walked in a stiff line down the cinder-block hallway to the visitor's area, listening to the high-pitched whine and whirling white noise that only she could hear. She hadn't seen Ally in nearly eleven months, not since embracing her that last awkward time in the courtroom. She hadn't wanted her daughter to accompany her to Rikers, where she'd agreed to turn herself in and begin serving the sentence set forth in her plea deal: five years for voluntary manslaughter.

Her defense hadn't worked as well as she'd hoped. Her lawyer had argued that battered woman syndrome was responsible for Jenny drugging her husband and pushing him down the stairs. Jenny had thought it the right move, given the prosecution's case. During the trial, the opposition had, thankfully, steered clear of any motive involving keeping Louis in the dark about her and Ben's affair, or pinning Rachel's murder on him—though Detective Watkins's interrogation had revealed that the cops considered both likely reasons for Jenny's actions.

For a sleepless month, Jenny had feared that the prosecution might admit Detective Watkins's sworn testimony about the words of a man about to die, opening the door to charging her with Rachel's murder. But the prosecution had ultimately decided it was too risky. Instead, they'd focused solely on the well-established abuse and the drugs in Louis's system, arguing that Jenny's desire to punish her husband for years of beatings had led her to plot his murder.

Her defense had somewhat conceded the point. Sure, they'd argued, Jenny had drugged her husband and pushed him off a staircase, but only after the abuse had escalated to the point where she'd had reason to believe he would kill her if she didn't act first. Moreover, her attorney had maintained, the constant fear of physical attacks, cultivated over years, had damaged Jenny psychologically to the point where she could see no way out of Louis's violence other than ending his life.

For a while, Jenny had thought the jury was on her side. Several of them had become misty-eyed seeing the police photographs of her injuries. But Jenny had lost her allies once the prosecution had delved into her finances. Few could understand why a woman capable of supporting herself—one that, in fact, out-earned her husband—wouldn't have simply walked out the door with her daughter in tow.

Both Jenny and her lawyer had sensed the jury's growing inability to comprehend her actions, to grasp how afraid she'd been of her husband taking Ally and continuing the cycle of abuse. Rather than risk a felony murder conviction, Jenny had opted to take a plea midway through the prosecution's case: five years for voluntary manslaughter versus the fifteen-to-life she could have received for premeditated murder.

Jenny hoped some of her sentence would be shaved off for good behavior. She liked to think of herself as a model prisoner. She read books, volunteered in the hospital ward, and helped many of the new, young mothers learn techniques to parent a newborn. Some days, the latter work helped her miss her daughter less. Some days, it turned her longing for Ally into an acute pain that Jenny could only describe as a peeling of her heart's muscle fibers from its beating core.

She definitely didn't want Ally to see her locked up, even if it was Mother's Day. The idea of her soft suburban daughter emptying her pockets and spreading her legs for a paddle detector was unbearable. She never wanted Ally to wait for her beneath blaring fluorescents surrounded by the smell of incarceration: body odor, backed-up sewers, and bad cafeteria food. Better, she thought, that she not see her for the duration of the sentence.

Most of the women Jenny chatted with in the cafeteria or in the library felt the same way. They'd each wait in line for hours to talk to their children on the phone, but they all begged them not to visit. Protecting their kids from the reality of prison was the last parental act available to anyone inside. They couldn't mother here amid the stink and the sweat. Who could comfort a child during a timed good-bye hug or impart parental advice with the backdrop of bars?

But here she was with a visitor anyway. It was probably Jenny's own mother bringing Ally to see her. She should have known better, but Jenny figured that her mother had convinced herself an in-person talk would be best for both her daughter and granddaughter. Perhaps her mom had thought Ally might actually speak to her if she saw the daily punishment Jenny endured: shuffling in lines of downtrodden women, wearing a musty-smelling, ill-fitting prison uniform with *DOC* stamped on the back, unable to pee without permission, confined to a bleak island where the roar of departing planes drowned out any bird's song.

Jenny's mother was wrong, though. Showing Ally the treatment society thought fitting for her would only further strain their relationship. It would tell Ally that she was right never to talk to Jenny again, that Jenny deserved to be punished for murdering Louis. Even though Ally had seen the evidence of her father's violence, she still wanted to believe that the abuse had been a one-off related to Jenny's affair. Daddy, according to Ally, had been emotionally devastated and "lost it."

A heavyset female guard—Toni, if Jenny remembered right—stopped at the front of the slow-moving line. She shouted for the women to press themselves against the wall, wait for the door, and then "proceed in an orderly fashion."

The door buzzed open. Toni secured it against the concrete and then positioned herself several feet in front of it. She motioned for the women to file into the painfully bright area filled with cafeteria-style tables and plastic chairs. Jenny scanned the visitors for the slight shapes of her elderly mother and daughter. Aside from an older woman with a toddler in tow and a lanky boy who might have been a teenager, Jenny didn't see any children.

"Jenny?"

A woman sitting in the corner seemed to mouth her name. She had near-black hair, flat-ironed straight to her shoulders, and brown skin, like Jenny and the majority of the prisoners, ninety percent of whom were Black and Hispanic. She wasn't a member of Jenny's family and certainly not a friend. For a second, Jenny wondered whether the guards had made a mistake and brought the wrong Jennifer to the visiting room. A moment later, though, the face came back to her: Gabby Watkins, the detective who had put her inside.

Jenny hadn't thought about her since her plea. Ensuring that Ally got settled with her parents and that her folks had all the information to enroll her in a new school had been her primary focus. Seeing the detective, however, brought back the memories of her arrest with a stinging clarity. She'd felt, that day, like Wile E. Coyote at the moment he realized there was only air beneath his running feet. She'd run off the cliff a long time ago—perhaps since forgiving Louis that first time. It was only when the officers had arrived to arrest her, though, that she'd realized she would have to fall.

"Officer Watkins?"

The woman stood and motioned to the seat across from her. Jenny started to turn away. Why should she volunteer to be interrogated again? Before she took a step, though, she saw the yellowed cinder-block wall of the visiting room, the same walls that confined all the inmates into four-hundred-foot squares. Anywhere was better than her tiny cell. At least in here she had company. And she should, she supposed, find out what Gabby wanted. If the police had uncovered some new evidence, they might try to make her stand trial for Rachel's murder.

Jenny settled into the offered seat. "I'm surprised to see you."

She let the fact hang rather than connect it to any pleasantry. The detective's presence wasn't auspicious.

"I brought you a . . ."

The ring in Jenny's ear muffled the detective's final word. "You brought something? I'm sorry. You have to speak up. I'm nearly deaf in one ear and I have tinnitus."

Detective Watkins brow wrinkled. She leaned over her chair arm toward the floor and grabbed a small brown paper bag, which she placed on the table. Jenny controlled her hands and her curiosity. For all she knew, it was evidence that the detective hoped she'd coat with her prints. "What is it?"

Her visitor pulled the bag toward her and removed the square contents: a bound journal with a black-and-white drawing of Virginia Woolf on the cover. Above it, in a stylized script, was a quote from the author: *A self that goes on changing is a self that goes on living.*

"I always liked that one." The detective said, passing the book across the table.

Jenny eyed the woman as she accepted the gift. Did she feel guilty for putting her in here? Was she afraid that Jenny might kill herself spending Mother's Day away from her daughter, and did she believe some life-affirming quotes might stave off any tying together of the bedsheets? Jenny flipped through the book's pages, expecting to find a bunch of inspirational and unintentionally mocking words to live by. Instead, the pages were blessedly blank.

"I figured that you might like to write down some of what happened to you." Detective Watkins's closed-lipped smile made Jenny feel like there was something behind the woman's teeth.

"Why? What do you think I'll write?" The question shot out more barbed than Jenny had intended. She was too anxious for the detective to get to the point of her visit to make their conversation sound like anything other than automatic fire.

"I don't know." Gabby folded her hands atop the table. "There might be things you need to get off your chest."

Like my affair with Ben. Fortunately for Jenny, the press had never uncovered the relationship. Jenny supposed they'd been too busy focusing on the Killer Doc, as they'd named Louis in the tabloids. The lurid story of a respected emergency room surgeon harboring murderous desires had been sufficiently newsworthy that the media hadn't snooped around Ben and Rachel's marriage. As far as anyone outside the East Hampton Detective Bureau was concerned, Louis had killed Rachel because of his anger over the lawsuit and its potential impact on his career.

"Um, I'm sorry, but why are you here?"

The detective's eyes fell to her hands. Jenny was shocked to see her rubbing her knuckles as though she were the nervous one. "I need to know. I know I won't prove it. There's no DNA. Ben denies that you two were ever more than friends. But . . ."

Jenny stiffened in her chair. She knew the question Detective Watkins would ask. It was the same one all prisoners faced down daily: *Did you do it?*

"In my mind, I keep seeing Louis fall back at the sound of the gun and then you pushing him. I want to know what role I played in everything." The detective shook a hand through her straightened hair. "Was Louis trying to save himself from being arrested, or was he telling the truth that day I shot at him?"

Detective Watkins looked at her, as though Jenny might be crazy enough to reveal the truth simply to give this strange woman peace of mind. Jenny stared back.

Gabby sighed. "Did you do it because you were sleeping with her husband? Did you kill Rachel?"

The sound of Rachel's name intensified the rushing white noise in her damaged ear and the impossibly high shriek that grew louder whenever Jenny's head hit a pillow. The sounds overwhelmed her brain, dragging it back to that night as they so often did—to when she'd run through the scrub forest to the beach, desperate to convince Rachel not to reveal the affair to Louis.

* * *

Rachel stood on the black rocks, haloed by the moonlight. Jenny removed her sneakers at the water's edge and stepped into the fizzing remnants of a wave. Cold froth splattered her calves. She hoisted herself onto the jetty, picking her way in the near dark toward the woman ignoring her advance.

As she drew within striking distance, Rachel whirled toward her as though she'd been waiting for Jenny to come close enough to land a punch. She'd removed her beach cover-up, perhaps realizing that a fight was coming and not wanting to give Jenny any opportunity to pull her down.

Tears stained Rachel's face, made paler and prettier by the white glow overhead.

"I'm sorry," Jenny shouted above the waves' repetitive crash. "It was a mistake. I never meant for it to happen. Louis beats me, Rachel. I went over one day to pick up Ally after a bad fight, and Ben saw my bleeding head. He realized what was going on and comforted me. I was so relieved to have someone's support that I acted foolishly. I'm so sorry. But it's over and—"

"You're pathetic, Jen!" Rachel's volume shot above the crashing surf. "And stupid, you know that? You really think Ben just magically figured it out? I told him what was going on a year ago. It was so obvious, the way you'd walk around town like a spanked dog with your head down and your makeup slathered on, wearing big sunglasses in fucking November. I told Ben that Louis hit you. I even asked him if I should talk to you. And what do you think Ben said to do? Call the police? No. He said we should stay out of it. Stay out of it, I guess, so when the timing was right he could get you to spread your legs simply by saying that you were too pretty to be popped in the face."

Rachel's tirade felt like a punch to the solar plexus. Jenny recalled her first time with Ben, how he'd seemed to know that Louis had caused her head injury before she'd even tried to stutter an explanation.

Rachel laughed. "Oh, what's wrong, Jen? You feel betrayed?"

The moonlight that had softened Rachel's features suddenly sharpened them, casting a triangle of shadow from her nose over the left side of her face. The dark side possessed a sinister quality, as though Rachel had peeled back her pale skin to reveal a demon beneath.

Jenny pleaded with Rachel's illuminated side. "I know you're angry, but don't tell Louis. Or, fine, tell him, just not tonight. You know he can be violent. I need a day to get Ally and take us someplace safe."

Rachel scoffed. She'd been so ridiculous with her makeup and strategic outfits, Jenny thought. She hadn't hidden anything. Rachel had known. Ben had known. Maybe everyone knew.

Jenny couldn't let her shame distract her from her begging. "Please, Rachel," she continued. "Hold off on telling him for twenty-four hours."

The ocean hissed and spit at the rocks, a chorus urging Rachel to show no mercy. "You think I'll help you? You slept with my husband! I can't wait to tell Louis that his wife is an unfaithful whore. And if you're worried about Ally, you should have thought about that before breaking up her best friend's family."

Jenny should have known her pleading would be futile. She'd slept with her supposed friend's husband in the woman's house. Her behavior was beyond forgiveness. Still, she couldn't let her daughter pay for her mistakes.

She launched herself at her neighbor. As Rachel raised her arm to block her hit, Jenny changed trajectories, instinctually curling her hands around Rachel's neck the way Louis had done hours earlier. Rachel coughed as Jenny squeezed her thumbs into the notch between Rachel's collarbones. The sound of the air escaping Rachel's throat only made Jenny squeeze harder.

"You can't tell him," Jenny screamed over the rushing waves. "You can't!"

Her bare feet suddenly hit a silken surface. She slipped on it, falling back into the water and dragging Rachel down with her, along with what she realized had been Rachel's kimono. Cold water enveloped her, sending a pain up her limbs. Her breath froze in her lungs.

A high-pitched sound pierced her shock. Rachel was screaming. Her suit had snagged a rock, ripping the shoulder strap and wounding her back. Jenny stood, pressing her feet against the sandy bottom. The water, she realized, barely reached the tops of her thighs.

"You bitch," Rachel shouted, seemingly loud enough for Louis to hear back in the house. "I hope he kills you. I hope he fucking kills you, you—"

Before she could say, Jenny grabbed Rachel's head. She shoved it beneath the surface, watching the unspoken words bubble around her. She didn't let go until all the bubbles vanished.

* * *

Jenny looked at her hands, at the jagged nails that hadn't seen polish and at the lines of dirt crusted underneath them. She fought the desire to pick out the grime. She knew that her awareness of what her fingers had done to Rachel, how they'd wrapped around her neck and pressed her beneath the waves, fueled the urge.

"Did you do it?" Detective Watkins asked again.

Jenny read her lips. The whooshing in her ear was so loud, the scream so high and unending. Sometimes Jenny thought it would drive her insane.

"Why do you care so much about Rachel?" Jenny asked, surrendering to her desire to pick the dirt beneath her thumbnail. "She wasn't the type to care about others. Do you know that she knew Louis was abusing me? For over a year, apparently. She'd talked about it with other people. But she never once asked me if I was all right. If I needed help. Sometimes, I think if I'd only had someone to snap me out of what was happening, to say to me, 'What's going on between you and your husband isn't something that should be rationalized' . . . I don't know, maybe things wouldn't have happened the way they did."

Detective Watkins nodded with a grave look, probably the same one Jenny had displayed when she'd been waiting for her to get to the point.

"But Rachel never talked to me like that," Jenny continued, sharing the silent justifications that helped her sleep at night. "It was always these shallow conversations. Who makes those jeans you're wearing? Do you know any good decorators in the area? Rachel was the kind of person that would realize your husband had beat the crap out of you and ask if you were going to a charity ball on the following Thursday."

Detective Watkins kept her look of strained interest. "So, you thought she deserved to die."

"Of course she didn't deserve to die." Jenny stopped

picking her nails and folded her hands in front of her, as in prayer. She couldn't let emotion lead her into a confession. "I'm sorry that Rachel is dead. I really am." Jenny's throat tightened around the harsh truth. A tear she didn't realize she'd shed tumbled from her cheek onto the table, leaving a damp circle on the surface. "All I am saying is that maybe we're all a little responsible when we turn a blind eye. I don't know. Maybe if Rachel and I had been better friends to one another, things would have been different for all of us." Jenny looked directly into Detective Watkins's brown irises, the mirror in many ways of her own eyes. "Maybe women should do more to help other women."

Detective Watkins stared at her like she could see the words materializing in the space between them. She seemed to look through them to Jenny's face, trying to decipher some coded message. Jenny knew, though, that she'd said nothing definitive. As much as she wanted Detective Watkins to understand, she couldn't risk the courts holding her responsible for Rachel's death, too. She had her daughter to get back to.

Jenny palmed the book and then pushed the chair back from the table. "Thanks, Detective."

Detective Watkins stood. "Wait. I need to know . . ."

Jenny looked directly in the woman's face. "You know how Rachel died. Louis killed her. He couldn't control his anger. He went out to talk to her about his case. They clearly fought and he killed her. Then, when he realized that Ben wasn't going to be his patsy, he decided that he could make up a contemptible story and pin it on me." Jenny shrugged.

"You shot at the right man, Detective. Rachel's murderer is dead."

Detective Watkins blinked, seemingly processing the picture while simultaneously scanning for signs that it had been altered, perhaps sensing something off. In her own way, Jenny decided, she'd told her the truth.

She turned toward the guard and pointed to the door, asking permission to leave. The steel door buzzed open. Its loud alert heightened the wail of white noise in her head. Jenny closed her eyes and counted to ten, like she was waiting out a contraction. The worst of the sound would subside. But, for the rest of her life, she would hear that scream over the waves.

ACKNOWLEDGMENTS

Some stories develop for me like a dream. It's as if my subconscious saw the film and spoiled it all for my waking mind. The beginning, major plot points, and ending are all known. The characters seem like people I've cried with. I settle down to write feeling like a typist transcribing each vivid scene.

Other stories start with a sense of something or someone. The characters are hazy, and I see the setting through oil-smeared sunglasses. I know the inciting incident that will set events in motion. But I don't know my imaginary people well enough to understand all they will feel, nor what they will do to each other. These stories are more painful for me. I enjoy being the sole creator of my imagined world, and relinquishing control to these developing people is anxiety producing and rewrite inducing.

I am fortunate to be surrounded by wonderful real human beings who help me negotiate with these characters and regain my sense of what I'd like to say, while being honest about the natures of the folks populating my story.

ACKNOWLEDGMENTS

I would like to thank my husband, Brett, who listens to me talk about fictional people as if I am sharing the secret problems of dear friends I need to help. I don't know how he puts up with me half the time, but I am deeply grateful for his patience and love. I would also like to thank my daughters, Ellie and Olivia, who have to deal with Mommy being stressed about a rewrite and getting them to tennis on time. I wish I could say I easily switch from penning a murder scene to the school pickup line, but I know I don't. I am very fortunate to have such loving children who can understand that sometimes Mommy needs a minute.

I would like to thank my agent Paula Munier, who held my hand many times when I needed it with this story and restored my confidence to continue writing it through various permutations.

I would like to give a special thanks to the Bloomfield Police Department and especially Detective Shonah Maldonado, who spoke with me at length about her job as a female detective and dealing with domestic violence cases and crimes of sexual abuse. She inspired me to write the detective in this story—my favorite character in this book—and she is a true hero for so many. The dedication and caring that she brings to her work are truly inspiring, and I am thankful that there are women like her protecting all of us.

I would also like to thank all the other people who believe in me and give needed counsel. You help me believe in myself. Mom, Dad, James, Tara, Grandma Gloria, Grandmother Maddy, Linda H, Galit, Gia, Jen, Julie, Joanne, Karin, Karly, Linda K, Lisa, Madeline, Margot, Mina, Nadine,

Saundra, Shana, Shelley, Soroya, Tamiko, Nafiz, Jeff, John, Vic, Garth, Trey, Uncle Paul, Uncle Philip, Aunt Julie, Aunt Elayne, Aunt Sharon, and Aunt Kim.

I'd like to thank the team at Crooked Lane—Matt, Nike, Sarah, and Jenny—for all your hard work helping to get this book out. I appreciate what you do and know that trying to get a writer to tell the best story she can (and then putting that story in the best possible package) isn't easy.

I am also thankful for Westley, my faithful dog who keeps me company when I write. #puglife

I am forever grateful to my grandfather, Poppy, who inspired me to be a writer in the first place. Sometimes I swear I feel his presence and energy when the writing is going well. And when it's not, I remember his work ethic and buckle down.

Last, but never least, thanks to God. In my stories, bad things happen. But there is always a character or two who gives of himself to try to make things better or who learns to appreciate what she has once she sees the bigger picture. I believe God is most present in our efforts to be good to one another, and when we stop thinking about how we feel and refocus on how we can make others feel. I try to remember this in my writing.